THE RAVEN THRONE

Books by Stephanie Burgis

The Dragon with a Chocolate Heart
The Girl with the Dragon Heart
The Princess Who Flew with Dragons

The Raven Heir
The Raven Throne

THE
RAVEN
THRONE

STEPHANIE BURGIS

BLOOMSBURY
CHILDREN'S BOOKS
LONDON OXFORD NEW YORK NEW DELHI SYDNEY

BLOOMSBURY CHILDREN'S BOOKS
Bloomsbury Publishing Plc
50 Bedford Square, London WC1B 3DP, UK
29 Earlsfort Terrace, Dublin 2, Ireland

BLOOMSBURY, BLOOMSBURY CHILDREN'S BOOKS and the Diana logo
are trademarks of Bloomsbury Publishing Plc

First published in Great Britain in 2023 by Bloomsbury Publishing Plc

A catalogue record for this book is available from the British Library

ISBN: PB: 978-1-5266-1446-9; eBook: 978-1-5266-1447-6;
ePDF: 978-1-5266-5292-8

2 4 6 8 10 9 7 5 3 1

Typeset by RefineCatch Limited, Bungay, Suffolk

Printed and bound in Great Britain by CPI Group (UK) Ltd, Croydon CR0 4YY

MIX
Paper | Supporting
responsible forestry
FSC® C171272

To find out more about our authors and books visit www.bloomsbury.com
and sign up for our newsletters

For Jenn Reese, Holly Webb, Deva Fagan and Ying Lee,
with love and thanks for lighting my way through
this novel. xo

'Uneasy lies the head that wears a crown'

— William Shakespeare, *Henry* IV, *Part* 2

PROLOGUE

Ivy was sneaking up the castle walls again, because the Raven Queen was dreaming. In her dreams, all her waking shields slipped from her grasp. Then the land of Corvenne reached out to embrace her with every green tendril.

In the morning, castle guards would chop down the new growth, keeping those high stone walls as bleak and bare as they had stood for fifty long, violent years before Queen Cordelia finally came to the throne. For now, though, it grew, because the twelve-year-old queen still slept, her small body tossing and turning within her massive, canopied bed. All her ladies-in-waiting slept as well, so none of them noticed those affectionate tendrils of lush green ivy that curled through the cracks in Cordelia's wooden shutters and crept along the rush-covered floor towards her bed.

Nearby, both her triplet siblings slept too, in the luxuriant bedchambers they had been given six weeks ago, their high walls draped in the finest tapestries and silk. But in their dreams, the two of them were anything but regal.

Giles sang to the moon in the high, yipping voice of a young red fox, and the forest around him echoed with wild cries and howls of approval.

Rosalind battled every bit as fiercely in her dreams as she did in waking life, but instead of wielding her favourite sword or bow, she kicked out at her enemies with big, padded hare feet, sending animal intruders of all sizes fleeing from her family's burrow.

Their mother slept dreamlessly in her own royal chambers, content in the knowledge that her children were surrounded by her best spells and wards of protection as well as by their human guards.

Even the queen's older half-brother, Connall, the quiet and serious new Duke of Harcourt, slept through the night. For the first time in his life, his dreams were free of fear. The ancient spirits of the land itself had chosen his sister to be queen and gifted her full use of their powers. Every dangerous duke and duchess in the realm had been forced to accept her claim to the throne when she had magically mended the broken Raven Crown, bringing the land and its people back into unity. With the magic of the land itself at her disposal, his little sister could upend human battlefields and tear stone walls apart.

What fears could keep *her* family awake any more?

Inside the queen's royal chamber, dark green ivy curled over her bed and draped across her sleeping body in a loving, protective embrace that made her restless twitching finally slow and cradled her into a deep, restful slumber.

But not everyone in the castle was so innocently sleeping. Far below, in its dark and long-forgotten depths, an ancient mystery had been hidden long ago … and a new evil was about to strike.

1

Prince Giles of Corvenne woke with a new song in his head, which was entirely usual. He also woke with a wild animal snuffling around his feet, which was becoming *far* too usual nowadays.

Rolling his eyes, he pushed off his covers and sat up. 'Wrong room,' he told the little hedgehog through his yawn as it froze in sudden panic before him. 'You're looking for my sister Cordy, three doors down. The long-haired one. I just happen to smell like her.'

The hedgehog rolled up into a tight, prickly ball of fear, but Giles had had plenty of practice over the years in coaxing wild creatures to be agreeable. Next to handling his two triplet sisters, *this* was easy. It only took a few minutes of his softest, sweetest humming to persuade the creature into warily unrolling. After a further few minutes of careful petting, it even settled into the crook of his arm, where its hard prickles poked through the fine linen weave of his nightshirt.

'Your High—? Oh, *no*.' The Master of the Princely Bedchamber, a tall and harried-looking man named Wincester, grimaced as he opened the door of Giles's bedroom ten minutes later and saw them both. 'Not again?'

'At least this one hasn't left any droppings on the bed,' Giles said cheerfully. 'I quite enjoyed the company.' A hedgehog was a far better surprise than a snake or a rat, when it came to the various wild visitors who'd come slithering or scampering to pay court to Cordy over the last few weeks – and it *had* been awfully nice to have an appreciative audience for his music again for the first time in too long.

Wait, no! He couldn't let that traitorous thought take root even for an instant.

Once upon a time, it was true, Giles had dreamed of becoming a famous bard. He'd spent years training for it in his family's enchanted forest before unexpectedly becoming a prince six weeks ago – but on a battlefield full of terror, he had promised the ancient spirits of the land to support his queenly sister's reign and do everything he could to keep their kingdom safe. He meant to keep that promise.

Here in the outside world, bards were seen as '*common, hired entertainers*' – a phrase that had dripped with disdain when he'd heard it from his newly met adult cousin, the Duke of Lune, only four weeks earlier. Lune had overheard Giles singing a silly song to his sisters in the open street just after Cordy's coronation, but he'd been kind enough to wait until later, when the two of them could speak in private, before he'd launched into his cousinly chastisement. It had only taken a few words from the duke for Giles to realise, with a cold wash of humiliation, just how rash a mistake his thoughtless singing could have been.

Apparently, after all the rumours that had circulated about Mother for the past twelve years, at least half of the royal court was already convinced that their whole family was a bunch of outlandish sorcerers who couldn't be trusted for long with the Raven Throne. The *last* thing any of them needed was for Giles to prove the nay-sayers right by behaving in such an embarrassingly unregal manner.

Fortunately, hedgehogs couldn't care less about the rules of princely dignity, so he'd had a fabulous time singing his secret new song to his small, prickly visitor. Parts of the tune sounded almost like a wild fox yipping, which was utterly hilarious, although it might have worried some small animals. Oddly enough, the hedgehog had seemed to like those bits best of all.

The rest of the court would be waiting for Prince Giles, though, by this time of day – and his poor Master of the Bedchamber, who was not comfortable with wild animals in any situation, was giving the hedgehog a deeply pained look. 'It hasn't left any droppings *yet*.' Wincester shuddered. 'It must be crawling with fleas though.' Visibly bracing himself, he held out his hands in a brave display of willpower. 'Please allow me to dispose of it for you, Your Highness. I will simply put it out of the window and—'

'We're three storeys off the ground! The poor thing would be crushed.' Giles gave the hedgehog a reassuring stroke between its prickles. 'No, I'll take it to Cordy. We all know it was looking for her anyway.'

'I'm sure Her Majesty will be delighted.' From the gloomy tone of Wincester's voice, he wasn't sure of anything of the sort. 'However, she may have more important duties—'

'More important than a hedgehog? You really don't understand Cordy yet, do you?' Giles jumped off the high bed, ignoring the steps, and landed lightly on his peacock-blue-stockinged feet. 'Don't worry. I'll be back soon, hedgehog-free. One day, though, you *will* find yourself loving a wild animal. I'm sure of it!'

'Your Highness …' Wincester's sigh was not discreet.

'The archives of Raven's Roost are said to hold ancient scrolls that date back hundreds of years, to times long before even this castle was built ... and yet, I doubt that even their famous archivist could find evidence of such a miracle ever occurring.'

'Ha! It's a wager between us then.' Giles beamed as he strode out of the room, triumphantly cradling the hedgehog. Six weeks ago, when they'd first met, Wincester had hardly dared meet Giles's gaze. He had bowed and scraped and been so excruciatingly respectful that Giles could tell he'd expected to be sacked – or executed – if he said a single word out of place.

Now, he was teasing Giles just like Giles's own relatives did! So much progress had been made.

Giles knew this castle could feel like a real home one day, no matter what Cordy and the rest of their family thought. He just had to *make* it happen!

Humming under his breath, so no one else could hear, he strode into the antechamber, which was buzzing with activity. Half a dozen official gentlemen of his bedchamber, ranging from boys his own age to full adults, were busy sorting out a range of luxuriant outfits for him to wear at different times of day. They all stopped to bow when he entered the room, murmuring in respectful unison, 'Your Highness,' exactly as they had from the

8

beginning – but this time, the two boys closest to his age both snuck him real grins as they straightened.

Even world-weary seventeen-year-old Lord Lyffed, who was always publicly bored by *everything*, let his haughty features relax when Giles caught his eye and pointed to the elegant wooden box where the gilded deck of cards was kept.

'I'll finally win a game off you tonight before bed, Lyffed. Just wait and see!'

'Perhaps you shall,' said Lord Lyffed coldly … and then his lips twitched into a smile so small, it was *almost* impossible to see.

'When pigs fly!' said one of the younger boys, and a warm chorus of friendly laughter ran through the room, to Giles's delight.

Still grinning, he sailed through the next door and emerged into a second, much larger antechamber. There, four armed guards framed the four corners of the room, each standing tall, stern and unmoving under the painted dark eyes and triumphantly outswept wings of the massive ravens who covered the plaster ceiling. All the elegantly dressed ladies-in-waiting, though, were fluttering in an anxious, exclaiming crowd around a fiercely scowling girl in a nightdress who stood in the centre of the room with a red squirrel standing upright and chittering loudly on her shoulder.

'Good morning, Ros,' Giles said cheerfully to his triplet sister, over the combined noise of human and animal agitation. 'Did you find yourself a new pet too?'

'It's not funny.' As Rosalind pushed through the crowd to meet him, the red squirrel shifted to crouch on the back of her neck, hanging on to her short black hair with its sharp foreclaws. Its bushy copper tail twitched warningly back and forth as it glowered at the world around her. 'This rodent chewed half of the string off my bow!'

'Has it ever struck you that some people manage to sleep at night *without* keeping dangerous weapons in their beds?'

'My bow isn't dangerous to *me*.' Rosalind rolled her eyes. 'It's only dangerous to intruders.'

'Oh, really?' Giles smirked at the squirrel over Rosalind's shoulder. 'Your latest intruder apparently found it delicious.'

'Your Highnesses!' Their sister's official Mistress of the Bedchamber, Lady Hastings, bustled up and burst into their conversation as if she couldn't hold back her feelings any longer. 'Neither of you needs to worry about dangerous intruders! We have trained *guards* to deal with that sort of thing. You see?' She pointed to the closest corner, where a heavily armed woman gave them a sharp, respectful nod.

Giles gave her a friendly smile in return.

Rosalind glared at her. 'I can take care of myself.'

'But you don't have to. Not any more. You're a *princess* now!' Lady Hastings shook her head. 'It's just terrible that you were forced to fend for yourself in the wild, but that's all over now, thank goodness. You'll never need to do any fighting again!'

Rosalind's face reddened to nearly the same colour as her squirrel's fur. The comparison was hilarious – but, mindful of their observers, Giles swiftly grabbed her arm and steered her safely away from Lady Hastings, towards Cordy's closed bedroom doors at the far end of the room. 'It's been lovely to see all of you again, but just now—'

'Oh, but you mustn't disturb Her Majesty!' Lady Hastings swooped past them, flapping like a startled swan. 'She hasn't announced herself to us yet for the morning!'

'Don't worry.' Giles gave her an easy smile as he edged past. 'We'll announce ourselves to her instead.'

'No!' Lady Hastings flung herself before the closed doors, spreading her arms wide until her fashionably long, drooping sleeves hung like a rippling shield of purple velvet. 'Your Highnesses, with the very deepest respect, I *cannot* allow you to disturb Her Majesty's slumber! I am her Mistress of the Bedchamber. I must fulfil my duties! No visitors until she rises.'

Giles's eyebrows rose. 'But—'

'We're not visitors,' Rosalind snarled. 'She's our sister.' Her right hand dropped to the waist of her nightdress, as if seeking the sword that she so often carried. 'You can't stop us from seeing her!'

'Ros …' Giles hissed. Not everything had to be a battle!

'She is the *queen*,' declared Lady Hastings. 'No matter what your relationship may have been before Her Majesty took the throne—'

'*May have been?*'

Giles cringed. 'If we could all, please, just take a moment and—'

The outer door slammed open like a thunderclap as a new visitor swept into the room. 'What in the world is going on in here?' Giles's mother demanded.

Giles's shoulders slumped in mingled relief and resignation as the ladies-in-waiting gasped, the guards stiffened, and Lady Hastings visibly gulped. *So much for settling all this calmly.*

'Your Grace.' Paling, Lady Hastings swept into a deep curtsey. 'I'm afraid Her Majesty hasn't woken yet.'

'Then we had better wake her.' Mother strode briskly across the floor. 'She has to meet with the Council of Dukes in two hours, and I need to meet with her myself, first.'

Lady Hastings looked anguished. 'If she had only mentioned your appointment to me last night—'

'Her Majesty,' said Mother dryly, 'is only twelve years of age. I think you'll have to grant her a bit of leeway when it comes to remembering all the details of her schedule.' Raising her eyebrows, she gave the Mistress of the Bedchamber an expectant look from her fierce dark eyes. 'Well?'

For one anguished moment, Lady Hastings held firm.

Even here in the fortress of Raven's Roost, the centre of power for the kingdom of Corvenne, there were very few people who could out-stare Giles's mother … and even fewer who were brave enough to try. After all, she'd been known to the whole kingdom for more than a decade as a wicked and terrible enchantress.

Giles hated those old stories. Mother might be a powerful enchantress, but she was only really *terrible* when it came to singing. If only she'd try to act at least a *bit* sweet and harmless now that Cordy was finally queen! The last thing his family needed was for any of the courtiers to spread even more lies about all of them.

The truth was more than troublesome enough.

All throughout history, the rightful Raven Queens and Kings of Corvenne had bound themselves to the ancient spirits of the land when they'd each put on the magical Raven Crown. Each ruler had wielded the spirits' powerful land magic in exchange for their own promise to protect the kingdom.

Independent human sorcery, though? *That* was considered far more worrying. Until now, it had only ever been officially wielded by the six dukes' own few hired magic-workers, and even then only under the dukes' strict supervision.

That was why Giles had stopped practising his own magic on the very same day that he'd given up singing in public. As the Duke of Lune had so patiently explained, his family's powers made everyone nervous. It was far safer to forget that he had ever had them, for the sake of keeping the peace.

Mother would never pretend to be weak, though, no matter how sensible or diplomatic that might be – and as Giles watched, Lady Hastings slumped in defeat.

'Of course, Your Grace.' Bowing her head, the Mistress of the Bedchamber stepped away from the doors.

'Ha!' said Rosalind, who had no tact. The squirrel on her neck chittered in noisy agreement.

Giles gave Lady Hastings a sympathetic smile as his mother and sister strode past her, the squirrel's bushy red tail swishing tauntingly in their wake. *I'll fix this later*, he promised himself. He'd just make certain to chat with her again later in the day and listen, for the fourth time so far, to that story she loved about her older son's jousting triumph. *That* always seemed to cheer her up a bit.

Still turning over plans and strategies, he trailed a few steps behind Mother and Rosalind as he strolled into his queenly sister's bedroom …

And then he came to a dead halt, the breath choking in his throat as all his plans evaporated.

Cordy's body lay still and prone on the bed, wrapped in loving chains of ivy as usual … but the ivy had turned ominously brown and brittle-looking, and his sister wasn't sleeping after all.

2

Before she became the Raven Queen, Cordelia had been free to fly as a hawk or run as a wolf through the wild forests. Her own shape had been endlessly adaptable until she had traded it for the vast land magic of the kingdom, rooting herself forever to mend the crown, heal the land and save her family.

Now, she was trapped.

Numbing cold shot up from the roots of her spirit, far below her physical bed, and froze her limbs into place. The paralysing cold clenched the muscles of her jaw together. It stopped the movement of air in her lungs.

She couldn't move. She couldn't breathe. She couldn't—

'Cordelia!'

Heat exploded around her with the force of her

mother's magic. The paralysis snapped, and Cordelia's eyes flew open. Mother's face loomed above her, looking both angry and frightened. The echo of the spell that Mother must have used to wake her still lingered in the air, sparking with pins and needles like the aftermath of lightning.

Cordelia gasped for breath and struggled to sit upright, pushing away strands of dead, brown ivy. It was *wrong*, just like everything else about how her body was feeling.

How could this ivy look so ancient and forlorn? It had only grown overnight!

Panicky, inhuman voices filled her head in a chaotic, wordless jumble as the land of Corvenne reacted to whatever had just happened. *I'll talk to you later*, she promised all the different frightened pieces of her kingdom. Then she shoved her inner shields safely back into place to muffle their distracting, overwhelming cacophony. Nowadays, nothing felt more natural – or more comforting – than communing with the land that had chosen her as its champion. Still, she'd had to learn to block it out with mental shields, when necessary, to allow herself to pay attention to her surroundings and survive the perils of her royal court.

'Was that a dream?' she finally asked out loud.

'That was no dream.' Mother bit off the words. 'That was an attack – and if we hadn't arrived in time, it might well have succeeded.'

'An attack?' And *that* voice, unfortunately, belonged to Lady Hastings; Cordelia had grown to know that anxious, interfering sound all too well over the past six weeks.

Cordelia sighed and slumped back against the massive headboard as her Mistress of the Bedchamber surged into view. Beyond Lady Hastings, Giles was hanging back, looking pale and shaken, while Rosalind was braced in a defensive position at the end of the bed, ready to take on any invaders … except, unfortunately, this latest one.

When Cordelia had first accepted the Raven Crown, she'd never imagined that it would mean accepting a nosy group of strangers bustling and fussing around her all the time. But according to Mother, Alys, and everyone else who'd spent any time at court in the past, separating each family member into a different official household – and letting a noisy flock of ladies-in-waiting roost outside Cordelia's bedroom, crowding in between her and all the people she loved – was an unchangeable part of being royal. It was simply *the way things had always been done*, and she would have to get used to it if she wanted to be queen.

Sometimes, it was hard to remember why that sacrifice was worth it.

'You think Her Majesty was *attacked*?' Lady Hastings demanded. 'In her own bed, without any of us overhearing? Impossible!'

'Not now, Lady Hastings. Just this once, our family needs to be alone.' Mother didn't bother to look back as she spoke, her hawk-like gaze busy inspecting every inch of the bed around Cordelia. 'Send for Her Majesty's brother the Duke of Harcourt and Lady Alys, immediately – but don't speak a word of this to anyone else.'

'Lady Alys? The mistress of *your* bedchamber?' Lady Hastings gave an outraged gasp. 'I am in charge of Her Majesty's bedchamber! I hardly think she—'

'*Immediately!*' Mother flung out her right hand. A gust of wind shot from her palm, pushing Lady Hastings firmly backwards across the rush-covered floor towards the open doorway and the crowded antechamber beyond.

'What—? *What*—? Of all the—!' The heavy doors slammed in Lady Hastings's face, closing her safely outside the room.

Cordelia's shoulders relaxed, and Rosalind gave a grunt of approval, but Giles groaned dramatically. 'Oh, *Mother*! If you had taken just a minute to be polite about it—'

Mother whirled around, looking as fierce as a cornered bear. 'Someone's tried to murder your sister in her bed! If you think I care a jot about being *polite* right now to any of these—'

'I'm fine!' Cordelia said hastily. 'I can breathe again now. It's all right.'

'It is *not all right*.' Power crackled in the air around Mother's body, a gathering storm of fury, waiting for any excuse to break. 'You were supposed to be *safe* on the throne, now that the Raven Crown has finally been mended. That was the only reason I ever agreed to this absurdly reckless—'

'**Mother**.' This time, Cordelia let all the voices of the land around her bleed into her own in eerie chorus, until her words echoed with the full power of Corvenne itself, and the stone walls of Raven's Roost shivered around her with the impact. '**It is *done*. I am the queen, for better or for worse. And it was never … your … decision!**'

They glared at each other for a long moment, as Mother's barely withheld sorcery charged the air around her and the land's magic waited, poised and ready, for Cordelia's command.

Then Giles said brightly, 'I forgot. There's someone here who wanted to see you!'

Hurrying forward, he deposited something small and warm on to Cordelia's quilt-covered legs. 'You see? He made a wrong turn along the way, but I promised I'd help him get here in the end.'

Cordelia tore her gaze away from her mother and took in the sight of the snuffling hedgehog climbing up her covers. 'She,' she told Giles as her shoulders relaxed. 'She's a girl.'

Why hadn't Cordelia ever thought to turn into a hedgehog, back when she could still shift her shape? She would have loved to have all those protective prickles at her command now, to hold off every demanding stranger who'd clustered around her ever since she'd mended the crown.

For the first twelve years of her life, she'd only known five other people in the entire world, and she'd *still* needed regular flights into the wild to stay steady and calm in herself. Now, she was hardly ever alone.

And she had almost been killed in her sleep.

At that thought, a sudden wave of shivers swept up her spine, almost too strong to control – but then the hedgehog waddled purposefully on to her stomach and she let out her breath in a sigh of relief, closing her eyes and leaning forward to lightly brush noses in greeting. *Thank you.*

It wasn't exactly that she could *speak* with animals now; they never spoke to her in human words. But ever since she'd made her binding pact with the ancient spirits of the land, a hum of connection had thrummed, bright and true, between her and all the natural creatures of the kingdom. She didn't need words to know that this hedgehog was taking comfort in her presence – and offering her the kind of comfort in return that she hadn't been able to ask for from anyone else since she had first put on the Raven Crown and had the security of her triplets' constant presence stolen away for good.

She almost never had time alone with either of them any more. Either her ladies-in-waiting or the older ones were always there. If she let her mother see now how badly her chest still hurt, or how much of that terrifying, paralysing chill still lingered deep within her – only waiting for its chance to sweep through her once again, this time freezing her for good – Mother would lose all control. Then the perilous balance of safety in this castle and the kingdom would be shattered.

Cordelia opened her eyes to find her sister looking at her with wry understanding from the foot of the bed. 'You might as well have the other one too,' Rosalind said gruffly, and reached back to pull a red squirrel from behind her neck. 'He's been fussing for you all morning.'

This squirrel really *was* a he. He leaped from Rosalind's calloused hands to race up the bed and plant himself triumphantly on Cordelia's shoulder, jeering down at the hedgehog.

'Stop that!' Cordelia told him. 'She's allowed to be here. You'll just have to share.' Still, she leaned her cheek against his for a long moment and let herself luxuriate in the silky softness of his fluffy tail against her skin, while the hedgehog sniffed happily around her cupped hands.

Like every animal she'd met in the last six weeks, these two found happiness in simply being with her; they thought if they were in her presence, they were safe.

That was the promise that she'd made to the ancient spirits of the land six weeks ago: to protect it, unlike the last several kings and queens, and to uphold the oldest contracts between humanity and nature for the sake of *all* the living creatures of Corvenne. Giles and Rosalind had added their own promises of support to seal the crown, but they all knew the greatest responsibility was hers.

Now here she was in this smothering, crowded castle, surrounded by powerful nobles who acted as if every attempt she made to protect the land or help the common folk of the kingdom was an outrageous personal attack – not to mention the gaggle of interfering ladies-in-waiting who never wanted to leave her alone for an instant.

Still, the creatures on top of her were the reminder she needed: there had been a reason she had made that promise in the first place. The wild creatures of Corvenne depended on her.

Just stay strong until everyone else leaves the room, she ordered herself. *It's not too long to wait.*

At that moment, the door burst open once again, and her older half-brother ran into the room, dark eyes wide with alarm in his light brown face and elegant green velvet tunic askew. For once, he looked distinctly young and unducal, despite the impressive new title Cordelia had given him six weeks earlier. 'What's happened to Cordelia?'

'I'm right here, Connall,' said Cordelia. 'I am *fine.*'

'She nearly died from a magical attack while she was sleeping,' Mother said.

Connall said, 'But all the protective wards and warnings that we set on the door and window and bed—'

'Haven't been touched. The attack must have come from some other direction.'

'But—'

'I'm *fine!*' Cordelia growled, loudly enough to make the hedgehog freeze in place on her lap, alert to sudden danger. The squirrel on her shoulder stood up tall to chatter in her defence – but beside her, her triplet brother let out a derisive snort.

'A few minutes ago, you couldn't even breathe!'

'Don't worry,' Rosalind told Connall, ignoring both Cordelia and Giles. 'I'll be sleeping in here from now on to keep her safe.'

Mother shook her head. 'That won't be necessary.'

'Oh, *thank you!*' Cordelia said fervently.

Her mother spoke over her. 'I'll be sleeping in here from now on, actually. And Cordelia will have someone with magical training by her side at every moment of every day.'

'What?' Cordelia's jaw dropped open. 'But—'

'I've *had* magical training!' Rosalind protested.

Mother rolled her eyes. 'Only three months' worth before you gave it up to play with swords.'

'I do *not*—'

'I can probably—' began Connall, frowning thoughtfully.

'*Stop it!*' Cordelia yelled at all of them. Panting, she glared from one member of her family to another as the tapestry-lined walls of her bedchamber squeezed tighter and tighter around her. '*No one's* staying with me for every minute of the day. I need time alone to breathe and to listen to the land!'

'And I need you not to be *dead,*' Mother snarled. 'So if you think I won't—'

The door opened before she could finish her threat, and Lady Alys stepped into the room.

Thank goodness.

Until a month ago, Cordelia had had no idea that Alys

25

was *Lady* Alys, nor that she was the sister of the powerful Duke of Arden (even if he was too stubborn to admit to their relationship any more). She was only *Alys*, the wiry, red-haired and wonderfully safe woman who'd helped to raise all four children as Mother's dearest friend and partner in everything. She had fled with Mother into hiding years ago, to keep infant Cordelia away from the battles over the throne.

Alys was entirely non-magical, strong, kind, reliable, and by far the most sensible person Cordelia knew. Better yet, *no one* could manage Cordelia's mother as effectively as she did. No matter how hysterical anyone else ever became, Alys could always be counted on to stay calm.

So it was a horrible shock when, after listening to the story of what had happened, Alys said, 'We'll be guarding her better from now on then?'

'Alys!' Cordelia stared at her, aghast at the betrayal. 'I *can't* have someone hovering over me all the time. You *know*—'

Alys fixed her with a steady green gaze. 'Do *you* know how they managed to attack you without setting off any of your mother's protective wards? Or who the attacker was?'

Cordelia swallowed. 'Well ...'

'It has to have been one of the other four dukes or else the Duchess of Solenne,' Giles said. 'Doesn't it?'

'Of course it does!' Mother took a quick, angry step, her gown whirling around her. 'Who else in this kingdom has a group of hired magicians at their command, to order a magical attack upon their queen? And who else could hope to seize the throne for themselves afterwards?'

'Hmm.' Connall crossed his arms, his eyes narrowing. 'The Duchess of Solenne went to war to fight for her nephew's claim to the throne through their family's alternate path of succession. She may have kept him out of sight ever since Cordelia mended the Raven Crown, but I'm sure she hasn't forgotten that scheme – and she's not the only one who could benefit from our sister's death. The Duke of Lune was expecting to rule Corvenne along with the Duke of Arden until Cordelia refused their regency – and Lune is the closest in *our* family's line of succession. He could easily seize the throne for himself if Cordelia was gone, without the power of the land to protect Giles or Rosalind.'

'Not to mention she's been antagonising the whole Council of Dukes at every turn,' Alys said grimly.

'What?' Cordelia stared at her. 'I have not—'

'Ah ...' Connall coughed. 'Cordelia,' he said gently, 'you must know how angry the others all are. Every council meeting we have is full of shouting.'

'That's only because the others are unreasonable!'

Connall sighed heavily. 'It's not that I disagree with you,' he said, 'but you *are* asking a good deal of them. You want to take away all the lands that they claimed in battle and hand them over to peasants they despise. Of course they're angry.'

'I'm just making them give back the land they stole.' Cordy looked to her triplets for support. '*You* remember all those displaced farmers who helped us when we were running for our lives. How could I not help them in return?'

Giles and Rosalind both nodded in agreement, but none of the adults in the room looked convinced.

'The point is, my girl,' said Alys heavily, 'you've spent the last six weeks doing a fine job of making enemies out of five of the most powerful nobles in Corvenne. T*hey* all had a grand old time dividing up the kingdom's power and treasures for decades without a hitch. Now, here you come with the power of the Raven Crown behind you, forcing them to answer to someone else for the first time in their lives. The question isn't *why* one of them wants you dead. The only question is *which one* is behind this attack – and how they managed it in the first place.'

'Please, Cordelia,' Connall said softly as he moved to stand beside her, tall and steadily protective. 'Can you remember anything about the way it started? We need to work out how they managed to attack you without setting off my or Mother's protections – or being prevented by the land itself.'

Cordelia didn't want to remember. She never wanted to think about it again.

But for the sake of her gentle older brother, and under his patient gaze, she took a deep breath and forced herself to think back to that awful, terrifying moment when the cold force had seized her in her sleep.

'Actually …' She frowned, trying to think through the haze of remembered helplessness and fear. 'I'm not sure I *was* the one being attacked.'

'Oh, for goodness' sake!' Mother threw up her hands in despair.

Connall's voice was steady as he put one hand on the mattress beside Cordelia, his dark brown gaze intent. 'What do you mean, you weren't attacked? Everyone saw—'

'I mean, I don't think the attack was *aimed* at me. I felt something …' She ran to a halt, breathing hard. She'd never been good with words like Giles; wordless, animal communication was just so much easier! And on that instinctive level, it felt deeply dangerous to let herself think too much or too carefully about this – because even though Mother's spell had woken her, that paralysing cold had *not* been fully banished. She could feel it, still malevolently lurking deep inside her bones; it felt horribly possible that she might unleash it and sink back into its grasp.

Still, she looked up at her older brother, who had braved so much over the years to protect her, and she made herself keep on trying.

'It felt as if the attack hit something else first,' she said, 'somewhere deep underneath me, and then it caught me like an echo. It came from so deep underground, it felt as if it were coming from the roots of the castle itself.'

'So you're saying the attacker was underground?' Connall's frown deepened.

'I don't know. I think the attack might have happened there. But I felt something else too. Something *really* old.' She could almost taste it again for one fleeting moment – an ancient, inexplicable sense of *presence* in her head that was subtly different from the jostling voices of the land that she heard every day.

Different but ... somehow linked?

Then the memory was gone, leaving her shivering with aftershock and exhaustion ... and even the voices of the land, muffled behind her mental shields, sounded strangely fainter than usual. Cold crept at the edge of her consciousness, trying to suck her back down into its darkness. 'I can't tell you any more.' Cordelia sighed, massaging her aching forehead, as the hedgehog burrowed protectively against her stomach and the squirrel stood guard upon her shoulder. 'It's all a haze.'

Maybe the land could tell her more, if she asked. She needed time to be alone and quiet with it first, though, to actually *listen* and hear its answers.

If her family ever let her have any breathing space again.

'So, there's still only one thing we know.' Alys crossed her thin arms, her pale face set and grim. 'However this attack took place, at least one of the dukes or the duchess was behind it – and *you* are due to face the Council of Dukes in less than two hours. You tell me, young lady. Does it not make sense to strengthen our guard?'

Cordelia's throat closed tight enough to choke her.

She looked around at her family: the five stubborn people she loved most in the world, all united, for once, and waiting for her to admit the truth out loud.

'I *am* the queen now, you know,' Cordelia finally muttered.

Alys rolled her eyes. Rosalind made a rude gesture. Giles smirked. One corner of Connall's mouth quirked upward, while their mother let out an exasperated sigh.

'As you say,' said Alys, '*Your Majesty*. Now let's tidy you up so you look less like a haystack when you meet with the subjects who most want to murder you.'

3

Rosalind *knew* she should have put on her sword-belt before leaving her room that morning, no matter what her ladies-in-waiting might have said. Still, she'd spent years training to become a knight, using sticks instead of swords in the enchanted forest where she and her triplets had lived their first twelve years. She was more than capable of defending her sister even without a standard weapon ... if only any of the adults in the room would let her.

'Go on,' Alys ordered as she nudged Rosalind firmly towards the door. 'Get dressed and make yourself look like the respectable princess you are now.'

Rosalind dug in her heels, her gaze still fixed on Cordy, who looked much too pale as she stroked the animals on top of her and argued in a low voice with Connall and their mother. 'I can stay here and guard—'

'We have plenty of guards already.' Alys put one hand under her chin to firmly divert her gaze. 'Trust me, young lady. I know you've had a fright – we all have – but you can relax now and let the adults take care of this. Your mother and older brother will take care of the spell-work, and your sister's soldiers will do the rest. All *you* have to do is go and enjoy yourself with your ladies-in-waiting. Who knows? You might even like them, if you gave them half a chance.'

'But—'

'Come on, Ros.' Giles slid her a wink out of Alys's sight. 'I'll walk you to your rooms.'

'As if I need help finding the way.' Despite her grumbling, Rosalind fell into step beside him as they opened the door together, leaving Cordy and their wild visitors behind. She tried not to let herself feel guilty when the red squirrel sent an angry chitter after her. She *wasn't* abandoning anyone, no matter how it felt. She knew both of her triplets, even now. That hidden wink meant that Giles had a plan.

She only hoped that it would involve bashing someone, *hard*. It had been so long since she'd had the opportunity. She wasn't even allowed to practise sword-fighting with Mother's magical shadows any more!

Unfortunately, her least favourite people in the world were all lying in wait for her in her own antechamber, less than twenty feet away in the crowded honeycomb of interconnected royal rooms. Worse yet, her distractible brother seemed to have already forgotten what mattered.

'What are you thinking?' she whispered under her breath to Giles as he waved and grinned to all their sister's ladies-in-waiting. He kept on calling out greetings and friendly small talk as they walked, as if it were any ordinary morning at Raven's Roost. 'Are we going to sneak back around, or—?'

'Shh,' he whispered back, even as he smiled and nodded at the servant who pulled open the next door. 'Before anything else, we're going to do exactly what Alys wanted. We'll dress to look like the fabulous prince and princess that we are.'

'You want to preen like a peacock *now*?' She slowed her walk to a trudge, grabbing hold of his arm to keep him by her side as they passed into Mother's antechamber, already much too close to her own. 'I know you like showing off your new wardrobe, but—'

'I'm doing it for a *reason*,' he said. 'Trust me! Just get dressed and meet me alone at the east stairwell. You tell your ladies that Mother wants you for some private lessons, and I'll tell my gentlemen the same. That way, no one will dare to come with us – and we can go on a hunt for answers.'

Finally, a plan that made sense! 'Fine.' Rosalind nodded sharply, bracing herself for the room and the confrontation ahead. 'You can turn around now.'

'I don't mind walking you all the way to your room – all right, all right!' He put up his hands in mock surrender as she narrowed her eyes ominously at him. 'The mighty Princess Ros shall walk everywhere on her own! No *one* could ever be allowed to imagine that she needed any help from her puny brother!'

Ha. He had *no* idea what she was really thinking ... which was exactly what she wanted. None of her family could ever find out, or the humiliation would be unbearable.

Rosalind waited for him to finish cheerfully greeting Mother's ladies-in-waiting and finally turn around before she squared her shoulders and strode forward.

Enough. Everything was going to change *today*!

Rosalind had tried so hard to be what her family and the kingdom needed. She'd sworn to the ancient spirits of the land that she would support her sister's reign, so for the last six weeks, she'd done everything that had been asked of her. She'd followed the stupid royal rules, worn nothing but awkward, floor-length courtly dresses, and smiled over her clenched teeth – for *what*?

None of it had protected Cordy after all ... which

meant she wouldn't put up with it for a single minute longer, no matter what any of the adults around her expected.

'I need leggings and a tunic. *Now!*' She snarled the command as she strode into her antechamber, before anyone else could say a word. *Strike before your enemies can attack!* It was one of the first lessons she'd learned in her martial training.

Unfortunately, her enemies here used weapons she'd never been taught.

'*Leggings*, Your Highness? Really?' Her Mistress of the Bedchamber, Lady Fauvre, was tall, willowy and effortlessly elegant, and as she gracefully rose from her seat in the centre of an admiring crowd of ladies-in-waiting, she spoke with a sickly-sweet tone of amusement that scalded Rosalind's skin. 'I'm sure you don't really mean that. Even you couldn't be *that* ignorant of courtly fashion! Perhaps you've got your words mixed up again? We all understand how tricky it is for a girl of *your* background—'

'I know exactly what I'm saying.' Rosalind braced her bare feet on the floor, ignoring the heat that was creeping up her skin under all those avid, hungry gazes. 'I want to wear something that lets me *move*.' How else could she hunt down Cordy's enemies – or fight off the next attack? 'If you don't give me the clothes I want, I'll rip the skirts of all my gowns right now to make *them* work.'

'No!' Lady Fauvre's forget-me-not-blue eyes flared with sudden alarm as she started forward, all her followers among the other ladies-in-waiting twitching and whispering behind her. 'Princess Rosalind, even *you* could never be so brutish as to ruin those lovely, priceless gowns!'

Oh, yes, I could. Rosalind crossed her strong – oh, fine, *brutish* – arms and let cold steel fill her chest, just as she would if she were preparing for any other battle.

She'd never understood, before she'd left her family's home, just how much damage could be done by a poison-tipped tongue. She'd never learned how to defend herself against the kind of attack that slid under her skin with a smile and made her burn with misery and self-doubt every time.

She'd never been surrounded by people who truly *loathed* her before.

Nothing mattered more than her family's safety, though, so she'd endured it for six agonising weeks – and now, she finally let herself stand firm. 'I won't have to ruin the dresses if I'm given what I've ordered.'

Lady Fauvre, draped in expensive silks from head to toe and scented like a delicate rose, stared down at Rosalind. Rosalind, small, stocky, and bare-legged under her thin nightgown, glared back up at her, unmoving.

Between them, unspoken, lay every mocking word and careless sneer that Lady Fauvre had tossed at her for weeks, whenever Rosalind's family hadn't been there to overhear it.

But one other truth sat between them too: everyone in the room knew perfectly well that Lady Fauvre was not allowed to openly refuse any order given by Rosalind in public.

At last, Lady Fauvre sighed and dipped a shallow curtsey. 'Within ten minutes, Your Highness,' she said, her voice sour. 'Of course.'

Rosalind kept the scowl on her face, but she had to half run to her bedroom door to reach it in time. She shut it firmly behind herself just before her legs finally gave out with relief.

She'd actually won the first battle. She could do this! All she had to do was gather up the weapons that were still waiting for her despite every attempt Lady Fauvre had made to wrest them from her.

The very day of the battle that had won her sister's crown, a mysterious benefactor had sent Rosalind a glorious crossbow and quiver of arrows to accompany the sword that she'd won in an earlier combat. Unfortunately, she'd made the mistake of leaving her sword, bow and arrows in the big cedar chest that sat beside her bed on the first night that she'd slept here in Raven's Roost. The next morning, she'd woken to find them all missing and Lady Fauvre fluttering her eyelashes in sweet-voiced confusion.

'But, Your Highness, it never occurred to me – how could it? – that any true princess would ever wish to keep such common, unladylike things!'

Rosalind had bellowed so loudly that day that Mother had heard from her own chambers and stepped in – and Lady Fauvre had never again attempted outright theft. From that day onward, though, Rosalind had slept with her weapons safely tucked up with her on her mattress or else buried in a secret compartment underneath her bed whenever she had to leave the room without them.

That was the day she'd first learned that she and her weapons weren't safe in this castle, any more than her comfortable old clothes had been. By the time she'd woken on that first morning, Lady Fauvre had ordered all her tunics and leggings to be burned as 'rubbish'. Rosalind had been furious – but at least she had taken comfort, back then, that Cordy and the rest of their family were out of danger.

She wouldn't make that mistake again.

The door opened exactly ten minutes later, just as Rosalind was scooping up the first unbearably stiff brocade over-gown, laced with glittering gold thread and pearls, to make good on her promise. It was far too thick to pull apart with bare hands, even with strong muscles; luckily, she had more than her own physical strength to work with.

Mother was wrong to think that she'd forgotten all her magic. Out in the mountains and on the battleground outside this city, she had finally learned how to use it in a fight. She hadn't called upon her power for weeks, not since that final battle had drained all her magical reserves. They'd had more than enough time to refill in the meantime. Now they rose within her with an exhilarating tingle that raced across her skin, gathering power in her arms as the door swung open.

Lady Fauvre stood in the doorway, arms empty.

Let the battle commence.

'Where are my clothes?' Rosalind demanded through gritted teeth.

'Don't be absurd.' Lady Fauvre let out a scornful huff of air as she stepped into the room, closing the door behind her ... so that no one else could hear them. 'I thought it best to give you time to calm down from your little temper tantrum, Your Highness. Now that you have, though, I expect you'll want to apologise to everyone for how embarrassing—'

Ri-i-ip!

With magic roaring through her grasp, the over-gown

ripped so easily that Rosalind wondered why she hadn't done it weeks ago.

Rip! Seed pearls went flying. So much for all those nit-picky royal rules!

'You bumptious little fool!' Out of sight of all her admiring followers, Lady Fauvre's ever-present smile finally disappeared, her face contorting with rage. 'Do you have *any notion* of how much money each of those gowns costs?'

Rip!

'Do you know how many people have killed and died for the *chance* to stand where you are now, you *ungrateful little peasant*?'

Rip! Rosalind wouldn't back down. Not this time.

'Do you really think you're fooling anyone?' Lady Fauvre stalked closer, her voice hissing through the air. 'I knew from the first moment I saw you that you don't deserve to call yourself a real princess. *Everyone* knows it, no matter how hard you try! You are *laughable*. You're an embarrassment to this whole kingdom!'

Rosalind wouldn't let words hurt her any more. She *would not*. Breathing hard, she grabbed the second dress from the pile. *Rip!*

'Oh, *you* may not be clever enough to care what the finest families in Corvenne all think of you, but do you really imagine the rest of your family *doesn't*? How long do you think they'll keep you here if you make fools of them as well?'

Rosalind's hands shook so hard, she lost control of her magic. It scattered, draining away from her skin, and the cloth in her grip held firm, refusing to rip.

'My family would *never* send me away,' she gritted.

'You are so naive.' Lady Fauvre's nostrils flared with disdain. 'Even after all this time, you still don't have *any idea* what it takes to be royal, do you? It's not enough to claim the crown. You have to show everyone that you deserve to keep it. Your sister has the power of the land. Your brothers, at least, understand how to behave in public. But you?'

Her lips curved into a derisive smirk as she looked Rosalind up and down. 'Perhaps if you'd grown up at court, you would have been trained as the rest of us all were in preparation for the moment we might be called upon to lead. But as it is … it's like putting one of Her Majesty's wild animals in a dress. You're not fooling *anybody*.'

It took every ounce of Rosalind's strength not to double over at that blow.

A *wild animal in a dress* …

No one outside her own family knew about her true origins. No one! And yet …

'You can't even argue, can you?' Lady Fauvre shook her head gently. 'Even *you* know it's the truth.'

Rosalind bit down so hard on her lower lip that it went numb. But her stupid, frantic heart refused to do the same. It just kept on pumping panic and despair through her transformed-again, no-longer-good-enough body.

'Maybe you *were* of some use to the rest of them out in the wilds,' Lady Fauvre said softly, 'but what use do you think you will be now if you can't even try to fit in?'

If she'd attacked with a sword, Rosalind could have defended against it. But Rosalind had no words to fight back with now, only memories and images that had been burned into her brain.

Only six and a half weeks ago, on the magical, mist-covered slopes of Mount Corve, she and her triplets had uncovered their family's deepest and darkest secret: she and Giles had both been born as wild animals but transformed into humans to keep their newborn royal sister safely hidden in their midst.

She *had* only become a part of her family in the first place to keep the others safe. That was the goal of every single transformation that had been enacted on her … and no one had ever asked her permission.

What would they do now if she finally took a stand and refused to be the princess they all wanted?

43

Mother loves me. Our family loves each other. The words whispered, sweet and hopeful, at the edge of her consciousness ... but they slipped away like broken dreams under Lady Fauvre's contemptuous gaze.

The heavy gown slipped from her fingers to the bed.

'I thought so.' Lady Fauvre's lips curled. 'I'll leave you to tidy up your own mess, *Your Highness*. Just call once you've finished and you're ready to be dressed in a proper gown – with none of your little play-weapons attached to it, if you please – so we can all carry on with this charade a little longer.'

4

Giles knew he was on show whenever he stepped out of his bedroom. That was why he was so grateful for his helpful new costumes, like the rich-blue velvet doublet, studded with pearl buttons, that he wore now with luxuriantly quilted breeches, diamond-patterned hose, and a single pearl earring that dangled from one earlobe. He looked magnificent, like the perfect prince, and usually, he rather enjoyed performing the role.

Now, though, as he waited for Ros by the busy grand staircase, he had to force his legs to stay still and his lips to smile instead of letting himself physically shrink from the nobles and servants who passed him on their way to or from the maze of royal rooms. Worse yet, several stayed, loitering in casual groups on the broad landing, to watch him like an animal in a menagerie. Of course, they all smiled and bowed to him as they passed … but who knew how many of them might have secretly been part of this morning's murderous attack?

Cordy had looked so pale and still on her bed, as if she were already—

No! He jerked his mind back from that image, fingers rattling a frantic beat against one leg. It was the rhythm of a song he couldn't possibly let out in public – *especially* not now, when his family was already in danger. Still, the wild tune seemed to vibrate through his skin in its urgency to get free, to gather up all the fear and the horror that he'd felt and turn it into beauty. The magic that he'd tried so hard to forget for weeks now was whispering in his ears once again, suggesting all the different ways that he could share his song with the world around him, just as he'd shared a different song six weeks earlier. T*hat* song, a call for peace, magically amplified, had brought hundreds of soldiers to their knees, weeping, on the battlefield.

It had felt so right, his music and magic finally mingling as one …

But my family needs a prince, not a bard!

Giles tipped his head back, struggling to swallow down the powerful surge of music and magic, and found dark, knowing eyes unexpectedly staring back at him from a shadowy corner.

I *should have known*. Giles huffed out a laugh as he shook his head in baffled recognition. Even here, in the middle of a simple thoroughfare, yet more ravens had been sneakily painted into the nooks and crannies of the archway overhead. Whoever had built and named this castle Raven's Roost – not to mention naming the Raven Throne, the Raven Crown, the kingdom of Corvenne itself *and* Raven's Nest, where the ancient spirits of the land kept their deepest secrets safe on the mist-protected slopes of Mount Corve – had been *obsessed*.

There were so many different animals in the world. Over a dozen different types had visited Cordy since her coronation. Couldn't the designers of this castle have used at least a *bit* of variety in their decorating plan? A hedgehog or a squirrel here or there? Symbolism was one thing, but—

'What are you grinning about?' Ros's tone was hardly friendly as she stepped up beside him, but Giles didn't mind. Ros *always* got grumpy whenever she'd been scared.

When he turned and saw her expression, though, he sucked in a breath. His sister's usually ruddy face was a sickly pale above her elegantly ruffed bronze gown, and her brown eyes looked wounded. 'What's happened to you?' He started forward.

She jerked back before his fingers could touch her. 'Nothing!' She clenched her square jaw. 'What could have happened? Just ... *you know.*' She tipped her head meaningfully in the direction of their sister's chambers.

Ros had always been a terrible liar. 'Don't be stupid.' She'd been fine when they'd left Cordy's room together. 'Did you hurt yourself? Is that why you're not carrying your sword? Or—'

'I'm *fine.*' She gritted out the words. 'Are you ready to start our hunt or not?'

Giles could feel the hungry interest of their onlookers intensifying with every moment they spent arguing in public. 'All right.' His breath whistled out in a sigh. 'But I *will* find out the truth later, and you know it.'

'Hmph.' Snorting, she started marching down the stairs ahead of him ... which was utterly typical of *both* of his sisters.

'*I'm* the one who knows where we're going, remember?' Rolling his eyes, Giles darted around her down the broad stone steps to lead the way himself.

The truth was, he still hadn't seen most of Raven's Roost, even after a month and a half of living here. This castle was hundreds of years old, and it sprawled across the highest point of the busy capital city, its massive wings stretching wide on either side of its hulking main body, and its high towers punching towards the sky. Before Cordy had claimed the throne, Mother had been held prisoner by the Dukes of Lune and Arden in one of those tiny tower rooms, her magic stifled by a wickedly enchanted golden collar made by one of Lune's mages. Giles remembered *that* sight only too well.

Ever since they'd freed her, though, the family had spent almost all their time in the luxuriant third storey – the *royal* storey – of the outspread east wing. Only the family and their personal attendants were allowed private rooms there; all the nobles with apartments of their own in the castle were spread across the other storeys and wings, along with multiple dining halls, dozens of reception chambers, and so much more. He had no idea of what went on in most of them.

Luckily, his Master of the Bedchamber *did* – and something that Wincester said earlier had given Giles the perfect idea for where to start hunting for clues about Cordy's attack. He'd casually teased out directions while being helped into his princely attire, so now he led his sister confidently down the first wide flight of steps and through the grand, echoing banquet hall, where they would eat supper later. Half a dozen servants were busy laying fresh mats made of rushes across the vast stone floor. With a smile and a nod, Giles strode briskly past them all and then through a whole succession of tapestry-lined reception rooms and smaller, curving stairways.

'Are you *sure* you know where we're going?' Ros

muttered as they started up the third stairway. This one was barely wide enough for them to walk side by side, and a low din of conversation emanated through the walls from a room nearby.

'Trust me.' After all the years he'd spent memorising lengthy ballads from Mother's precious books, a simple list of directions wasn't a challenge to remember. Giles pushed open the door at the next landing and strode into a long, sunlit room lined with windows and full of tables covered with inkwells and scrolls. Black-clad scribes took up every seat at every table, heads lowered and pens scratching busily as they copied out new laws, proclamations and leaflets to be distributed across the kingdom of Corvenne. A silver-belted supervisor on a stool in the far corner bowed deeply at Giles and Ros's entrance, but the scribes all kept their heads down, quill pens racing without a pause.

Giles loved that busy hum. It set off a lively rhythm in his chest, bright and confident and full of purpose. He and Ros were on a quest once again, and just like their last quest, to Raven's Nest on Mount Corve, this quest would *definitely* end in a ballad-worthy triumph. How could it not?

At the far side of the room, he pushed open the door with a flourish. 'Ta-da!' he carolled as he gestured his sister through.

Then he froze as he took in the symbol that faced him from only fifteen feet away.

To his left, a deep and dusty cavern of a room, dimly lit and filled with the scent of ageing ink and paper, was stacked high with wooden drawers, like a shadowy forest of records marching into the distance. He'd found the castle's famous archives, just as Wincester had promised – but straight ahead, the next door bore the House of Solenne's snarling boar on a blood-red pennant. It hung like a warning against the chambers ahead, revealed by the rich but flickering lights of a single brace of candles set in a sconce on the right-hand wall.

Suddenly, he wished that Ros had brought her sword after all.

'We're interrogating the duchess? Excellent!' Ros started forward with a swagger in her step, sounding more cheerful than she had in weeks.

'Don't you dare!' Giles grabbed her arm to hold her back. 'We're not going anywhere near that door.'

Six weeks ago, the Duchess of Solenne had led an allied army against their family, fighting for her nephew to become the Raven King. Giles would never forget the sight of her towering figure striding across that battlefield, topped with a spiked helmet, brandishing a brutal axe – and bellowing the order for the lethal cloud of arrows that had shot directly at him and his sisters. All three of them would be dead now if Ros hadn't used her martial magic and her sword-play to hold those arrows off in a ferocious blur of motion.

Giles still found himself dreaming, far too often, about the terrible moment when he'd first seen the arrows coming at them – and then he'd lie awake for hours afterwards every time, panting and staring up at the high canopy of his bed in the darkness, fighting to believe that it was over and they were safe at last.

If it were up to him, he'd never come within ten feet of the duchess again, but Ros stared at him as if he'd spoken gibberish. 'I thought we were on a hunt for answers.'

'We are!' Giles flung out his free arm to indicate the towering stacks of wooden drawers. 'We're looking in *there* – the castle archives.'

'You brought me all the way here to visit a *library*?' Ros's voice rose with mounting outrage. 'Our sister's in mortal danger, and you want to sit around *reading*?'

'Shh!' Giles hissed, his gaze darting frantically around them. He couldn't *see* anyone between those dim and shadowy stacks, but who knew how many of the duchess's guards might be lurking on the far side of that door? The last thing they needed was for anyone even *remotely* connected to the duchess to overhear them and guess what was going on. He lowered his voice to an urgent whisper. 'Don't you remember what Cordy said about the attack? She said it started deep underneath the castle with something *really old*.'

'So?' Ros shrugged, frowning.

'Well, Wincester told me that the archivist has scrolls here that are hundreds of years old. Some of them were written even before Raven's Roost was built! This is the *perfect* place to find out what kind of ancient magical weapons might be hidden underneath our feet.'

'You think Cordy was talking about a weapon?' Ros's eyebrows rose with sudden interest.

'Well—'

'Your Highnesses.' A woman's calm voice spoke just behind them, and Giles spun around, letting out an embarrassing squeak of surprise.

A small, grey-haired woman with dark brown skin and a midnight-blue gown had stepped out from the shadows between two stacks of drawers, her hands clasped before her. Humour glinted in her brown eyes, but her tone remained gentle. 'Forgive me for intruding upon your private conversation. I am Margotte, the archivist. May I be of any service to you?'

Ros began, 'I still think it would be faster to—'

'No.' They were *not* going to charge into the terrifying

Duchess of Solenne's family quarters and start interrogating her without any protection, *especially* when no one else knew where they had gone!

Giles's face was still hot with embarrassment, but he drew a deep breath and pasted on his best performer's smile as he stepped swiftly between his sister and the archivist. 'Thank you! Yes, we would appreciate your help. We've heard so much about your wonderful archives.' Thank goodness he was a good four inches taller than Ros; with luck, the archivist wouldn't even glimpse her expression. 'We were hoping to find the answers to a few small questions.'

'Of course I'll be delighted to help.' Margotte tilted her head, and polished onyx beads glinted from within her tight grey curls. 'What sort of questions did you have?'

'It's … well, it's really just curiosity. We'd like to learn more about Raven's Roost, now that it's our home. Do you have any of the old, original plans from when it was first built? Maps of all its, ah, underground cellars and so forth?'

Margotte's eyebrows rose. 'Raven's Roost has been expanded time and time again across the centuries. Would you like to see all the different plans that were used by different rulers and their architects? It should only take a few days for me to find and prepare them all for you.'

A *few days*? If they didn't work out what was happening soon, Cordy might well be attacked again.

'What about the very oldest plan of all?' Giles fought to keep his voice light instead of desperate. 'How long would it take you to find just that one?'

'So you're interested in the deepest history! Well, in that case ...' Smiling, Margotte gestured them forward into the shadowy walkway between the closest stacks. There were dark, painted patterns on the tiles of the floor, but Giles couldn't make them out in the dim light. 'You're in luck. There's someone here who's been poring over those very oldest scrolls for over a month now. I must confess, it has been twenty years or more since I last made any careful study of them myself, but this young man should be able to guide you to exactly the right section of my archives. If you'll just follow the path towards the north-west corner ...'

Ros shouldered past Giles without a word to step before him into the shadows. This time, he didn't argue; there was never any point in trying to dissuade Ros from guard-duty whenever she thought there might be peril. She strode forward, shoulders squared and one hand falling to her hip where her sword would usually be fastened to a makeshift belt.

Even without her sword, Ros still had her magic and all her skills. With his sister on alert, Giles had no fear of any attackers surprising him within those shadows. Still, he couldn't let go of another worry. *'Young man?'* he repeated as he trailed behind Ros, looking back at Margotte. 'What do you mean … ?'

'Wait. What's *he* doing here?' Ros's outraged voice boomed through the shadows. She was already out of sight.

Giles broke into a run.

At the far end of the winding pathway through the stacks, sunlight broke over a wide, clear area of the room. Floor-to-ceiling windows lit the archivist's small bed, tucked neatly into the left-hand corner, a small wooden desk in the centre, and a large round table with warm, natural light …

… and exposed the tall, blond boy scrambling to his feet from his chair at that round table, his pale eyes wide with alarm and two scrolls clutched defensively to his chest.

'Ros!' Giles grabbed his sister's arm before she could say another word – or lunge to attack.

He'd seen that thin, clever face before too, shadowed by the looming figure of the duchess at Cordy's grand coronation.

'Have you all been properly introduced?' Margotte spoke from behind them, her voice perfectly serene. 'Your Highnesses, this is the helpful young man I was speaking of: Lord Edmund de Vore, nephew to the Duchess of Solenne.'

… The boy who'd tried to steal the Raven Throne from their sister six weeks earlier.

5

Magic raced up and down Rosalind's arms with a rush of pins-and-needles energy, only waiting to be released. Swiftly, she took stock of every weapon within reach. There were thousands of wooden drawers piled high in the stacks behind her; she was almost certain she could fling half a dozen of them at once with her powers if she focused hard enough.

If he made a single move towards her brother, she'd—

Giles's hand tightened warningly on her arm, and Rosalind stifled a groan. Why did her family always make it so difficult to protect them?

'Lord Edmund,' Giles said, and smiled as brightly as if he were greeting a new friend. 'We're delighted to meet you at long last!'

Ha. Rosalind set her teeth together in a snarl, and the

light green eyes of the boy before them widened even more. He looked about the same age as them, but he was even taller than Giles, and the way he clutched those scrolls to his narrow chest made it look as if he actually suspected her and Giles of trying to steal them. Under Rosalind's glare, he backed swiftly away from the table, his brown half-cape tangling with the tall chair he'd just been sitting on. He had to kick it away awkwardly, his hands still gripping – or was he trying to hide? – the scrolls.

'Your Highnesses.' His gaze veered away from hers, pale cheeks colouring. 'I'll leave you to speak with the archivist in privacy.'

We'll see about that! Rosalind shook off Giles's hand and narrowed her eyes, preparing to make certain that he didn't linger among the shadows in the stacks to sneakily eavesdrop.

'Oh, but you don't have to go,' said Giles sweetly … because *of course* her brother could never resist trading pleasantries with anyone, even a boy foolish enough to think he'd be a better ruler than their sister. 'Margotte was just telling us that you're an expert on the history of Raven's Roost. We've been wanting to learn more about it ourselves. Can you tell us where the oldest map is kept?'

'Oh, no, I'm not … I mean …' Lord Edmund slid a furtive look over his shoulder, as if he were searching for someone to rescue him. 'I'm not an expert on the castle.'

'Margotte told us you've been studying all the oldest scrolls about it for weeks.' Rosalind scowled at him, crossing her arms. 'Was she wrong? Or was she not telling us the truth?'

Giles hissed out a frustrated breath through his teeth, and her jaw tightened, heat creeping up the back of her neck. She'd learned to hate that sound from her brother ever since they'd first moved into this stone maze full of unspoken rules that seemed so obvious to everyone but her. She kept on banging into new ones without meaning to … and Giles kept on *noticing*, every single time.

It was bad enough that her ladies-in-waiting sneered at her; it hurt so much more when her own triplet brother acted as if nothing she did was good enough for him either any more.

'*How long do you think they'll keep you here if you make fools of them, too?*' Lady Fauvre's words slithered through her memory.

'What my sister *meant* to say—' began Giles.

But the other boy was already speaking, his eyes still wide and worried. 'Oh, no, Margotte wasn't wrong. And she would never tell any untruths!'

'Thank you, Lord Edmund,' the archivist murmured, amusement rippling through her tone. Rosalind had almost forgotten that she was still there, watching them all with her hands clasped and her expression untroubled. 'I do appreciate that endorsement.'

'Then what is the problem?' Rosalind demanded.

Edmund sighed, his shoulders slumping, as he seemed to finally give up on finding an escape. 'I have been studying those scrolls, but not the history of the *castle*. I've been studying the history of the *magic*.'

'The … magic?' Giles's voice sounded strange, but Rosalind barely even noticed. She was too busy letting out a scornful huff.

'Raven's Roost isn't magical!' She *knew* magic. It had twined around every inch of their beautiful, beloved first home, where Mother's and Connall's enchantments had guarded and helped them all. Rosalind had trained in sword-fighting with Mother's clever shadows while Giles had warbled away the hours with his lute, using songbooks that Mother had magically summoned for him, and Cordy had prowled or flown around them in all her different animal forms.

It had all felt so natural and so *right* … when they were there. Here, everyone acted as if magic were a terrifying threat to whisper about, not a strength in which to take well-earned pride. The dukes and duchess might have trained mages in their pay, but all *their* magic was supposed to be saved for battles. Only plain candles, torches and ordinary fires in the big stone fireplaces lit this castle's rooms whenever sunlight faded.

There was *nothing* magical about any of it.

'Oh, no, what I meant ... Not that I would ever – I mean, I only wanted to learn – that is ...' He broke off, his gaze darting past Rosalind's head. 'I have to go!'

'Lord Edmund!' Of course Giles was desperate to make peace, as always – but this time, he failed.

The other boy was already thrusting the two scrolls that he'd been holding into an open drawer set underneath his table. The moment they were safely in place, he lunged into a run and fled as desperately through the shadowy stacks of the archives as if he were being pursued by the venomous water snakes from Mother's moat back home. A moment later, the sound of a crashing door signalled his retreat into the safety of his family's quarters.

Pitiful. Rosalind blew out her breath in a snort. *So much for that threat!* Shaking her head, she turned to the archivist ... only to spot a much graver danger prowling towards them.

'Cousins!' Flanked by four lesser noblemen from his house with long swords glinting at their sides, the elegant and untrustworthy Duke of Lune stepped out of the shadows. Smiling widely, he held out his arms in welcome.

'My dear young cousins. How delightful to come across you so unexpectedly!'

Ha! This was no accident. It was an *ambush*.

Rosalind instinctively grabbed for the hilt of her sword ... and closed her fingers on empty air. *Curse it!* Once again, she flung her senses outward, searching for other weapons she could use – but Giles was stepping forward with another brainlessly delighted smile.

'Cousin! What research brings you to the archives?'

Was her brother blind? Rosalind ground her teeth. They'd been watched the whole way here, hooded eyes following them through every room they'd crossed. *Obviously*, Lune's spies had told him where they were headed, so he had hurried to cut them off with his guards here, well away from any armed protection of their own.

We are not *defenceless, no matter what he thinks!* Rosalind shouldered past Giles to stand guard in front of her brother ...

And a door swung open from the opposite direction, followed by loud footsteps ... *many* loud footsteps, marching from the Duchy of Solenne's castle quarters directly towards them.

Oh, no.

The two most likely suspects behind Cordy's murderous attack were both converging upon her and her brother at once ... and even Rosalind couldn't think of any way to keep her eyes on both sets of approaching enemies. She shifted slightly to the left, trying for a better angle – and caught the swish of dark skirts in the corner of one eye as the archivist retreated swiftly into the shadows of the stacks. Apparently, even the gentlest of professional scholars could recognise the scent of impending battle.

'Your Grace!' At least her brother hadn't missed *this* menace. Giles's voice was high and bright behind her, but Rosalind felt the tremor in his left arm as it brushed against the back of her right shoulder, and she knew that he was preparing for his own kind of battle too. 'What a coincidence,' he said. 'You were also in a mood to visit the archives?'

'Your Highnesses.' The marching feet came to a halt, and the tall and muscular Duchess of Solenne – by far the most impressive fighter Rosalind had seen on the battlefield six weeks ago, looking just as powerful now in a crimson gown edged in pearls – lowered her head with brisk respect. Five sword-carrying noblewomen and noblemen from her own house took position behind her as she spoke. 'My nephew warned me that Lune had you two directly in his sights. I thought I'd better come and lend you my support. You should always have a set of reliable shields behind you whenever you have to deal with this treacherous worm.'

'You were warned by your nephew? The *young pretender*?' Lune's voice dripped with contempt as he drew himself up, and his scowling followers closed in around him, their hands already resting on the hilts of their swords. 'If I'd known my poor young cousins would be forced to endure *his* company, I'd have run to get here sooner. They're lucky he didn't attack them in his constant quest to steal the throne from my family – or was he too busy stammering and stumbling to try?'

'You dare—!' The duchess's face contorted into a terrifying scowl.

Metal scraped against leather in a lethal chorus as every supporter's sword was yanked out of its scabbard at once, only waiting for a ducal command to attack.

It was exactly the kind of moment when Giles *always* started singing to break the tension with his bell-like, irresistible singing voice. Then he'd follow up the song with some performer's joke or nonsense that made people forget for a crucial moment about their anger.

So Rosalind felt a rush of relief at the sound of his preparatory in-drawn breath just behind her …

But then he stopped himself, which made no sense. 'Everyone,' he said instead in an ordinary speaking voice that cracked on the word, 'if you'd all just, please …'

No one even turned to look at him. It was up to her.

Rosalind summoned up her magic. If she had to aim each drawer in a different direction, with so many opponents closing in from all sides, she would only be able to control three wooden drawers at once. Of course it wouldn't be enough, but—

The archivist spoke from the shadows, her calm voice echoing with eerie weight around the tension-filled room. 'I *need not* remind Their Graces of Lune and Solenne of the Law of the Archives, agreed by every duchy in Corvenne centuries ago. As these archives sit above the heart of Raven's Roost, so our nation's history forms the heart of our people, made tangible in these ancient records. No blood may ever be spilt among them. Any family that breaks that law shall be banned from Raven's Roost forever after.'

'Of course.' The Duke of Lune smiled thinly and gestured for his followers to resheathe their swords. Breaths were released all around, but his brooding gaze still didn't fall away from the duchess. 'My family desires only to respect the throne we hold, and to protect our shared kingdom.'

The duchess sneered at him as she gestured her own followers back with a flick of one strong hand. 'You're no closer to the throne than I am nowadays, Lune. Remember? Her Majesty has declared *all* duchies equal in her favour and all old enmities at an end now that the Raven Crown has finally been restored.'

'How could I forget?' Lune's upper lip curled. 'My innocent young cousin still has faith in the possibility of lasting peace. But then, she doesn't know your brutish house as well as I do. Fortunately, she has me at her side to protect her.'

At the word *brutish*, Rosalind had had to fight not to flinch. His last words, though, made her spine stiffen with hot fury.

Protect Cordy? How could he even mouth those words without choking on his lying tongue?

The Duke of Lune's mages had hurt Alys terribly when Lune and the Duke of Arden had first attacked. He'd agreed to let them heal her only on the condition that Mother surrender their home to his and Arden's soldiers. Then he'd kept Mother and Connall in tiny, dirty cells as prisoners until the triplets had jointly freed them.

Rosalind would never forget the sight of the cruel gold collar that Lune's mages had created to drain Mother's magic, leaving her sick and weak and helpless in that awful prison cell.

Lune had given Giles the key to unlock Mother's collar only when Cordy had forced him to do it, using the overwhelming power of the land. Ever since then, he'd played the part of a smiling, kind relation as if it were all that he had ever known, but Rosalind would *never* forget the truth.

If she was a wild animal in a dress, as Lady Fauvre claimed, then *he* was a slithering, venomous snake in human form – and she would never trust him with her true family.

If she'd had a sword, she would have drawn it. Since she didn't, she'd have to do what Giles was always nagging her about and try diplomacy instead. 'Don't you *both* have somewhere else to be?' she growled. 'You *must* have some duties that don't involve bothering us!'

Giles's breath huffed through his teeth in horror. The Duke of Lune's eyebrows soared upward, but the Duchess of Solenne let out a booming laugh and grinned down at her. 'Well spoken, Your Highness. It's good to see there's still *someone* here at court who doesn't endlessly beat about the bush! I like a girl who's not afraid to speak her mind.'

Rosalind knew all the way down to her bones that, behind her, her triplet brother was rolling his eyes in despair at her uncourtly behaviour ... but just for one brief moment, she couldn't help cracking a tiny smile as she looked up at her family's oldest enemy.

She would never be fool enough to turn her back on the duchess in any undefended situation ... but still. She had forgotten how good real approval could feel, lightening every inch of her body.

The Duke of Lune, on the other hand, sounded decidedly sour as he murmured, 'Indeed. We shan't interrupt you two any longer in your – ah, what *were* you here to study today, cousins?'

'History,' said Giles, before Rosalind could even open her mouth. 'We want to learn more about our family's history, now that we're finally living here.'

'Aha. Now, *that*, you don't need any tedious archival help to learn. I happen to be an expert on our family's history, and I would be delighted to share the details with you myself ... but, perhaps, a little later?' Lune cocked his head, locking eyes with the duchess once more. 'At the moment, I'm afraid Princess Rosalind is quite correct. We are *both* expected at the Council of Dukes. Unless you'd prefer to excuse yourself from today's round of decision-making, Solenne?'

'In your dreams.' The duchess snorted. 'But I'm not leaving these children without shields around any of *your* courtiers.'

'No more than I ever would with yours.' The duke smiled thinly and looked back at Giles. 'Perhaps, for the sake of kindness, you might allow us *both* the honour of jointly escorting you back to the safety of your own apartments? At least until your sister can spare one or two of her royal guards to accompany your next trip?'

They didn't need any royal guards, and they certainly didn't have time to waste … but once again, Giles spoke without consulting Rosalind. 'Thank you,' he said, and nodded with courtly grace. 'We'd be delighted. And …' He turned to Margotte, who still stood in the shadows, observing everything. 'Of course there's no rush on our family history, as the duke is being so generous and helpful, but do you think we could visit you again sometime soon? Just to look at some of those old scrolls we were discussing, out of curiosity?'

'Of course, Your Highness. I would be honoured to meet with the two of you at any time. You will always find me waiting here, day or night.' Margotte's expression was as serene as ever, but Rosalind felt uncomfortably exposed as the archivist's keen gaze landed on her face, seeming to see far too much. 'I hope you may both find these archives to be a welcoming place where you may feel at home and free to be yourselves, always.'

Ha. Rosalind hadn't been free to be *herself* in weeks … but her shoulders slumped with resignation as she heard Giles say brightly, 'Of course. We always are, now that Raven's Roost is our new home! Aren't we, Ros?'

Rosalind might not be the clever one, but she knew

exactly what was required from her now. Unfortunately, she also knew, at that moment, that she couldn't speak that lie without gagging on it.

Instead, she tightened her lips and hoped that it would look like a smile of agreement. Thankfully, everyone around her seemed to take it as enough.

But as her triplet brother strode before her into the shadows of the stacks, talking cheerfully to the Duke of Lune and his retainers, she felt more alone and out of place than she ever had before.

6

An eerie chill emanated from deep within Cordelia's bones, growing stronger with every passing minute. None of the rustling courtly layers that had been laced and buttoned over her – from petticoats and chemise to corset, skirts, sleeves, over-sleeves and a gold-embroidered green damask gown over all the rest – could thaw that terrible cold or keep it from spreading as she walked through the maze of rooms in her new castle. The Raven Crown closed tight around her stiff headdress as a stream of nobles curtseyed and bowed on all sides and Cordelia kept her face a perfect, queenly mask over her panic.

This cold couldn't be natural. It felt *wrong* at a deep level, like those brown and crumbled leaves that she'd found upon her bedspread – but if she told Mother what she was feeling now, there would be an explosion of magic and fury at the worst, most public moment. She was expected at the Council of Dukes in only a few more minutes.

She'd accepted the Raven Throne. She had to be strong enough to hold it.

The Raven Queen doesn't break her promises!

So Cordelia gritted her teeth to hold back a shiver, lowered all her inner shields, and reached down with her mind through the thick stone walls of Raven's Roost to draw strength and warmth from the land underneath her.

For the first time in weeks, she couldn't quite reach it. She could only hear distant echoes of the land's various plaintive voices, as if they had somehow retreated too far away for her to make out their words any more. She could feel them all begging her to listen and *pay attention*, just as they had ever since she'd first woken … but they were drowned out by insistent human voices at every turn in the castle, as she forced herself forward to do her royal duty, walking perfectly upright with the help of her boned corset and never, ever allowing herself to hesitate.

Rosalind or Giles would have known that something was wrong – she could never hide anything from her triplets for long – but as usual nowadays, they were nowhere to be seen. Ladies-in-waiting surrounded her instead, as always, noisily fretting over the details of her royal appearance, while grim armed guards marched ahead and behind and her mother focused only on the dangers waiting for her.

'Oh, dear, Your Majesty's ruff still isn't quite right.' Lady Hastings tutted, trotting beside Cordelia on her right. 'Just let me tweak—'

'Remember, *don't* drop a single hint about what happened to you this morning!' Mother hissed into Cordelia's left ear. 'If the wrong person guesses that that attack nearly succeeded—'

A lady-in-waiting gasped behind her with as much shock and horror as if fountains of blood had suddenly erupted from the walls. 'Oh, *no*! Your Majesty, you've *lost an earring*. Let me—'

'Oh, but now there's a strand of hair coming out of your headdress!' Another lady-in-waiting reached for her with grasping fingers. 'Let me—'

If only she still had the hedgehog and the squirrel to ground her! They'd both disappeared soon after her triplets had left her room, even before her ladies-in-waiting could shepherd them safely out of the castle in the usual daily routine. These latest visitors had slipped quietly away while all the adults were busy arguing around her. Cordelia would have given almost anything to do the same.

'Don't admit *anything* in that meeting,' Mother ordered. 'You've *never felt better*. That's all you need to say, no matter what they ask! And—'

'Here – she can wear mine!' A new earring was jabbed firmly into Cordelia's right earlobe, making her hiss out a breath of pain as it scraped through at an awkward angle. 'If you'll just turn your head quickly, Your Majesty, we can replace the other one to match, and then no one will notice—'

'Let me just tuck in that stray bit of hair and—'

'Enough!' Cordelia batted away all the hands that were pawing at her, breaking free at last. 'We're here.'

Two of her guards were already waiting at the ancient oak doors that led to the dark stone trap of the windowless Moon Chamber, their faces cold and stern. Inside, the powerful dukes and duchess of Corvenne awaited her, plotting who-knew-what – but for once, Cordelia couldn't bring herself to care.

At least there would be rush-lights burning inside that stuffy room. Perhaps they might produce enough heat to make a difference.

She was just *so cold*. How much longer could she keep herself from shivering as the chill spread further and further through her body?

'Cordelia …' Mother leaned over her, dark eyes

haunted as they searched Cordelia's face. For a moment, Cordelia was afraid that she had finally been caught out – but Mother let out a heavy sigh and stepped back, nodding firmly down at her. 'Just remember: *show no weakness.*'

The Raven Queen never did.

The guards opened the doors wide, and Cordelia stepped through them, freezing in perfect, queenly silence.

The first thing Giles saw when he stepped back into his bedroom was the hedgehog he'd first met that morning, asleep in a curled-up ball of brown prickles on the floor beside his bed.

'Oh, for—What are you doing in here again?' Letting out a laugh of disbelief, Giles loped across the room and dropped to his knees beside her, running a careful fingertip along her quills. 'Were you trying to find your way back to Cordy, little one? I can't help you this time, I'm afraid. She's busy staring down the scary duchess and all the dukes right now.'

Thank goodness for that perfectly timed meeting of the council! Giles wasn't sure how much longer he could have kept up his performance of easy good humour under the Duke of Lune's too-knowing gaze.

Earlier, for one terrible moment, he had nearly lost control and sung in front of the worst possible audience; he'd only caught himself *just* in time, before he could put his family in even more danger. But then, bloody battle had almost broken out in the castle *archives*, of all the unlikely places!

Mother was right: despite the luxury and elegant courtly rules of this castle, none of their family would be safe until Cordy's would-be killer was caught. Giles had to find a way back to the archives – but *without* any ducal interference or oversight. This time, he didn't only want to see the oldest maps; he *needed* to see the scrolls Lord Edmund had been studying, the ones he'd tucked into the drawer underneath that table.

'I've been studying the history of the magic …'

The Duchess of Solenne's prized nephew wouldn't come to the royal archives to study the kind of magic his aunt's hired mages all practised. No, the archives of Raven's Roost stored only the records of this castle itself and its past rulers …

Those rulers who'd wielded the power of the land ever since the Raven Crown's creation. Could Edmund be trying to steal the land's magic from Cordy?

Giles let out a snort. *As if that could ever happen!*

At his snort, the hedgehog finally stirred in her sleep, opening her small, pointed pink snout in a wide yawn. She kept her eyes closed but uncurled her body enough to let him stroke the soft, vulnerable pink skin of her chest.

'That's right,' Giles crooned softly as he petted her. 'I'm safe to trust. You can smell my sister on me, can't you?'

The land *loved* Cordy and always had. Well before the triplets had mended the Raven Crown, it had called to her in a voice that no one else could hear, guiding her – with Giles and Ros trailing in her wake – all the way across the broken kingdom to Raven's Nest, where the ancient spirits of Corvenne lived on the slopes of Mount Corve, protected by a magical barrier of mist and channelling all the raw power of the land that had created them.

That land hadn't only spoken to Cordy; it had *cherished* her from the very beginning. As much as Giles hated to remember it, the hardest truth he had discovered at Raven's Nest was that he wouldn't be a part of his own family now if it weren't for the land's deep love for Cordy and its overwhelming desire to protect her. *That* was the only reason it had sent him and Ros, as a newborn fox and hare, to be transformed into human triplets – protective camouflage – for their royal sister.

It doesn't matter though. It can't!

Mother loved them all equally. So, why *should* it matter that Giles had ever been other than human? It wasn't as if he'd ever felt any urge to change his shape, the way that Cordy used to do before she took the crown. The only wild part of Giles's nature was the music that had sung through his veins for as long as he could remember – and he would never let himself be ruled by *that* again.

Nuzzling closer to his fingers, the hedgehog let out a happy clicking noise that sounded almost like a purr – and with a start, Giles realised that he had somehow stopped petting her and had begun tapping his fingertips against her soft skin instead, rattling out the exact rhythm of his dream-music from last night …

… The part that sounded just like a wild fox yipping.

Ugh! He lunged to his feet, breathing hard and ignoring the hedgehog's huff of disappointment. *No more distractions!* He had to follow the clues to keep his family safe.

The land would never willingly transfer its powers to anyone else while Cordy still lived – *especially* not to pale, scholarly Edmund, who looked as if he'd never stepped willingly into nature in his life. But if Edmund *had* found some sneaky way to try to steal it, and if that was connected to this morning's attack …

The hedgehog rolled to her feet and waddled grumpily away, but Giles ignored the snub. The answers *had* to be in the archives! If only he could go back now, immediately – but with all the dukes' and duchess's entourages loitering impatiently in the royal wing, waiting for their masters to re-emerge from the Moon Chamber, he couldn't sneak back without being observed by far too many dangerous eyes. He still didn't know the castle well enough to come up with any alternate routes …

But now that he thought of it, he knew exactly how to start fixing that.

'Ah … Wincester? And everyone else too, if you wouldn't mind?' He pulled his bedroom door open and smiled winningly at all the waiting boys and men in his outer chamber, most of whom had lived in Raven's Roost for years before he'd even heard of its existence. 'Do you think you might be able to put your heads together and draw me a proper map of the castle? Just to help me keep my bearings better from now on? You know how forgetful I can be.'

Wincester's eyebrows rose as he studied Giles's face for one long, unnerving moment. Then he lowered his head and bowed deeply. 'Of course, Your Highness.'

All the others echoed him, and a rowdy hunt began for quill pens and paper, with jests flying back and forth among the gentlemen-in-waiting as they competed over who would do the drawing of the map. Giles's practised smile turned real as he stepped forward to join in the noisy, companionable throng.

An unexpected *twang!* rang out from behind, stopping him in his tracks. *That* was the sound of lute strings jangling. The hedgehog must have blundered into the case that he'd placed on the floor underneath his bed, out of sight, weeks ago.

Giles gritted his teeth against sudden, horrifying temptation ... and then closed the door firmly behind him.

Rosalind groaned when she spotted the visitor waiting on her bed. 'Not you again! Didn't you do enough damage the last time you were here?'

The red squirrel didn't even have the decency to look ashamed of the chaos he had caused. This time, unlike last night, Ros's weapons had been safely hidden underneath her mattress, but a trail of discarded fluff and feathers marked the tunnel dug by sharp little teeth and claws into her bed, as he'd torn his way through to find them again.

'What does that bow even taste of that's so enticing to you?' she demanded. 'And – were you actually chewing on the *sword-hilt* too?' Rosalind stared in horror at the unmistakable toothmarks on her well-worn leather grip.

'*Kwaa! Muk-muk-muk KWAA!*' The squirrel scampered around the bed, scolding her furiously at the top of his voice.

'Oh, you and everybody else.' Rosalind rolled her eyes as she pushed the weapons safely back underneath the mattress, out of his reach. 'Believe me, *no one* approves of me any more. If you think I'll give in and let you ruin these, though, you're dead wrong.'

Still, she couldn't leave her room in such a state – not if she wanted to avoid another venomous tongue-lashing by Lady Fauvre in front of all the others. Right now, her Mistress of the Bedchamber was thankfully busy, teasing all the other ladies-in-waiting in the outer chamber about the powerful secret admirer she'd been courting, but Rosalind couldn't count on that distraction to last forever. Sighing, she knelt down to scoop up the scattered remnants of mattress stuffing and push them back into place. When she was finally done, she twitched her bedcovers over the telltale hole to hide it.

Pushing up the heavy mattress with one hand, she took one final peek at the sword, bow and arrows, just to make sure they were tucked in far enough to be safe … and then she frowned and cocked her head. *Wait.*

She'd never studied her bow from this angle before. That little mark at one tip – it was a miniscule set of carved lines that she had assumed to be random when she'd been gifted the bow by her unknown benefactor the day she'd moved into Raven's Roost, after fighting off a shower of arrows from the Duchess of Solenne's archers.

From this angle, though …

Could that actually be a tiny, stylised *boar*? The same

kind she'd seen snarling on the duchess's own house pennant earlier that day?

'No.' She shook her head firmly, ignoring the red squirrel, who was still shouting down at her from the raised mattress above her head, practically dancing on his paws with impatience. 'That makes no sense.'

Why would anyone from the House of Solenne have gifted *her* a beautiful bow on the same day as that battle?

For just a moment, she remembered the duchess's fierce grin in the archives earlier. '*I like a girl who's not afraid to speak her mind …*'

'*Definitely* not.' The duchess had been the one who'd ordered all those arrows shot at Rosalind and her triplets in the first place! She was an enemy, *not* a friend.

Still, Rosalind found herself feeling unaccountably cheered as she stood up and scooped the furious squirrel off the bed. 'Come on. We both know my sister's the reason you're here. *She* can be the one to cope with all your nonsense now.'

'*Kwaa!*' The squirrel wriggled out of her arms and scrambled upward, reclaiming his earlier alert perch on her shoulder and gripping her hair for balance with his sharp claws.

'Not too tight,' Rosalind warned him softly as she

walked across the room. Then she took a deep breath, braced herself … and opened the door into the battle arena of her outer chamber.

Every head swivelled towards her as she stepped forward. Breathing through her teeth, she fixed her gaze on the outer door ahead. *Just keep moving!*

But in these skirts, she could never move fast enough to escape.

'What an interesting new pet you've chosen to adopt, Your Highness,' Lady Fauvre drawled from the corner to her right. 'Are we to understand that you've taken this one in for good? It may well suit *your* tastes, but you may be asking a bit too much to expect the highest ladies of this land, gathered here in your chambers, to pick up after yet *another* untrained animal. We do quite enough of that already.'

A muffled laugh snorted out from Rosalind's left. She quickened her steps, her shoulders hunching.

'Or, I wonder …' Lady Fauvre *tsk*ed thoughtfully. 'Could this actually have been considered a *fashionable accessory* in the deep, dark woods where you grew up?' Rosalind could hear the malicious smile in Lady Fauvre's voice. 'Did you spend years parading around like this to all your animal friends, imagining yourself an actual—'

'*Muk-muk-muk*-KWAH!' In a sudden wild rush of

motion, the squirrel swarmed around the back of Rosalind's neck to berate her attacker with a series of loud barks that escalated to a shriek. '*Muk-muk-*KWAH!'

Gasps and giggles broke out all across the room – but it was the crash of something falling that made Rosalind finally jerk around and stare.

Lady Fauvre had leaped out of her seat and was flattened against the wall. Her embroidery hoop must have fallen along the way. Half of a howling black wolf had already been stitched on to the cloth; the needle and length of black thread lay discarded beside it, evidence of her panicked flight.

'Good heavens.' Lady Fauvre's voice didn't sound as controlled as usual; her blue eyes glinted with a furious light as she took a deep breath and stepped back towards her abandoned seat and all the followers who were staring at her. 'That creature really is almost as out of control and impolite as its new mistress.'

H*a*. Rosalind put one hand on the squirrel's back, warmed by the outrage that still vibrated through his small, furry body.

No one had *ever* stepped up to protect her from her Mistress of the Bedchamber's venom before. For the first time in hours, Rosalind dared to meet Lady Fauvre's gaze full-on. 'This squirrel's *mistress* is the Raven Queen, my sister,' she said flatly. 'Don't worry though. I'll be sure to tell her *exactly* what you think of him … and of *her* too.'

'Wait—No—Your Highness—!'

Rosalind crossed the rest of the room in three quick steps and was free.

'*Phew!*' She breathed out a sigh of relief as the door fell closed behind her, leaving her in her mother's nearly empty outer chamber. Fortunately, Alys wasn't there to see her. The two ladies-in-waiting who were still left in the room looked up with only mild curiosity from their needlework.

The squirrel, forced away from his field of battle, grumbled irritably to himself and then began to roughly groom Rosalind's hair with his claws and tongue. She reached up to stop him – and then shrugged and let her hand fall back to her side after all.

'Oh, go on,' she murmured. 'It can't look any more ridiculous than all the other courtly hairstyles.'

There would be a heavy price to pay for Lady Fauvre's embarrassment in front of all her followers – especially once her Mistress of the Bedchamber realised that Rosalind had issued an empty threat at the end. *Of course* she could never really tell her family about the cruel words Lady Fauvre had spoken; not without exposing the humiliation of everything else that had been happening in her outer chamber for weeks.

It was bad enough to have to live through all of it herself. But the thought of her family's reaction if *they* ever found out? Rosalind had to hold back a full-body shudder.

She could *never* let the others find out just how badly she was failing in her latest transformation ... and unfortunately, Lady Fauvre knew it.

Ugh.

Still, that moment had felt *so* satisfying. She could hardly begrudge the squirrel some reward. Raising her voice, Rosalind asked her mother's ladies-in-waiting, 'Is the Council of Dukes still in session?'

'We think so, Your Highness.' The older woman at the far side of the room – Rosalind had no notion of her name – nodded calmly, without pausing in her needlework. 'The Dowager Duchess will be waiting outside the Moon Chamber until it's finished.'

'Then so will we.' As the squirrel continued his grouchy ministrations, Rosalind strode to the next door and through the other rooms along the way, her shoulders tightening more and more with each new person she passed. Oh, they might all smile and bow or curtsey as deeply as they liked, but Lady Fauvre's words always echoed in her head with excruciating precision, telling her exactly what the rest of the court all thought of her.

Luckily, this time she had a perfect distraction. 'Cordy will be glad to see you again,' she told the squirrel on her shoulder, ignoring the courtiers around her and giving him an absent-minded stroke. 'She'll need cheering up after being trapped in a room without windows, being shouted at by dukes. By the time she gets out, she'll be dying for a piece of real nature to help her breathe.'

It was still hard for Rosalind to believe, even now, that her wild-hearted sister – who'd grown wings and shot off into the sky to free herself from every restriction they'd ever faced throughout their earlier lives – had settled now in just one body and place to be queen … but ten minutes later, when the doors to the Moon Chamber were flung open, there was no doubting it.

It was the Raven Queen, not Rosalind's familiar Cordy, who stood pale and magnificent in the doorway, flanked by four tall royal guards. Her dark eyes looked nearly black in her white face, the Raven Crown glinted an ancient, magic-infused silver around her head, and the gold embroidery on her overdress glittered. A sigh of appreciation rippled through her assembled ladies-in-waiting – the only courtiers allowed to wait in that private outer chamber until the queen had safely vacated it – as they sank into deep bows and curtseys to their mistress.

Beside Rosalind, Mother – who'd waited with all the

87

tension of a bow preparing to let loose at any second – let out a breath that sounded like relief.

But Rosalind left her far behind, lunging forward in as close to a run as her infuriating skirts would allow.

She had known her sister in every animal form that Cordy had ever taken, from bugs to bears and more … and she *knew*, with a sick tugging at her own gut, that something was terribly, dangerously wrong.

Cordy's glazed eyes blinked as Rosalind hurtled towards her. The guards stepped forward in alarm, two of them crowding together to fill the doorway behind the queen with their broad shoulders, blocking her from view of the dukes and duchess, who still waited inside the Moon Chamber.

'Rosalind!' Mother snapped. 'What do you think you're doing?'

Rosalind kicked up her speed as Cordy took a breath, blinked – and then crumpled helplessly forward into Rosalind's ready arms, like a marionette that had lost all its strings.

The squirrel on Rosalind's shoulder shrieked an ear-splitting alarm. Royal guards surged to surround them. Mother started towards them like oncoming thunder. But all Rosalind's attention was fixed on Cordy's ragged, almost-inaudible voice, as Rosalind struggled to wrestle her sister's limp body upright.

'It wasn't me,' Cordy whispered as chaos erupted all around them. 'I was right. It was the magic. The land … Ros, tell Connall, it's the *land* …'

'The land *what*?' Rosalind demanded. 'Cordy, *what*?'

Her sister's eyes rolled back in her head. The squirrel let out a low, sorrowful cry that echoed through Rosalind's stuttering heart.

The Raven Queen's physical body still hung in her arms, but her sister had just slipped out of reach.

7

The Raven Queen was dreaming.

In her dreams, the land always reached out to enfold her within its green embrace. This time, though, she couldn't find it, no matter how desperately she searched. The voices of the woods and fields and mountains were crying out with pain and fear, but she couldn't reach them to help.

Her sleeping body twisted and stretched in her mother's bed, low whimpers of distress slipping through her closed lips. Her eyes moved rapidly behind their lids.

In the bedroom, urgent human voices argued. Magic crackled through the air, again and again, calling her old name, trying to pull her from her dreams.

But the land needed her.

She needed it.

She sank deeper and deeper, searching, as her family's voices thundered around her.

'You're certain none of the others saw what happened?' Mother demanded.

'None of us could have seen it,' Connall said. 'It wasn't possible from our side of the Moon Chamber, not with Cordelia's guards blocking the doorway. We all heard you ask what Rosalind was doing, and then calls of dismay a moment later – but I was out before any of the rest, and even I couldn't see Rosalind or Cordelia through that phalanx of royal guards who marched them back here.'

'Thank the spirits.' Mother's footsteps moved restlessly back and forth around the bed. 'We've gained at least a little more time to solve this.'

'… If none of the ladies-in-waiting breathe a single word.' Alys's voice was sharp. 'None of the royal guards either. We'll have to trust Captain Godfrey to keep them in line – *and* keep her own vows to the throne.'

'We need all the time we can get,' said Connall. 'I still can't sense any break in the web of protective spells we laid upon her – or any other spells lurking underneath. Until we understand what's actually happening, we have no chance of healing her at all.'

Alys said, 'I thought she *had* been healed this morning.'

'That spell of waking that I cast on her barely lasted three full hours,' Mother said. 'I've tried it three more times already without any effect. It bounces off her as if it can't even find her spirit to wake it any more. However this attack was managed, it was no ordinary act of magic – but what can we tell the other dukes and the duchess while we search for the answers we need? Without any explanation for that uproar …'

'Wait a minute.' Giles finally spoke, his voice unusually tentative. 'They all think *Ros* caused the uproar, don't they? *She's* the one they heard you calling to. So …'

'Of course. That's it!' Mother's footsteps finally came to a halt. 'We'll let the word be spread that there was an unfortunate incident – a practical joke gone wrong. Rosalind did something foolish, accidentally knocked over her sister, and—'

'No.' Fury burned in Rosalind's voice as she started forward, footsteps scuffing against the floor. 'I would never – *ever!* – put Cordy in any kind of danger for a stupid joke.'

'Of course you wouldn't,' Mother said impatiently. 'That's not the point. If everyone else thinks it was a squabble between sisters, and Cordelia only twisted her ankle in the process, then they'll understand she'd need to rest in bed until it's healed …'

'And they'll believe it,' said Alys. 'I've already heard gossip from three different courtiers that Princess Rosalind ripped apart one of her beautiful gowns this morning in a terrible fit of temper and frightened all her ladies-in-waiting with her wildness.'

'What?' Rosalind's voice faltered. 'But that's … that's not how it happened.'

A growl erupted from Mother's throat. 'We don't have time for this foolishness. We *will* have a discussion later about courtly behaviour and self-control, I promise you … but for now, only one thing matters. Do you want to give us the chance we need to find a magical solution and heal your sister? Or do you want to choose *now*, of all the most impossible moments, to finally start caring what other people think of you?'

Rosalind didn't answer, but the air simmered with the force of all her withheld words.

Alys sighed heavily. 'The moment any other members of the council sniff out what's really going on, we will *all* be in mortal danger. No matter how great a fighter you may wish to be, Rosalind, you cannot stand against all of them any more than your mother and Connall can stand against all their mages. *You* swore to support your sister on the throne, remember? So you'll play the part that's needed, for all our sakes. Understood?'

'Understood,' Rosalind muttered.

'Good,' said Alys, 'because this throne was only ever safe when your sister could call upon the land to defend it. Right now, she can't protect anybody – least of all herself.'

The Raven Queen twisted unhappily in her bed as the words flowed ominously around and over her, twining a new thread of unease through her anxious, clinging dreams.

The land wasn't all that needed her now. So did her family – and she wasn't only a queen after all. Was she?

No. She was Cordelia, and she had to protect the others. She had to wake up now!

She surged with all her strength towards consciousness – and something shot up in answer from deep underground, freezing her restless body into place, freezing too that brief, hot spark of energy that had lit within her chest with the memory of her own name. Blackness swept her back under, even deeper than before.

The Raven Queen slept on and on, against her will, while her kingdom sobbed wordlessly through her dreams. Its voices grew fainter and fainter, even to her, with every minute that passed.

8

Giles saw exactly the moment that his sister stopped moving. Cordy's face had screwed up tighter and tighter with an anguish that had tugged him to her bedside as the hedgehog and squirrel stood guard at either end of her bed, their family argued, and she wrestled with whatever silent nightmares haunted her. Then her expression turned suddenly, horribly blank, and her whole body jerked into one stiff, unnatural line.

'Cordy!' He lunged forward, silencing the others' debate.

It was as if she'd been turned into a statue. Her fingers wouldn't even curve when he gripped them with all his might. They had stiffened into rigid, immoveable claws. Her arms clung as if pinned with heavy weights against her sides.

Mother's magic blasted over her body again and again, sending flares of heat echoing through the room and over Giles's skin until the hair on his arms stood on end. The hedgehog and squirrel both hunkered down, clinging to the sheets with their claws to withstand the magic's force.

But Cordy didn't move.

Connall muttered rapid, desperate spells. Alys nudged Giles out of the way to run her hands over Cordy's face and chest with ferocious efficiency.

Cordy didn't move.

Giles stood back, mute with panic – and Ros advanced to stand just beside him, her strong shoulder pushing against his arm and holding him upright. 'She isn't,' Ros said, '– *is* she—?'

'She's not dead.' The bones of Alys's face jutted out against her suddenly hollow cheeks, but her voice was firm as she answered Ros's question. 'Her heart is still beating.'

'But … how is she even breathing?' Giles couldn't look away from that blank, mask-like face. It didn't even budge as the red squirrel patted her cheek with frantic, clawed paws and the hedgehog nosed worriedly at her feet. His wildest triplet should *never* lie that still!

'I don't know.' Alys shook her head, her lips tightening as she straightened. 'I'm no mage – and whatever's holding her now is nothing natural. Who knows what rules apply?'

'She told me it was the land.' Ros's burning gaze was fixed on their sister. 'That was the last thing she said: "Tell Connall it's the land. And the magic."'

'The *land*?' Connall frowned. 'That isn't possible. She and the land are linked in an unbreakable connection; the ancient spirits of Corvenne gifted her with its power. Even they cannot break that connection while she lives.'

'And the land *loves* her,' said Giles. 'It would never want to hurt Cordy.'

'Oh, she was just confused.' Mother shook her head impatiently. 'It's no wonder; she never had any real magical training. But what *we* need to do——'

'Wait, the *magic*!' Giles slapped his head. 'Of course. We need to get to the archives now.'

'Not again!' Letting out a harsh half-laugh, Ros stepped away from him, leaving him off balance and his arm suddenly cold. 'We already tried that, remember? It brought the Duke of Lune *and* the Duchess of Solenne down on our heads, *and* we didn't even get anything useful out of it. We're not going there again!'

Alys's eyebrows rose ominously high. 'You did *what*, exactly?'

'You two aren't going *anywhere* from now on,' Mother

snapped. 'If I had any choice in the matter, I'd keep you both right here where I could see you for myself – but the only way we'll survive the next few days is if the rest of the court believes our family hasn't a care in the world. That means you two need to go back to your households now and act perfectly normal for the rest of today – *without* taking any unnecessary risks! As long as no one knows that your sister is powerless, they won't risk attacking either of you in public. You should be safe if you keep yourselves surrounded in this wing of the castle.'

Giles shook his head desperately. 'But—'

'Didn't we already have this argument, only a few minutes ago?' Alys sighed, rubbing her forehead with the back of one hand. 'Never mind. Giles, I've explained this to your sister, but I'll explain it you, as well—'

Why wouldn't they listen? 'I understand the politics of it already,' Giles said. 'I'm not like Ros! I've always—'

'*What?*' Clenching her hands into fists, Ros took another step away from him. 'I may not be the clever one, but I'm not *stupid*.'

Giles groaned. 'That's not what I was trying to—'

'If I have to let everyone think I hurt Cordy, then *you* can let go of your stupid fixation with those crumbling old manuscripts! The last time we went to the archives,

98

I almost had to fight nine people. And you didn't even try to help!'

'**Enough**.' Mother's voice boomed inside their heads as well as into their ears, and Giles's lips sealed shut against his will. 'Do you want every eavesdropper in that outer chamber to hear our family squabbling now? Just when we *most* need to stand together? Think, both of you, about what your family needs of you right now!'

When, at any point since they lost their first home, had Giles *ever* let himself forget for an instant everything that his family needed from him? The injustice sent a howling wave of music through his ears, trying to crash over his defences and sing out his piercing outrage to the world … but right now, he had no voice left even to speak. His mother's magic pressed his lips closed, keeping every relevant fact and important theory locked away and useless to everyone.

In the corner of his vision, he caught sight of the hedgehog bumping against the end of Cordy's bed with sudden urgency, clearly searching for an escape route, while the red squirrel stood up on its hind legs and chattered angrily in Ros's direction. Even those little creatures couldn't fail to notice the tension that crackled like soundless lightning through the air. Beside him, Ros's face had turned so red, it neared purple as she struggled against her own magical silencing.

Alys stepped between them and put her hands on one shoulder apiece. 'It's all right.' Her fingers squeezed Giles's shoulder with a firm warmth that might have felt comforting in any other circumstance. 'I know,' she said quietly, 'you had to step up and fight adult battles for yourselves when everything went wrong at our first home. We all *know* that you're frightened now … yes, even you, Rosalind, like it or not. But this time is different. No one's taken the adults away from you. Remember?'

She smiled wryly as Ros wrenched free of her hold and Giles stared at her with unhidden outrage and betrayal. 'You don't *have* to manage family disasters any more,' she finished. 'You can remember that you're still children and leave the hard parts to us.'

Was that a joke? He hadn't been able to relax and act like a child for a single minute since they'd moved into this castle full of watching, judging eyes. The last thing he wanted was to leave Cordy's rescue to the adults – especially when he *knew* they didn't have all the information that they needed!

There was only one thing left to do. For the first time in weeks, Giles reached deep inside himself for the dangerous energy of his own magic, to break Mother's spell and reclaim his voice, to force the truth upon them …

But the only way he'd ever learned to use that magic

was by channelling it through the music that had always sung through his deepest and wildest soul. Even now, he wasn't reckless enough to put his family at risk that way. The Duke of Lune had been more than clear enough in his warnings; Giles could *never* sing like a common, hired entertainer whenever other people might overhear.

So instead, he gathered up all the scattered power that he could, threw it all in one awkward and desperate, music-less mass against the force of Mother's spell – and felt it shatter on impact, leaving him physically rocking with aftershocks.

'Go on.' Alys shooed him and Ros towards the door as Giles's chest rose and fell in rapid, shuddering bursts. 'We need to leave your mother and brother to focus without interruptions. They'll work to untangle whatever spell has captured your sister *and* keep her protected from any more attacks. Meanwhile, I'll keep an eye on her ladies-in-waiting and make certain that none of them slips out for even a moment, *or* sneaks any messages outside. If we're all very careful and very clever … *well*.'

The sigh that Alys let out, as they neared the door to the outer chamber, sounded shockingly like a sob. 'No more bickering, please, either of you. We haven't enough time left to waste on arguments.'

No more time.

That realisation chilled Giles's shuddering chest into stillness.

As he stepped into the crowded outer chamber, all Cordy's gathered ladies-in-waiting, led by Lady Hastings, leaped from their seats and erupted into a panicked surge of questions and demands, flanked by equally anxious-looking royal guards. Alys stepped forward to answer them all, and Mother's spell slipped away at last, leaving Giles's lips wonderfully free.

He almost turned to run back into the chamber and try again – but instead, he took a deep breath and let the door fall shut behind him, despite catching sight of the hedgehog who had found her way off the high bed and was waddling across the floor in his direction.

Alys was right: he didn't have any more time to waste, whether by holding that door open or by trying to convince his stubborn family of the truth. Ever since they had all been reunited, he had fallen back into his old habit of looking to the older ones for approval – but the truth was, he and his triplets had saved their family without adult help before. He *knew* that they could do it again.

'Ros,' he whispered. Taking her arm, he pulled his sister closer, away from Alys and her noisy, distracting group of questioners. 'I need to tell you—'

'No!' The word was a snarl. 'I *won't* listen any longer – and you've said more than enough to *everyone*.' Lunging forward, she wrenched free of his grip and plunged through the crowd towards the outer door without a single look back.

What was that? Giles stared after her, his mouth falling open. Why was she suddenly angry at *him*?

And why did his whole family have to be so unreasonable about everything?

Never mind. He didn't need approval from any of them any more. He was a prince, and he *would* save his family – even if they were all too stubborn to admit that they needed his help for anything.

Now, he just had to find a way to escape the protective net of his royal household without letting himself be captured by a far more dangerous trap.

He knew exactly where to start.

9

Unfortunately, when Giles walked into his antechamber, he found Wincester and his other gentlemen-in-waiting fully occupied with a female visitor.

She was talking in a low voice to Wincester with her willowy back turned to the door and one hand laid in appeal upon his stiff-looking right arm, while Wincester listened with an expression of chilly civility. The other gentlemen-in-waiting had gathered around, all eyes appreciatively upon her – but the moment that Wincester spotted Giles, he stepped back to bow, forcing her hand to fall away.

'Oh!' She turned in a flurry of scented silks and velvet – the most luxuriant fabrics permitted to anyone outside the royal family – and swept into a deep curtsey of her own. 'Your Highness! *What* an honour.'

'Lady Fauvre.' Giles forced a welcoming smile, shoving down his frustration at the interruption. Being friendly to his sister's Mistress of the Bedchamber was the least that he could do to help Ros at court – and of course, Lady Fauvre had never been anything but pleasant and helpful since they'd met. As one of the most established ladies of the court, she could have forced the younger ladies-in-waiting to do all her work for her. Instead, he'd frequently seen her visiting both his antechamber and Cordy's too, generously offering to run simple errands for the others.

So it really wasn't fair that he'd never felt entirely comfortable around her – and it was even more unfortunate that there had been some kind of misunderstanding between her and Ros on their first day together. She'd been so distraught about her own part in it that she'd insisted on personally apologising for her mistake to every member of Ros's family – so Giles had felt more and more guilty every time he'd seen Ros glowering at her after that. It wasn't as if she'd done anything wrong since that one innocent mistake – and hadn't Alys said something about Ros scaring Lady Fauvre earlier today?

Swallowing a sigh, he forced his shoulders to relax and his smile to deepen. 'It's always a pleasure to see you, of course. Did you need any assistance?'

'From *you*, Your Highness?' She let out a beautifully trilling laugh as she straightened, and two of the older gentlemen-in-waiting trailed closer, smiling hopefully at her. 'Oh, no. I would never dream of taking up your valuable time that way! No, I was hoping to offer assistance of my own. So many awful rumours have been spreading! Can it be true that your dear sister the queen has suffered a terrible accident? Or been struck ill? No one seems certain of exactly what's happened. Of course, I tried to offer my help to her own ladies-in-waiting, but they wouldn't even allow me inside, so I worried—'

'There is no need to worry, Lady Fauvre,' said Giles. 'Cordy's fine. It was only a tiny accident, with no serious damage. She has a twisted ankle, that's all.' He shrugged. 'She's been prescribed rest for a few days to keep from straining it.'

'*Only* a twisted ankle? Are you sure?' Her eyebrows rose over her worried gaze. 'I confess, there was *such* an outcry reported, I did think it must have been more than a trip over her skirts.'

'Ah ...' Giles glanced at the group of gentlemen-in-waiting around them, all of whom were avidly listening in. 'I didn't say that she had tripped.'

She gasped, one be-ringed hand flying to her mouth. 'Don't say that someone actually attacked her *on purpose!*'

The story that they had all agreed upon in private was still the only one that made practical sense. Somehow, though, Giles hadn't anticipated how it would feel to repeat it to his sister's own Mistress of the Bedchamber, who'd been frightened by Ros once already today.

How much worse was he about to make that relationship?

'It was only an accident,' Giles repeated weakly. 'I swear, no one *meant* for Cordy to be hurt.'

'But then, who—? *Ohhh*. Oh dear.' Her blue eyes narrowed. 'I did hear that your lady mother had called out to my own mistress in some alarm when it first happened. But surely ...' She glanced pleadingly at the gentlemen-in-waiting, biting down on her lip for a fraught moment. 'No matter how Princess Rosalind may struggle to control her ... unfortunate temper, as we all know by now ...'

'Ros would *never* hurt anyone on purpose!'

'Of course she would never *mean* to.' She sighed deeply. 'We all understand how difficult courtly life is for my mistress. Poor girl! It isn't really her fault, is it? If only ...'

This was spiralling out of control. 'Please don't bring it up with her,' Giles said hastily. 'It was only a simple joke gone wrong, and she feels terrible about it.'

'Oh, I'm sure she does.' For just one instant, he

thought he saw Lady Fauvre's lips curve upward ... but then she made a sound of deep distress, and he was sure he must have imagined that flash of an unsettling smile. 'What a distressing day this must have been for all of you, Your Highness. Her poor Majesty the Queen! Can I be of any help at all, do you think? I'd be more than happy to help her ladies acquire any special treats for her recovery, or—'

'She's fine,' said Giles, 'only frustrated that she can't be up and about. She's communing with the land right now, though, so she's still keeping busy for the kingdom. And besides ...' He winked, trying to lighten the atmosphere. 'She has a squirrel *and* a hedgehog in her room. Knowing her, she'll be more than happy enough with that company.'

'Of course.' Lady Fauvre nodded, her eyelashes sweeping back down to hide her eyes. 'Her Majesty is so understanding of the lower animals.'

Uh ... Giles felt his eyebrows draw down. Had there been some sort of jibe hidden behind her sweet tone? Or was he being unfair and imagining things?

'Well, if I really can't be of any more help, I suppose I'd better return to my own chambers,' said Lady Fauvre. 'My mistress will be in *such* a mood. If I'm not there for the sake of my poor companions ...' She shook her head dolefully.

Giles wished *so much* that they weren't being overheard by so many people! 'You truly don't have to worry about Ros,' he said gently. 'I know she can sometimes seem a little gruff, but she has the kindest, most loyal heart of anyone I know. If you only take the time to get to know her—'

'It is *so* good of you to try so hard to help your sister, Prince Giles.' Lady Fauvre curtseyed even deeper than she had before. 'You mustn't worry about me though. I know my duty, and I would never allow anyone to frighten me out of doing it.'

'Ah … good?' Giles blinked. 'Ros *isn't* frightening, though – that's what I was trying to explain, so—'

'*Such* a good brother and prince!' Smiling brilliantly, she swept across the room, trailing rose scent in her wake. She was gone a moment later, the door falling shut behind her.

'Well!' Giles blew out a breath, shaking his head briskly to release his own confusion. 'I hope you haven't all been too worried by those ridiculous rumours.'

'Ahem.' Wincester cleared his throat, giving a stern look over Giles's head at the other assembled gentlemen-in-waiting. 'Fortunately, none of those rumours had reached us until Lady Fauvre's own arrival a few minutes ago. I am sorry to hear of Her Majesty's injury though.'

'Oh, that's nothing.' Giles forced a light laugh. 'She's more annoyed than injured, honestly. Cordy's always hated being stuck in one place.' *And now she was trapped inside her own body.*

A sudden vision of her stiff, pale face swirled before him, filling up his vision and making his throat clench with fresh panic as the truth bore down on him again. It was too horrible; too wrong; too …

No! He swallowed hard, forcing himself back into the present moment, and found Wincester's eyebrows lowering sharply into a frown of concern. 'Anyway!' Stepping back, Giles clapped his hands together and turned a beaming smile upon the rest of the room. 'I'*m* not stuck in bed, thank goodness, so what would you all think of mounting a scavenger hunt around Raven's Roost for today's entertainment?'

The younger gentlemen-in-waiting all shouted out their immediate consent. Even painfully sophisticated Lord Lyffed nodded in agreement after a first, pointed sigh of resignation.

But Giles's Master of the Bedchamber only looked at him for a long, considering moment of unnerving silence. That probing gaze made Giles's palms start to sweat and his legs want to fidget … until Wincester finally lowered his chin in grave acceptance. 'Of course, Your Highness. We are at your disposal. Have you any thoughts about what the objects of this scavenger hunt should be?'

This time, Giles's grin was sincere. 'Oh, I have *plenty* of ideas.'

Of course, his ideas weren't the only ones that went on the list in the end. Giles insisted that all the gentlemen-in-waiting contribute to it, and when he suggested that they allow a few royal guards into the day's fun, those guards were reluctantly persuaded into contributing their own ideas to the list too.

So it was a large and noisy crowd that finally streamed out of his private royal quarters and through the crowded maze of the third storey, gathering even more curious courtiers along the way. Giles took care to ensure they didn't parade through his mother's or Cordy's chambers, but they did pass into Ros's outer chamber, where his sister sat red-faced, silent and miserable-looking among her ladies-in-waiting.

'Something made of lace!' It was Lord Lyffed, of all people, who shouted out the announcement of one of the top items on their list. He lunged for the needlework held by one of Ros's younger ladies-in-waiting.

Giggling, she wrestled him for it with vigour. The others descended around them in a laughing, cheering crowd, and Giles seized the opportunity to sidle over to his sister, who sat stiff-backed on an uncomfortable-looking chair, jabbing her needle like a knife into a tangled piece of embroidery. 'Do put that aside and come along with us, Ros. We're adventuring all around the castle! You'll love it, I *promise* you.'

He didn't dare be any clearer when so many people could overhear them. Luckily, he knew perfectly well that Ros would *never* turn down any opportunity for adventure – but his sister looked over his head instead of meeting his eyes, and then she shook her head with a grim, decisive jerk. As his eyebrows shot upward, she turned away from him without a word.

'Oh, dear.' Sighing delicately, Lady Fauvre swept forward from behind Giles while Wincester stepped up on his other side, a silently looming observer to the scene. 'Perhaps another time?' Lady Fauvre suggested. 'When it's been a less … *disappointing* day for my poor mistress? She must be dreadfully tired by now, you know, after all the excitement and upsets earlier.'

Ha. Lady Fauvre had no idea how to handle his sister! Biting back a victorious grin, Giles waited for Ros to leap into action after all, just to prove to the world that she could *never* be slowed down by anything.

Instead, as he watched in mounting disbelief, she

hunched even more tightly over her needlework. Gaze fixed firmly downward, again she jabbed her needle into the delicate embroidery cloth so fiercely that it should have spouted blood.

Giles's mouth fell open into a gape of shock. How could she *still* be so angry at him that she'd choose needlework – which she hated – over adventure?

Or Lady Fauvre's company over his?

'Ahem.' Wincester cleared his throat gently behind him. 'If Your Highness is ready to move on to the next item on our list …'

'Of course.' It was harder than usual to summon up a cheerful smile when his insides felt as miserably knotted as Ros's poor embroidery threads. But the others were already bustling towards the door – and no matter how wounded Giles might feel, he couldn't wait for item number nine on their list: *Something older than the castle.*

It took almost an hour to tick off the first eight items, but by the time they finished, Giles knew he was perfectly protected. His household had gathered up more and more courtiers along the way, until well over two dozen of them, flanked by multiple armed guards, hurtled in a loud and laughing mass through the long, quiet room of working scribes and into the hushed stillness of the archives beyond. The Duchy of Solenne's boar still snarled fiercely from the facing door, but this time, Giles rolled his eyes at the threat. Even if the duchess herself came marching out now with all her attendants, there would be nothing she could do with so many witnesses.

'Margotte?' he carolled as he strode ahead of the others towards the forest of stacked drawers. 'I'm back, and my friends and I are playing a game. Would you help us with it, please?' He peered through the shadows of the closest winding path through those towering stacks, searching for her upright figure.

Not even a whisper came back in response to his call.

Wincester stepped up behind him. 'Perhaps the archivist has left on an errand.'

'Perhaps,' Giles agreed.

An irrational ripple of unease washed over him, though, as he remembered her earlier words: '*You will always find me waiting here, day or night …*'

Nonsense. Taking a breath, he shook off the worry before it could sink its claws into him. 'She should be back soon.' Even now, there was no reason to imagine danger in every shadow. As Margotte herself had pointed out, the archives were officially neutral ground. No blood had ever been shed here through all the wars and bloody upsets of the past. 'We'll just have to wait for her return.'

But he wouldn't wait for the most important part of

his plan. *Almost there!* A lively marching tune played in his head as he started down that first pathway through the stacks, leaving the others to choose their own paths behind him.

'Come on!' shouted one of the younger gentlemen-in-waiting. 'Let's see if there's anything we can find for ourselves.'

No chance of that, Giles thought wryly as he glanced up at the closest stacks. They all loomed several feet above his head, and none of them were labelled in any way he could understand. Only the archivist herself would ever be able to find anything in that mysterious domain.

Luckily, he knew exactly where to go. His pace quickened with every step until he was half running by the time he burst into the clear, sunlit area by the floor-to-ceiling windows at the end of his path. While the others laughed and chatted in the shadowy stacks behind him, he raced past the archivist's tall, empty desk to the round table where Lord Edmund had sat a few hours earlier …

And found the floor underneath it empty. The scrolls that Lord Edmund had been so carefully studying – and the drawer that they'd sat in – were gone.

'No!' Spinning around, Giles stared wildly back at all those hundreds of unlabelled drawers piled into towering stacks. Had the drawer been removed on purpose? Or had

Margotte simply put it away since he had left? It could be anywhere in that enigmatic forest. He would never find it on his own.

But how much longer could he stall to keep the others here, waiting, if the archivist didn't return soon? Already, he could hear a few people arguing over whether they should give up and search somewhere else in the castle rather than wasting more time here.

He couldn't raise anyone's suspicions. He had to keep them all convinced that this was no more than a meaningless game and his family wasn't fighting their most desperate battle yet.

Untuned pipes shrieked jangling warnings in his head. If he didn't find those scrolls in time …

'Your Highness.' Wincester's voice made him jump – and then curse himself for that betraying move. When he turned, Giles found that his Master of the Bedchamber hadn't been looking at him anyway. Instead, Wincester was kneeling underneath the archivist's tall desk, while the others from their group were still hidden from view within the forest of the archives.

'I think you may want to see this.' Wincester's voice was quiet and perfectly controlled, but something in its edge made Giles's stomach sink with sudden dread.

A moment later, he knew why.

Dark red drops – still fresh enough to be wet when he reached out to touch them with trembling fingers – stained the tiled floor just beneath the desk. An irregular fragment of ancient-looking parchment lay nearby, as if it had been ripped from a larger scroll by a hasty, desperate hand.

Blood had finally been spilt in the archives after centuries of neutrality … and Giles didn't think the archivist would be returning today after all.

10

Rosalind knew her duty, and she would not break.

It didn't matter how hilarious Lady Fauvre thought it was to repeat the story again and again – full of lies and dramatic re-enactments – of how Rosalind's 'childish prank' had injured her own sister *so badly* that poor Cordy had had to retreat to her bed.

'At least you weren't toting around any of your little play-weapons this time. Can you imagine how disastrous *that* might have been? Her poor Majesty could have lost her entire leg instead of merely twisting an ankle!'

It didn't even matter that Giles, who was loved and admired by *everyone*, had spent the afternoon gallivanting around the castle with a whole pack of his admirers while Rosalind was left to bear the brunt of the story he had devised for her.

'Poor Prince Giles,' Lady Fauvre had sighed, 'was so mortified to admit what had happened to Her Majesty. He is such a kind-hearted boy, a true prince – you should have seen how hard he tried to pretend that he wasn't embarrassed by your clumsiness! I'm afraid there was nothing he could do, though, to stop all his gentlemen-in-waiting from sniggering about the incident. They thought it was hysterically funny – and of course, the whole court will be laughing over it by now!'

After hearing *that*, Rosalind hadn't needed Lady Fauvre's pointed look of warning to make her turn down Giles's invitation to join in his silly games. She couldn't imagine any torture worse than being surrounded by even *more* people who knew what she'd supposedly done to Cordy. Rosalind was supposed to be a knight. A *protector*.

She'd kept her mouth shut and held her spine rigid. She would not let Lady Fauvre's taunts break her.

She had felt like a vat of boiling oil, hot and desperate to overflow.

The only way she'd survived the trial of supper in the great hall, sitting at the royal high table in full view of every noble in the court, was to duck her head low over her plate, eat as swiftly as she could, and pretend she was invisible and couldn't hear anyone else no matter *what* they were sniggering about. For once, even Giles seemed to know better than to try to pull her into conversation.

But there was no stopping Lady Fauvre once they'd all returned to their private quarters. She lingered close to Rosalind, talking and talking, while another lady-in-waiting changed Rosalind into her nightdress and washed her face, as if Rosalind wasn't trustworthy enough to handle even those duties herself. Lady Fauvre talked and talked while Rosalind climbed into bed and the other ladies-in-waiting closed the window shutters, curtseyed, and finally left her for the night, taking their candles with them …

But Lady Fauvre took a seat at the end of Rosalind's bed as the door fell shut behind the others and darkness swallowed the room. Only her candle was left burning, turning her blue eyes into hollow-looking shadows as she kept on talking. 'It just seems so impossible to believe, even now, that a *royal princess* of Corvenne, no matter *how* brutish, would fling herself at her sister, the queen herself, in an actual physical attack—'

'I *didn't attack Cordy.*' Rosalind had held her tongue all night, but at that claim, the words gritted through her teeth like arrows twanging from a bow. 'I would *never* attack my sister!'

'Our dear Prince Giles did pretend he *thought* you had

only meant it as a joke, didn't he? He tried so desperately to convince everyone else of that too. But I wonder ...' Lady Fauvre's voice lowered; shadows flickered across her face as she leaned forward. 'Could it be that you were actually jealous? Because ... if you really *didn't* attack her ... what other explanation could there possibly be?'

The air was horribly thick and still around them. Only silence seeped in from the outer chamber; the other ladies-in-waiting were long gone. Only Lady Fauvre had a bed in that outer chamber, and as Rosalind watched, her lips curled into a mocking smile. 'I see. If we both know the truth, I expect your family must as well. I wonder how much longer they'll agree to keep you after this disaster?'

They're the ones who made up the whole story!

Rosalind *burned* to spit out that truth and wipe off Lady Fauvre's smile. Her fingernails bit into her palms as she opened her mouth, the words roiling within her. Lady Fauvre cocked her head, that infuriating smirk stretching wider. Rosalind took a deep breath ...

And then she lunged forward and blew out Lady Fauvre's candle.

'Ahh!' As blackness swallowed her, Lady Fauvre jumped off the bed with a shriek. 'You little—! Oh, I *give up!* Keep your ridiculous secrets for one more day, if you insist. I've done enough!'

Hasty footsteps shuffled away through the darkness, followed by a muffled thump that sounded like a collision. Snarling, Lady Fauvre finally wrenched the door open. Light from the outer chamber streamed through for just an instant, framing her furious figure – and then she slammed the door behind her, leaving Rosalind in darkness.

Alone. Finally!

Rosalind collapsed on to her mattress, heart thundering hard enough to shake her whole body apart. Every emotion she'd numbed herself against for hours swept through her in a roaring wave. There were no thoughts in her head, only wordless rage and fear and panic and a whole succession of images flashing unstoppably behind her eyelids:

Cordy collapsing, limp, into her arms; the whole family turning on her at Cordy's bedside; Lady Fauvre sneering down at her again and again; that desperate moment in the archives when so many armed adults had converged upon her and Giles, and she'd known she couldn't defeat all of them on her own, she couldn't protect her family or …

'Ugh!' She jerked upright, panting. She couldn't stay here for a single minute longer, lying helplessly – *uselessly* – in the dark while all these *feelings* buffeted her.

Her body needed to move. She wanted to fight. She had to *do something*!

Lady Fauvre was still lurking in the outer chamber, but if Rosalind didn't find a way to let out this boiling energy somehow, she'd never make it through another day without breaking.

Only one door led out of this room for an elegant princess, but Rosalind hadn't always been royal. She loped across the room as swiftly as she could on the quiet tips of her bare toes. When she yanked the wooden shutters of the window open, the cool night air of early autumn brushed her hot cheeks with the promise of freedom.

Back at home – her true home – when the grown-ups had been occupied, she and Giles had often raced each other to climb the flat stone walls of their castle, using a combination of strong ropes and clever legwork. He had been nimble and fast, but her arms were stronger – and the walls of Raven's Roost were a different kind of challenge. This castle was hundreds of years old, built in a completely different era, back when people had used large, round, stacked stones to create fantastically bumpy walls. Any of those stones could form a useful handhold for a really determined climber. That was why guards patrolled the ground below every night – to stop intruders from taking advantage and creeping up the walls for a surprise attack.

In this pitch darkness, though, with only their own torches to light their way, those guards would never glimpse one mutinous royal climber a full three storeys above them.

She doubted they would even think to try.

A grin stretched Rosalind's lips for the first time in weeks as she pulled herself up on to the wide stone window sill. Moving with muscle-clenching control, she rose to her feet, gripping the upper edge of the window frame – and then she carefully stretched out her left leg, wrapping her bare toes tightly around the top of a cold, round stone as the night breeze blew through the thin linen of her nightdress.

She had to bite down on her lip to hold back a laugh of pure exhilaration. Oh, she had *missed* this kind of challenge so much!

The magic inside her loved it too. As her mind finally turned blessedly quiet, forced to shut out everything but the essentials for survival – *hand here, foot there, feel the wind, balance, go!* – prickles of golden power lit up underneath her skin, racing through her muscles and then hovering in an excited, invisible cloud around her body like a second, backup set of limbs and immense strength. She could have powered her whole climb with the force of that family-bestowed magic and removed all her risk – but no.

She *wanted* to fight for this climb herself. She needed it!

So Rosalind was gasping and sweating with physical effort by the time she finally stretched her right arm high to grab the closest gap in the stone parapet at the top of the east wing's main battlements. *Almost there … No!* Her fingers slipped and lost their grip.

Her bare feet slid along the curves of the stones below as she frantically scrabbled to regain her handhold. She felt her magic readying itself to catch her if, no, *when* she fell – but Rosalind gritted her teeth and *lunged* with all her might, swinging her full weight with bruising force against the stones to catch herself. For one perilous instant, she hung suspended from the battlements, her toes dangling in the night air.

Her arm muscles ached with a dull fire, out of practice and tired before she'd reached her goal. The wind blew cold through her short hair and against her sweat-drenched skin. For one shameful instant, she closed her eyes to retreat from the fight … and then she saw Lady Fauvre's smirk once again behind her eyelids.

'Gnarr!' Rosalind gathered her strength and *moved*.

The next few moments were a blur of blunt force and pain and movement and …

'Ha!' She tumbled over the parapet on to the long flagstones of the castle's battlements and landed hard on her back, panting and laughing painfully up at the sky. It was the first time in weeks that she'd seen it from this angle. It felt *amazing*. Stars glittered high and white across the endless night sky as the cooling breeze swept over her sticky skin and her pulse thrummed wildly through her wrists and neck and chest.

She had done it. For the first time in six weeks, she was free. No one was watching her. No one was judging her. She was herself, gloriously alone and unroyal and—

'Ros?'

She jolted upward ... and found her triplet brother staring at her from the shadows of the parapet only ten feet away.

Rosalind let her head fall back against the low wall with a thunk of protest against *everything*.

For weeks, she'd been craving more time with her family. Now, when she most needed time alone – especially from *him* ... !

'What are you doing here?' Giles's shocked voice emerged from the shadows where he sat with his arms wrapped around his drawn-up legs. She couldn't make out his expression in the darkness, but she just *knew* it was judgemental.

Her shoulders braced for battle. 'What are *you* doing

here?' she retorted. 'Shouldn't you be off playing stupid games with all your friends?'

The night air thickened with bristling silence. Rosalind's muscles hardened more and more with the building tension, ready to endure whatever he said next ... but it all felt sickeningly *wrong* under the cover of those bright, familiar stars. She and Giles had spent so many nights together under the stars on their trip across the kingdom!

Some nights, during that long journey, Cordy had joined them in human form; just as often, she had chosen to stay animal, finding her own food and leaving conversation to the two of them. Either way, Giles had always been by Rosalind's side as their sister had dragged them both across Corvenne with a mysterious fervour that had baffled them at the time.

Cordy's bizarre behaviour had been explained when they'd finally reached Raven's Nest on the slopes of Mount Corve, where the deepest secrets of the kingdom were guarded by the ancient spirits of the land behind a shimmering wall of mist. Of course, they'd still had plenty to worry about afterwards, as they'd all sat together under that sparkling canopy, planning out how to rescue the rest of their family from imprisonment.

But at least, back then, Rosalind would never have

doubted for an instant that Giles would always be on her side when it mattered.

Enough! She pushed herself up from the hard floor of the battlements, ignoring the protest from her aching muscles. She'd come here to escape, not to feel even worse! Now, though, the dark, shadowy line of mountains on the horizon, with Mount Corve rising at their centre, felt like a taunting reminder of everything she'd lost. She jerked her gaze away from them, grabbing hold of the parapet and ready to escape.

Just as she was starting to boost herself over the low wall, though, something about the outer wall below finally caught her eye with its eerie wrongness … and then Giles's voice, low and despairing, broke into her thoughts.

'The archivist's been taken.'

'*What?*' Rosalind turned back to him, peering through the darkness and still balanced halfway across the parapet. 'What do you mean, "taken"? By whom?'

His shoulders rose and fell in a shrug; his face remained tipped against his knees, his voice muffled. 'There were drops of blood under her desk, and Lord Edmund's scrolls were gone. This was all that was left.' He unclenched his hands and revealed the fragment of parchment that had been hidden between his palms.

Frowning, she dropped back on to the battlements and

strode over to snatch it up. Of course, it was ridiculous to try to read anything in the middle of the night, without a candle; all she could make out at first was a dark smudge, part of a drawing – the wing of a raven, maybe, echoing all the other pictures in this castle? But scribbled just beside it …

She gave up. 'What do those words say?'

'They're only fragments.' Giles sighed. 'I think this must have been ripped out of her hand when they took her – or maybe she even ripped it herself, to leave a clue for us to find whenever we came looking. But it just doesn't make enough sense on its own. 'Connection between the land and … the transfer … a barrier only family can …'

He grimaced. 'I've spent all night trying to make sense of it. If we only had the rest of the scroll … but the duchess probably has it locked up tight in her chambers right now, and Mother and Connall won't listen to me about anything.'

Frowning even harder, Rosalind sank down on to the flat stones beside him, worrying the fragment between her fingers. 'What if it wasn't the duchess who took it?'

He snorted. 'Lord Edmund was the one studying those scrolls, remember? He said he was studying the history of *the magic*, but I think he was really trying to steal Cordy's connection to the land. That's the only explanation that makes sense.'

'But this says *a barrier only family can*,' Rosalind said. 'That sounds like a barrier that only family can pass. He and the duchess aren't part of Cordy's family.'

'No, but—'

'Who else is always going on about what *dear* family members we all are to him? Even though he absolutely wants the throne for himself and couldn't care less about any of us?'

'You mean Lune?' Giles finally lifted his head from his knees. 'You think *he's* the most likely one? The duchess tried to *kill* us only six weeks ago. He's tried to help us ever since then.'

'Ha!' This time, Rosalind was the one to snort. 'The duchess might have fought against us in battle before Cordy mended the crown, but that was just regular warfare.' And if that mysterious gift of bow and arrows really *had* come from her after all ... but Rosalind wouldn't share that possibility until she was absolutely sure of it. 'He's so slippery, he'd definitely try to attack behind our backs – and he doesn't care about helping anyone except himself.'

'He helped me when Cordy was crowned. He warned me ...' Giles tipped his head back against the parapet, swallowing visibly. Dampness glittered against his cheek in the darkness as he gazed up at the stars, and his voice lowered. 'Whichever one of them did it, we can't reverse it now without getting hold of the rest of that scroll. And since we can't search their chambers without assembling the royal guard to force our way inside ... which would let the whole court know that Cordy's been attacked ... and since Mother and Connall won't listen to a word I try to tell them anyway ...' He let out his breath in a half-sigh, half-sob. 'We don't have anywhere else to look for answers.'

'So what *do* you want to do?' Rosalind demanded. 'Give up the fight? Just let Cordy *die*?'

'Of course not. But—'

'Have you even looked down there tonight?' Surging to her feet, she pointed over the rise of the parapet at the bare and bumpy walls below.

With unmistakable reluctance, Giles unfolded his long legs and joined her by the parapet, leaving behind the coil of rope that he had used for his own climb and keeping a careful few inches away from her. 'What am I supposed to be looking at? There's nothing down there.'

'Exactly.' When he didn't answer, Rosalind let out a growl of impatience. 'Cordy's been asleep *all day*. What always happens when she sleeps? Every single time?'

'Wait ...' He leaned perilously far over the parapet, his head turning back and forth. 'Where's the ivy?'

'It's not growing up the wall to find her,' Rosalind said. 'Not any more.'

'But the land *can't* be separated from Cordy! Not until ...'

... *Until she's dead.* The words hung, unspoken, in the darkness between them ... and every true part of Rosalind – everything that could *never* be transformed, no matter who demanded it of her – rose up in a sudden furious rebellion.

I will not let that happen!

She was done with following other people's plans and trusting anyone – even their own family! – to protect her sister for her. 'We can't depend on archives and crumbling old scrolls for answers any more. Cordy's connected to the *land*, not to the castle, and obviously –' she stabbed a finger towards the empty outer wall beneath them – 'something's gone horribly wrong with that connection. *That's* what she was trying to tell us earlier! So if we actually want to understand how to make her better ... *Oh!*' The realisation pierced through her like a lance.

How could she not have seen the truth before?

She'd been trapped inside that suffocating maze of a castle, full of adults so certain of their own rules that they'd made her believe her own knowledge and experience didn't matter any more. They'd been *wrong* ... but she'd had to escape and stand under these stars and in front of that line of mountains once again to realise: 'There's only one place we can go to find real answers.'

Giles sucked in a breath, eyes flaring wide – and then they both turned to look at the highest mountain in the distance as they spoke the answer together:

'*Raven's Nest.*'

11

The land of Corvenne was not sleeping. It was screaming with all its might, with all its many and desperate voices, for the one who was meant to protect it above all else, the one who had *always* listened and cared for its pain before ...

But the Raven Queen couldn't even hear it any more – or recognise her own name when it was called nearby, with less and less hope, by those who loved her.

She couldn't move. She couldn't think.

And neither could the *other*, deep within the earth below, who lay as still and trapped as the queen in her bed, as their magic began to slowly, inexorably wither ... and poison both of them along with it.

12

Giles had given up his magic weeks ago, but now it roiled through him, howling a tune that wanted to fill the entire castle with its urgent power. He kept his mouth clamped shut with all his might, but his fingers wouldn't stop trembling as he frantically crammed supplies into the soft leather case that usually protected his precious lute. The last time he and Ros had fled a castle together – Alys's scream of pain echoing through their home; Mother's panicked warnings raging with magical force as she ordered them to run for their lives and find Cordy – he hadn't had time to bring anything along.

But back then, he'd thought that he had already lost everything that could be taken. He'd had no idea just how much he could still lose once they finally arrived at Raven's Nest, where the ancient spirits – and their unbearable revelations about his family and his own past – were lurking behind a dangerous, magical barrier of mist.

Terror, mist, magic and the awful truth like a dark and endless chasm that had nearly sucked him down until Cordy grabbed his hand and saved him.

What new secrets would be revealed to upend his world this time?

Last time, he had wished so often along the way for his lute, for the simple comfort it could bring. Now it lay bare and unprotected on his bed, waiting to be woken from its six-week-long sleep – but music couldn't help anyone along this journey, no matter what the desperate magic inside him might believe. All that his magic understood were his own feelings, and those couldn't be allowed to matter any more.

When a throat suddenly cleared behind him, he jumped so hard, the linen undertunic in his hand slipped from his grasp and fluttered to the floor as he spun around.

'Ahem.' Looming in the newly open doorway of the outer chamber, his Master of the Bedchamber's long face was lit from below by the candle that he carried, and his thick eyebrows had lowered into a frown that added even more shadows to his eyes. 'May I be of any assistance, Your Highness?'

'Wincester.' Giles slumped with relief, putting one

hand on the raised mattress of his bed for support. 'I'm so glad it's you.'

Wincester's brows lowered even further. 'Who else would it be? I am the only one who sleeps in your outer chamber.'

'Ahaha. Yes. Good point. I only ...' Taking a breath, Giles forced a bright performer's smile, even as the warning music inside him ratcheted up to a near-deafening volume. *No time to waste, no time, no time ...*

With what he hoped was a casual-looking move, he stepped forward to block Wincester's view of the open lute case and the crumpled-up clothing that spilt out of it on to his luxuriant bedcovers. 'Was there something you needed from me?'

'At this time of night? No, Your Highness.' Wincester shook his head, his shadowed gaze steady. 'I came because I heard movement inside – and while I was relieved that you had returned unharmed from tonight's perilous expedition, I did hope I might convince you to allow me to help with the rest of whatever you've planned for tonight.'

'*Perilous expedition?*' Giles's laugh came out much too high; even he could hear its horrible falseness. He clenched his fingers together behind his back to hide their trembling from those too-perceptive eyes. 'I don't know what you're talking about, but I've been here all night. Really, you should know that better than anyone – I couldn't walk through that door without you seeing me.'

'Indeed,' said Wincester. 'I had assumed that *that* was why you took care to acquire a rope strong enough for climbing earlier today.'

As Giles took in the weary understanding in Wincester's deep voice, every excuse that he summoned shrivelled hopelessly on his tongue. He had acquired that rope as part of his scavenger hunt ... which had been *meant* to seem like a trivial game to everyone around him.

His shoulders slumped. 'Was I that obvious?'

'No, Your Highness. You were excellent – as always – at performing the role of a carefree youth for the pleasure of your court.'

Giles frowned. 'Then how ... ?'

'I have served many princes in my time at Raven's Roost,' Wincester said gravely. 'To be the master of a royal bedchamber can be a dangerous role, for all the honour that it carries. It requires great care and the utmost caution, and it has taught me to look for the hidden truths behind many different types of mask.'

Hidden truths ... There were so many truths Giles was hiding. Now, they all felt as terrifyingly exposed as the lute that lay openly on his bed after six weeks of being hidden in its case, safely out of sight.

Could Wincester tell that he hadn't really been born a prince, only brought here through his family's transformations? Had Wincester been able to see all along that Giles was only playing a royal role with all his might?

Giles's pulse beat hard against his throat, and the heavy darkness seemed to close in around him as he asked, 'What kind of truth do you think you've seen in me?'

'I have served many princes,' Wincester repeated, 'but *not one* of them took the care you always have to make their dependents feel safe and respected in their household. Not one of them ever worked so hard to look after the happiness of everyone around them, even to the detriment of their own. Not one of them made me feel so truly proud to serve my prince.

'I would not care to lose you as I have lost too many princes before, when whispers raced through Raven's Roost as swiftly as they have today. I have learned, over the years, to sense that kind of danger in the air. So …' He regarded Giles gravely over the flickering flame of his candle. 'If I may be of any use to you and your safety, I am asking you to trust me tonight – as I have learned to trust you – and tell me how I may help. My loyalty is yours, and I will not shy from peril.'

Giles opened his mouth … but couldn't speak. Tears stung his eyes as he swallowed over the sudden knot in his throat.

He had worked *so hard* ever since he'd first arrived at this castle, but he'd been so certain that no one else had noticed. He'd never realised just how much it would mean to hear that someone had.

Trust no one but family! It was the first and most important order that Mother had given them all when they'd moved into Raven's Roost. At the time, Giles had nodded along with all the rest.

Unlike the others in his family, though, he had always hoped that that order wouldn't have to last forever. He had believed that they could build a safer future, and he had worked to make that happen. Now, just as his family's lives were teetering over the most lethal precipice of all …

Could he actually trust that it had worked?

Or would it be an even greater risk to refuse the only possible help he had?

'Thank you,' he said at last, his voice hoarse. 'If … if you're truly willing to take a risk, I would value your help tonight so highly. Ros and I have to get out of this castle somehow, without anyone else knowing. It's the only way to save our sister's life … and probably ours too.'

Wincester's eyebrows rose. Then he stepped forward,

closing the outer door carefully behind him. 'I think you had better tell me everything.'

It was *such* a relief to pour it all out to a trusted ear at last, after holding all his panic and fear inside all day. Giles collapsed on to the bed as he explained every detail of the dilemma that they faced – from Cordy's initial attack to the enigmatic clues on that fragment from the archives. Wincester had been with him for its discovery, of course, but at the time, Giles had tried to cover up his horror, making excuses for the bloodstains that they saw and sneaking the parchment into his tunic unread. He had cheerfully insisted that they leave to carry on with the rest of the scavenger hunt, and he'd succeeded before any of the others could grow suspicious.

Now, Wincester's frown deepened further and further as Giles explained the desperate plan that he and Ros had concocted on the battlements.

'So you see,' Giles finished, 'we need to get out as quickly and quietly as possible. You will help us, won't you?'

Wincester didn't immediately answer. He had agreed to sit, stiff-backed, at the end of the bed at the beginning of Giles's explanation, but now he studied Giles in silence, shadows shifting across his long face. A heavy hush hung in the air of the room as he made his deliberations. In the thin, flickering candlelight, his face looked like a stranger's.

'Your Highness,' he said finally, 'my loyalty is yours … which is why I have a clear duty now to go immediately to your lady mother and share your plans with her for the sake of your safety.'

'What?' Giles's mouth dropped open in horror. 'But you promised you'd help me! You said you wouldn't shy at peril—'

'My peril,' said Wincester, 'not yours. I did say, did I not, that I would prefer not to lose another prince?' He shook his head with finality. 'Helping you and your sister ride into danger will not keep either one of you safe now.'

'But it will!' Giles protested. 'If I stay here, we'll *all* be in awful danger in a few more days. The *only* way to stop what is going to happen is to leave tonight.'

'Perhaps you are correct, but you cannot expect me to help two royal children on to the open road without any protection. Even if I came with you myself, I have no training in warfare. If either of you were hurt or abducted, your mother would blame me for it, and rightly so.'

'Ros and I can take care of our own protection,' Giles said. 'We've done it before. Really, we have!'

But he could see Wincester's expression hardening into deeper certainty with every desperate word he spoke. Just like Mother and Connall, Wincester hadn't witnessed their earlier adventures – so none of them understood just how much it had changed him to survive danger without adults before. Wincester had only met Giles as a prince, and Giles had done his utmost to play that part to perfection, laughing and peacocking for the court in his new finery and *always* taking care not to frighten anyone by doing magic.

He'd been so careful never to spark any fear or intimidation that even his loyal Master of the Bedchamber had never guessed at his most scandalous hidden truth.

Please don't make me prove it!

'Wincester,' Giles said, knotting his fingers together, 'even if you can't bring yourself to help me, at least promise not to go to Mother with this news tonight. Pretend that we never had this conversation. Please! You can be as surprised as everyone else to discover my disappearance tomorrow morning.' He smiled weakly. 'Can't you do that much for me? If I beg you?'

Even the flickering candlelight seemed to still in anticipation between them as he waited for Wincester's answer.

'I *could* do that,' said Wincester with grave precision, 'but I could not live with myself afterwards if anything happened to you or Princess Rosalind on your reckless journey. It would break every oath I swore when I first took this position with you.'

Giles closed his eyes. He had been right about one

thing, at least: his Master of the Bedchamber *was* a good man. He could be trusted. But that made this part infinitely worse.

Saving my family is worth one more sacrifice, he told himself as he summoned up the tingling magic in his blood. It came gladly to his call, after six weeks of repression. It was ready. It had been waiting.

He'd already given up his music and his first dreams weeks ago; he could give up this one, sweet point of trust and safety too.

But as he cast his voice, with the power of his magic, to surround Wincester from every side – hypnotic and drugging and utterly overwhelming – he opened his eyes and forced himself to witness every instant of shock, hurt and betrayal that passed across Wincester's face before his Master of the Bedchamber finally surrendered to Giles's power and slumped, unconscious, on to the bed, just beside the discarded lute.

Giles didn't bother packing any more supplies. He only buttoned his lute case closed with shaking fingers and fled, shivering, into the darkness of the castle beyond and whatever lurking dangers awaited him.

Family *was* worth any sacrifice. He knew it.

But sometimes, sacrifices felt unbearable.

13

Rosalind was waiting in the royal stables for a groggy stable boy to saddle two horses on her command when a soft, scraping sound came from the shadows behind her.

Luckily, she was prepared for danger. She spun around, drawing the sword that she had reclaimed from her room in a lightning-fast visit that had stretched her nerves close to their breaking point.

She hadn't dared sneak past Lady Fauvre on her way to freedom, so she had gritted her teeth and used magic to power her climb back up to the battlements just as soon as her feet were safely shod and the sword was hanging from her belt. Any route through the castle had seemed better than passing through Lady Fauvre's lair, even if it did use up more of her magical reserves than she would have liked.

Still, if any spies had spotted her along the way in the various darkened rooms she'd navigated …

She squinted into the shadows past the circle of the stable boy's lantern, searching for tall, lurking figures.

The attack came from a different angle.

'*Chukka*-KWA!' With a high-pitched cry of fury, an all-too-familiar creature launched himself out of the shadows and landed on her lower leg with all four sets of tiny, painful claws. Scolding her fiercely all the way, he scrambled up her thin nightgown, undeterred by the lethal weapon in her grasp.

'For goodness' sake!' Rosalind lowered her sword with a groan, and the red squirrel gave her short hair a firm yank as he settled back into his earlier place on her shoulder. From the tone of his scolding, he seemed to think that that particular spot was *his* by right of conquest, and she had been unjustly withholding it from him for hours. 'I'*m* not the one being unreasonable,' she snarled, craning her neck to try to look him in the eyes. 'I brought you to Cordy *twice*, remember? I have other things to do besides ferrying you around all day!'

'*Kuh-kuh-kuh*-KWA!' the squirrel retorted, and set to grooming her hair with fierce determination, teeth and claws.

Rolling her eyes, Rosalind looked away and found the stable boy staring, open-mouthed, in her direction – obviously as scandalised by her unregal behaviour as everybody else at court. Well, she was only minutes away from freedom and in *no* mood to deal with that nonsense! She narrowed her eyes in warning.

He didn't say a word … but a horribly familiar voice spoke close behind her.

'My dear young cousin! What a fascinating time and place to come across you.'

Curse it. The stable boy hadn't been staring at her after all – and in her distraction, Rosalind hadn't even heard the stable doors open.

Tightening her grip on the hilt of her sword, she drew a deep breath and turned to face the smiling Duke of Lune. On her shoulder, the squirrel's tail puffed out to twice its size in sudden menace as he let go of her hair and hunkered down to focus on the looming predators ahead. Freedom might be beckoning, but there was a new set of obstacles in the way.

The duke had four armed men in the black-and-silver uniform of his household standing ready behind him in the open stable doorway, embroidered black wolves howling across all their tunics. Rosalind had her own sword, her aching muscles, her fading reserves of magic … and, apparently, a small red squirrel.

At least I have someone at my side.

Where was Giles? He was the one who knew how to talk people around. Everybody *liked* listening to him! All that Rosalind knew how to do was fight ... but if she wanted to save Cordy and get out of here tonight, she couldn't afford a noisy battle.

Gritting her teeth, she sheathed her sword. 'What are you doing here?' she demanded. 'These are the royal stables. You have your own, remember?' All six duchies kept their own private stables at Raven's Roost.

'Ah, but we are family, are we not?' The mocking note in the duke's voice made her shoulders tighten. 'Doesn't family count for anything with you, my dear cousin?'

'Not when it comes to our horses,' Rosalind said flatly. 'You have plenty of your own. Did you get lost along the way?'

'Actually,' he drawled, 'I worried *you* might have. I know that stories have been circulating through the court for some time now, about your little ... *eccentricities*, shall we say? But when I heard that a royal princess of Corvenne had disappeared from her bedchamber in the middle of the night and then been spotted skulking through the castle in nothing but her nightdress ... !' He raised one elegant eyebrow. 'What could I do but summon my guards and hurry to your aid?'

Snake, Rosalind thought fiercely. *Snake, snake, snake!*

148

She pressed her lips tightly shut, but she couldn't stop humiliation from prickling hot against her skin as everyone in the stable turned judgemental gazes upon her and her outfit.

She had withstood every barb from Lady Fauvre. She would withstand this as well – and she *wasn't* only wearing her nightdress. She had put on her stockings and shoes too, not to mention her makeshift sword-belt. Her stiff and bulky court gowns would have been useless on a race across the kingdom, and she hadn't any more practical clothes to wear. Lady Fauvre had seen to that when she had burned Rosalind's comfortable old tunic and leggings.

Lifting her chin, she planted her feet even more firmly on the hay-strewn floor, even as her head began to throb with exhaustion and the after-effects of all the fear and anger that she had already endured across this endless day. 'I am *fine*. So you can all go straight back to your own chambers and—'

'Oh, no. We couldn't possibly leave you unprotected. What would your sister, the queen, think of such shameful neglect?'

'She would tell you to *trust me*,' Rosalind gritted through her teeth, her headache intensifying, 'and I'*m* telling you, right now—'

'Shall we go and ask her together?' The duke cocked

his head, his gaze cool and calculating. 'Or, perhaps, would it be better for me to ask your lady mother?'

'You—!' She'd managed to lock down all her rage and her fear from today's attacks, but at his words, a different memory suddenly surged forward against the fragile shreds of her control: her mother trapped in a tiny prison cell, terrifyingly pale, sick and desperate, wearing that choking golden collar that had drained her of all her magic …

… The collar that the Duke of Lune's mages had created and that *he* had placed around her neck.

'Don't you *dare* talk about my mother!' The hilt of Rosalind's sword was suddenly in her grip, although she didn't remember reaching for it. Her fingers dug into the rough, squirrel-chewed leather in furious anticipation as the squirrel on her shoulder chattered his teeth in warning.

The guards behind the duke all stiffened as one, shifting their own hands to their sword-hilts in answer … but the duke only smiled wider. 'Why, Princess Rosalind,' he murmured. 'Even you wouldn't be so foolish as to lose your temper and attack your own loving cousin in front of multiple witnesses, would you? Especially –' his voice lowered into a nearly soundless hiss as he leaned towards her – 'not in defence of the most notoriously wicked, shameless, untrustworthy and traitorous magic-worker in the history of our kingdom?'

'Ahhh!' There were no words in Rosalind's bellow of rage, or in her head. She yanked her sword free from its scabbard as he leaped swiftly back, and—

'Ros!' Giles's eyes and mouth were wide with horror as he tumbled through the open stable doors, carrying his lute case over his shoulder and sliding frantically between the duke's guards to hurry towards her. 'What's going on?'

She froze, still only halfway into her first lunging step. What *was* she doing?

Under Giles's appalled gaze, she found herself suddenly, horribly conscious of the lethal weapon in her grip … and of the Duke of Lune's smooth, bare hands, held out before him now in exaggerated supplication. Had she really been about to attack an unarmed man?

Rosalind stumbled back, almost dropping the sword in her fumbling attempts to shove it hastily back into its scabbard. She couldn't look Giles in the eye. She couldn't look at anyone. On her shoulder, the red squirrel chittered frantically, but it was meaningless noise to her.

'I am afraid,' said the Duke of Lune, 'that there seems to have been an unfortunate misunderstanding. As my own men and this young stable hand can all attest, I was deeply concerned for your sister's safety. Unfortunately, something I said in my humble attempts to help her must have sparked that notorious temper we've all heard so much about.' He shook his head sorrowfully. 'Perhaps it's best if I leave you to draw your own conclusions.'

'Ros?' Giles asked. She could feel him angling to try to catch her gaze – expecting her to defend herself. Ready to hear her side.

Her head hurt. Her heart hurt.

'He said ...' Rosalind stopped to swallow down fresh nausea. 'He said that Mother ...' But it was no use. She faltered to a halt, still staring down at the sword she had been so proud of, now hanging from her belt.

She was supposed to be a knight: a *protector* of the innocent. No matter how vile the duke's words had been, it was unbearable to imagine how badly she might have hurt him – an *unarmed opponent* – if Giles hadn't arrived in time to stop her. And, oh, the disgrace *that* would have brought down upon their family, just when Cordy's life depended upon her and Giles sneaking out without any notice!

Nothing mattered more than her family's safety ... but her lack of self-control had just put all of them at risk. She clamped her jaw tightly shut and breathed through her nose to stop herself from being physically sick.

Lady Fauvre was right: she *was* a brute.

'I confess,' said the duke regretfully, 'I did suggest that

we visit your lady mother to confirm that your sister was indeed safe on her own without any guards for her protection. I am afraid she did not take well to the notion, as you saw when you arrived.'

Rosalind's jaw ground together ... but she couldn't deny a single slippery word *or* bring herself to look at her brother's face.

Was he ashamed of her? Furious at how badly she had handled the duke's interruption and mangled their attempted escape?

Or, worse yet ... was he not even surprised?

Letting out a long sigh, Giles turned his back on her to face the duke. 'Obviously, this was all a terrible misunderstanding,' he said. 'You have nothing to worry about though. Our sister, the queen, has entrusted us with a private errand. She felt that it would be best for us to slip out quietly tonight, without any pomp or ceremony, because speed is of the essence.'

'Of course,' murmured the duke. 'Quite understandable.'

'Mother will be glad to hear of your concern for our sister,' Giles added, making Rosalind's jaw grind even tighter, 'but now that you understand what's really going on—'

'Oh, now that I understand,' said the duke, 'I can be of much greater assistance to you both. As you see, my men are ready and waiting. There is no need for any delay. We will happily escort you on your errand.'

'No!' Rosalind's mouth fell open in horror.

Giles's shoulders twitched. 'What my sister *meant* to say …' he began.

Over the last six weeks, those had become her least favourite words, and some of the ones she'd heard most. Now, the Duke of Lune ruthlessly spoke over them.

'My dear cousin,' he said, 'if speed is of the essence, then you'll certainly want me by your side. I can help you change horses along the road, I can clear your path in a thousand different ways – and you can hardly rely upon your *sister* when it comes to personal protection. Not after the behaviour we've all witnessed tonight!'

Rosalind refused to physically react to his words … but deep inside her, something shrivelled when Giles didn't speak up to deny them.

Lune continued, his voice soft and persuasive. 'There are bandits on the road, you know, there are sly, hidden enemies lurking even here at court, and—'

'Oh, you know all about sly, lurking enemies, don't you, Lune?' As the duke and his men all spun around, the Duchess of Solenne stood squarely in the centre of the open stable doorway, strong arms crossed before her cloaked chest, and smirked. 'I *knew* I'd find you here when

I heard the whispers. You saw an opportunity to try to snatch hold of the prince and princess away from anyone else's notice, didn't you?'

The duke's left hand was hidden from the duchess behind his back, but Rosalind watched it tighten into a fist. 'I came to help and advise my young cousins,' he snapped, 'as is my duty. You have nothing to do with this matter.'

'Oh, no? Well, I swore my loyalty to the Raven Throne. So I will *not* stand back when I come upon an attempt to abduct—'

'There is no abduction! I promise!' Giles's voice came out higher-pitched than usual. 'We're just—'

'They are fulfilling a private *family* errand,' the duke snapped. 'I am lending them my escort and assistance. That is all.'

'Oh, that is never *all*, not when it comes to your sneaking schemes.' The duchess looked past Lune to Rosalind as her own armed followers spread out in the darkened courtyard behind her, clearly making ready for battle. 'Did *you* ask this weasel to be your personal escort, Princess?'

'No,' Rosalind said flatly, and ignored her brother's cringe.

'I thought not.' Solenne nodded to her followers. 'In that case—'

'Wait!' Giles begged. 'Wait. No one needs to fight over us. We just have to leave, *quickly*, on an errand for our sister. We can't afford to wait while everybody argues about it. So if you'll all just step aside and—'

'Neither of you are going anywhere without my escort!' Lune's words might have been aimed at Giles, but he didn't look away from Solenne.

She sneered back at him. 'I'm certainly not letting these children go anywhere alone with *you*.'

Swords rasped free from their scabbards on both sides.

'So …' the duchess began.

'You can come with us too,' Rosalind told her.

Everyone turned to stare at her, including Giles. Even Rosalind could hardly believe the words that had just come out of her own mouth. Still, she didn't take them back, because she'd taken a good look at the mascot who snarled from the tunics of all the duchess's followers, male and female alike.

It was definitely the same boar that had been inscribed in miniature on her mysteriously gifted bow.

'Ros!' As the adults erupted into a brand-new debate, Giles grabbed her arm and hissed his words into her ear. 'What are you doing?'

'You know we won't get out in time if they start a

battle now!' she whispered back. 'They'd bring down the royal guard and everyone else. Our only way out is to let them come with us!'

'But she's the one who ordered Cordy's attack!'

'Or *he* was.' Rosalind's gaze narrowed on the Duke of Lune. 'Either way, they can guard us against each other – and we're not getting past him now. Trust me, I *tried*.'

'If it weren't for—!' Giles broke off, pinching his lips together, but angry colour stained his freckled cheeks even in the dim light of the stable.

Rosalind's hands squeezed into fists as she watched him visibly bite back the rest of his sentence.

If it weren't for how badly she'd fouled up their whole escape?

If it weren't for how disastrously she'd handled the duke?

Of course she knew that this mess was her fault. Did he really think she had missed that detail? But it didn't – couldn't – matter that her clever, courtly brother had been embarrassed by her ineptness yet again. Cordy's life depended on them getting out *tonight* to ask the spirits for their help, no matter what sacrifices that required ... so fourteen horses, not two, streamed out through the castle gates once all the debates were done.

The red squirrel clung tightly to Rosalind's hair for

balance as the cool night wind blew past her shoulder. Rosalind clung to her new horse's reins, refusing to lose her unaccustomed seat *or* let herself be intimidated by the grim-faced ducal guards who flanked her and her brother on all sides, leaving no room for either of them to escape.

She'd failed her family once already tonight. She *would not* fail them again when it most mattered.

Together, they raced down the winding, cobblestoned street into the sleeping capital city. That winding street would lead them out into the wide countryside, towards the wilderness beyond and the looming mist-shrouded, magical mountains.

Secrets and answers were all waiting for them there. Rosalind would not turn back before she'd found them.

But she couldn't bring herself to meet her brother's gaze as they rode into the night, away from the court, into the dangerous unknown … under the care of the two most likely suspects in their sister's attempted murder.

14

Giles woke, as was usual, with a song in his head. This time, it was full of such overwhelming heartbreak that it threatened to sink him into despair ... until something soft and ticklish suddenly bumped against his nose, making his eyes fly open.

'Oh, *you*!' Half laughing, half sighing, he reached out from under his piled covers to pet the small and pointed chin of the nosy little hedgehog who stared expectantly at him from the cloth floor beside his head. She had waddled up to him in the royal stables last night, just as he'd been about to finally mount his horse for the journey, and had insisted with a series of noisy grunts and snorts that she ought to come along.

In that moment, he hadn't had the heart to turn her away, no matter how foolish he might look to all the adults around him. He had *needed* the comfort of her steady presence, tucked snugly against him as he and Ros rode away from the castle, leaving the rest of their family behind.

Now, though … 'I thought you'd leave once I fell asleep,' he whispered. 'Don't you want to be wild and free?'

She snorted in his face and then turned to waddle purposefully across the small tent that the duke had given him, coming to a stop at his lute case.

'Sorry,' he told her as she nosed hopefully at it. 'No music for you today. My lute isn't even in there any more.'

His fingers tingled with the old, familiar yearning to start his morning by strumming a chord; he shook them out, as he had every morning for nearly six weeks, and then pushed himself upright, tossing aside his covers. He might only have had a few hours of sleep, but there was no more time to waste – and outside, he could hear brisk footsteps and adult voices already sounding through the thin black-and-silver tent walls.

'Right,' he said. 'No time for singing *or* despair. Let's find food and my sister.'

He and Ros needed to talk. Last night, when he'd arrived at the stables too late and found chaos erupting, he'd fumbled everything. He'd been so wrecked by his confrontation with Wincester that he'd faltered and failed to find the right words for that perilous moment. Even if he'd dared to use magic on the duke or the duchess, by then, he couldn't have managed it. His magical reserves had been trickling away, like sand in an hourglass, to maintain his first casting and hold Wincester safely unconscious.

Of course, he hadn't been able to explain that in front of the others, though, so who knew what Ros had made of it? Even beforehand, she'd spent so much of the day being inexplicably angry at him. He'd hated to leave his failure unexplained – but by the time their whole party had finally come to a halt, hours later, the sun had been creeping up over the horizon and his head had been spinning with exhaustion. He'd barely even managed to slide off his horse and fall into the tent he'd been given.

He was awake now, though, and more than ready to make plans, so he untied the straps that held his tent shut and pushed through the new opening – just as another tent opened five feet in front of him.

The Duchess of Solenne's nephew, Lord Edmund de Vore, stared out at him with startled green eyes. 'Your Highness.'

'Lord Edmund?' Giles's own eyes widened. How had he missed the other boy in the duchess's entourage last night?

Edmund must have joined their party at the very end, hidden among all the others in the darkness and confusion. But *why* had the duchess bothered to summon him? As far as she was supposed to know, they were only going on a minor royal errand. What was she scheming?

There was only one way to find out … so his sister would have to wait for explanations after all.

Giles smiled brightly as he stepped out of his tent on to the grass. 'I've been hoping to talk to you again!'

'You have?' Edmund's pale eyebrows rose in unhidden surprise. Then his lips curved tentatively upward. 'Did you want to ask more about – oh!' He gave a start of surprise as his gaze fell on the ground by Giles's feet. 'Is that your pet?'

'Ha! No.' Giles shook his head ruefully as he looked down at the determined little creature trundling after him. At this time of day, he was fairly sure, any reasonable hedgehog ought to be fast asleep, but this one was forcing herself to stay awake by his side, blinking furiously against the too-bright sunlight of early afternoon. 'Silly beast.' He knelt to carefully scoop her up from the dandelion-strewn grass, cradling her soft, warm belly in his hands. 'Why don't I give you a ride so that you can take a nap? I won't leave you behind while you sleep, I promise.'

Meeting Edmund's wide-eyed gaze as he rose back to his feet, Giles shrugged his right shoulder, keeping the curve of his left arm still as his prickly, grumbling burden busily padded her way into a more comfortable position. 'Wild animals love Cordy, that's all there is to it. To them, Ros and I both apparently smell like her.'

'How fascinating.' Brows lowering into a frown of concentration, Edmund finally stepped out of his tent. 'Was it always like that for your family? Or did it change after your sister mended the Raven Crown?'

Actually, all three of them had mended the crown together; Giles and Ros and Cordy each had to make their own personal vows to the ancient spirits of the land before that mending could be completed. But Giles wasn't surprised that Edmund didn't know that part. After all, it wasn't as if he or Ros had ever tried to argue over who should wear the crown.

The ancient spirits to whom they'd made their vows on that terrifying battlefield had never deigned to show themselves to any of the triplets. Still, their choice of ruler had been crystal clear: *Cordy* was the one the spirits had chosen to hold all the power of their land, and Cordy was the one the land had always loved … as was obvious from even a cursory look at the countryside around him now.

The last time Giles had journeyed between Mount Corve and the capital city, no sunny yellow dandelions had burst through lush grass underfoot. Back then, all those rolling hills in the distance had been brown and lifeless, a sign of the land's despair; now, they were covered in vibrant, happy green as the land rejoiced in its new ruler.

The last time Giles had passed farmers' fields in this kingdom, barely any seeds had managed to take root in the broken, barren earth. Last night, every field along their journey had been crammed full of tall and thriving shadows in the darkness – eager plants rising high for an abundant harvest.

Giles and Ros might both have done their part to mend the crown, but it was Cordy who'd mended the land itself when she'd put that crown on to her head and sacrificed her own magic for everyone else's sake.

He *had* to save her now, in return. He would never have a better chance to find out what those old scrolls had really said – *and* what Lord Edmund and his aunt had been plotting together.

'Everything changed after Cordy became queen,' he said in answer to Edmund's question, 'but then, you probably could have guessed that yourself. Didn't you say you were studying the magic of the crown?'

Luckily, their tents were in the centre of the makeshift camp, shielded from any dangers or witnesses beyond. Every adult voice sounded at least fifteen feet away, all coming from the area where a trail of smoke rose high over the triangular tent roofs, carrying with it an enticing scent of cooking food. Giles stepped closer to Edmund anyway, so that he could safely lower his voice. 'How long have you been interested in the history of royal magic?'

'Oh ...' Edmund ducked his head, colour rising behind his pale cheeks. 'The truth is, I've always been obsessed with history. I know it's not what I'm supposed to care about, but ... well, Aunt Solenne would tell you I've been hopelessly lost in books and ink ever since I was born. She did try to help me master more appropriate pursuits, to be moulded into a better future king for Corvenne, but—'

'But you're not going to *be* the king, are you?' The sharp words slipped out from Giles's lips before he could snatch them back. He cursed himself for the mistake ...

But Lord Edmund's face lit up with pure joy. 'I know!' he said. 'Isn't it *wonderful*?'

Giles stared at him, for once lost for words.

This was the boy who'd tried to seize the throne of Corvenne through bloody battle six weeks earlier? Was he the most brilliant performer Giles had ever met? Or had they all been wrong about Edmund from the beginning?

Before Giles could even begin to think it through, he heard adult voices coming dangerously closer. *No time left to beat around the bush!* 'Tell me about those old scrolls I saw you studying yesterday.'

'You actually want to know?' Edmund shook his head, letting out a half-laugh of disbelief. 'Everyone usually begs me to *stop* rambling on about old scrolls. I know they aren't very interesting to most people, but—'

'I'm interested,' Giles said firmly. '*Very* interested. Please tell me every single detail.'

'Well—'

'Aha! You're awake ... and apparently I am just in time to save you.' The Duke of Lune's voice lashed like a whip through the air, making Edmund jerk backwards even though the words were aimed at Giles. 'My poor young cousin. Did the Young Pretender catch you unawares? Don't be deceived by how limp and useless he appears. He'll betray you in a heartbeat if you give him the chance.'

Edmund shook his head frantically, his narrow shoulders rising to bracket his ears as he seemed to shrink into himself. 'I wouldn't – I mean, I'd never—'

Giles had never expected to protect his sister's most famous rival for the throne, but he found himself stepping between Edmund and his adult cousin after all, turning a placating smile upon the rapidly approaching duke. 'We were just having a pleasant conversation. We're both interested in history, so—'

'Was he regaling you with the history of his family's brutal schemes to steal what was never rightfully theirs, with no regard for how much blood they spilt along the way?' Lune sneered as he looked Edmund up and down, from his rumpled fair hair to his leather boots. 'I wouldn't put too much faith in any interpretation of the past that comes from *that* direction.'

'Cousin …' Giles began.

'No, it's all right.' Shoving his hair out of his eyes, Edmund flicked a quick, unhappy look at Giles. 'I understand. But it was an honour to speak with you again, Your Highness. I do hope you'll believe that.'

Shaking his head, Giles stepped forward to argue – but before he could say a word, Edmund turned and fled towards the fire in the distance where everyone else in camp seemed to be gathering.

The Duke of Lune sighed, placing a strong hand on Giles's shoulder. 'You have a kind heart,' he said gently, 'but you'll soon learn not to let unscrupulous characters prey upon it. The Young Pretender may not look like much of a threat to your sister's crown, but his aunt has been his only guardian since birth, and she has raised him with the unswerving belief that the Raven Throne belongs to him and their family by right. Why else do you think he would spend so much time buried deep in the archives, hunting up every source he can find to bolster his own personal claim to kingship?'

'Perhaps,' Giles said, 'but I still don't think—'

Lune's fingers squeezed tightly around Giles's shoulder, cutting him off. 'I happen to know that that harmless-looking *boy* has been privately researching the ancient bindings of royal magic that connect your sister to the land itself. Did he happen to offer you any innocent explanation for *that* in your "pleasant conversation" just now?'

'Well ... not exactly,' Giles admitted, 'but—'

'Of course not. There is none.' Lune snorted. 'Fortunately for you, cousin, I'm here now to guide you and protect you from being tricked by our worst enemies. Trust me: I will always stand by your side to protect our family from their scheming.'

As Giles watched, the other boy's thin figure disappeared behind a tent, taking with him every opportunity for useful information.

Clenching his teeth, Giles let out a long sigh and forced himself to stand still, not even trying to free himself from the heavy weight on his shoulder. 'How very fortunate.'

15

osalind was *not* enjoying herself, obviously. How
could she? Her sister was in deadly danger, and she
and Giles were surrounded by enemies. Only a true brute
would allow herself to be *happy* about any of it …

But, oh, it had been so long since she'd been allowed
to exercise outdoors in the sunshine! It felt amazing to
be using her muscles again now to ride on horseback
across the country after weeks of being cooped up inside
Raven's Roost. Better yet, when she'd first awoken to
the sounds of a busy camp, she'd found the perfect
travelling outfit – a plain bronze tunic and leggings –
folded just outside her tent, waiting. No, they weren't a
perfect fit, but who cared? For the first time in over six
weeks, she was wearing clothes that let her *move* – and best
of all, Lady Fauvre was miles away, with that distance

growing further with every minute of this journey.

Tipping her head back in the cool breeze as she rode, with the red squirrel balancing alertly on the pommel of her saddle, Rosalind sucked in a deep, invigorating breath and felt herself *glow*.

'Beautiful, isn't it?' The Duchess of Solenne deftly manoeuvred her powerful horse into place on Rosalind's left-hand side, nudging her guards out of the way, and surveyed the rolling landscape of vibrant green hills and fields with as much satisfaction as if they all belonged to her.

For all Rosalind knew, they actually might. Unlike Cordy, she hadn't spent the last six weeks poring over tedious maps and laws, so she'd no idea which of the six duchies laid particular claim to this portion of the kingdom. Still, that wasn't why she allowed the duchess and her guards to box her in now, all of them moving as carefully-casually as if they thought she couldn't tell perfectly well that they were working to close her in for a private conversation.

It gave her the perfect excuse to avoid any more attempts from her brother to get her alone for a conversation of his own. Ever since breakfast, Giles had been clearly bursting to lecture her for ruining their quiet escape last night with her failures in basic diplomacy and courtly manners. Rosalind didn't want to hear any of it – and she'd been waiting for this chance ever since yesterday's revelation.

So she ignored the duchess's opening parry about the view to focus on what really mattered. 'Why did you send me that bow?'

'Aha. Worked that one out for yourself, did you?' The duchess's lips curled upward in what looked, astonishingly, like real pride. 'Well done, Princess. I must admit, I'd rather hoped you would manage that.'

Rosalind frowned. 'You could have sent a note with it, to make sure.'

'Could I have, indeed?' The duchess snorted, keeping her horse to an easy, steady trot as she kept her gaze fixed on Rosalind. 'And what exactly do you think *you'd* have done if I'd sent a signed note along with my gift that day, with your blood still boiling from your first true battle?'

Well … 'I *might* not have smashed it.'

'You think not?' The duchess shook her head, smiling faintly. 'I expect, even if you hadn't broken it, you would have turned it over to your mother in suspicion of some devilish trickery on my part … and I'll have you know, that bow was crafted by my own personal weapons master. It was meant for good use, not for waste, and besides, you'd earned it. In all my years, I've never seen anything like the way you fought off all my archers. It was *beautiful*.' She hummed in unmistakable appreciation.

Warmth spread through Rosalind at the sound, loosening long-clenched muscles. Still, she forced herself not to smile. 'I *was* fighting against you, remember?'

'Oh, that.' The duchess waved off the reminder. 'You didn't grow up the way the rest of us did – that's the problem. This whole life is new to you. Once you've grown more accustomed to it, you'll understand the first rule of life at court: if we all hung on to grudges after every battle we fought, there'd be nobody left to talk to over supper.'

'Hmm,' Rosalind said. She hadn't noticed the duchess and duke letting go of any of their grudges against each other.

'It's all about the shifting game of power – really, that's all that courtly life ever comes down to, in the end, for all the pearls and glamour.' The duchess shrugged. 'If you want to make sure your own family stays safe, you'll play for the most powerful seat and fight to win – but of course, now that your sister's mended the Raven Crown, we can all finally relax and enjoy each other's company … Not that you've had much to enjoy so far.'

The duchess's upper lip curled into a sneer. 'When I heard you'd been landed with Lady Fauvre for your Mistress of the Bedchamber, I thought you might end up truly *needing* that bow. Frankly, I'm amazed you haven't lost your temper yet and whacked her with a sword in one of your official training sessions!'

Rosalind's jaw tightened. 'I don't have any official training sessions,' she said curtly. 'Lady Fauvre says princesses can't—'

'Lady Fauvre,' said the Duchess of Solenne, 'is a pathetic little worm who failed every weapons-training session she attempted when she was your age. Trust me; we were raised together, unfortunately.' Her nostrils flared with disdain. 'Has she been inflicting her peculiar theories about what makes a "proper lady" upon you too?'

Rosalind didn't answer … but inside her chest, a flicker of hot, desperate hope began to burn for the first time in weeks.

'She's never forgiven me for trouncing her on her own mother's training ground when we were both girls,' the duchess continued. 'But of course, she couldn't simply accept that she is terrible at fighting; no, she wants to convince everyone that fighting itself is somehow inherently wrong for *ladies*.' The duchess rolled her eyes expressively. 'I hope she hasn't managed to convince you with her particular brand of poison?'

'Never,' Rosalind vowed. Her fingers tightened on the reins for an instant, before she forced herself to loosen them; her latest horse was strong and sweet-natured and responsive, and he didn't deserve to be alarmed. In her own head, though, every perception was shifting so rapidly that she felt dizzy.

What if she wasn't a humiliating failure at court after all?

She *hadn't* let Lady Fauvre steal her weapons *or* poison her out of believing what she'd always known was true. She had kept on practising her sword-work in secret, hadn't she? It had been hard – sometimes impossible – to find enough moments of privacy in her own bedchamber when no one was there to see, but she had persisted, despite every taunt and every slippery, mocking word.

She'd spent her whole life being transformed again and again against her will … but in the end, she hadn't let Lady Fauvre transform her, had she?

'I'd like to see you on a jousting field one day,' said the duchess. 'I'll teach you the way of it when we get back, if you'd like.'

Rosalind swallowed hard to choke back a sob. 'I … would like that. I'd like it very much.'

'Good! It's settled then. And maybe you can do me a favour too and be kind enough to train with my nephew once or twice. He means well, you know – he's a soft-hearted lad – but he's as useless as a blade of grass when it comes to the training field, just waiting to be trampled.' The duchess shook her head, sighing. 'He's spent too much time buried in scrolls and archives. He could do with an example of someone who really knows what she's doing.'

Really knows what she's doing ... Rosalind blinked at the unfamiliar description. 'I don't mind practising sword-work with anyone.'

'Excellent. I *knew* I was right about you.' The duchess's teeth gleamed in her fierce smile. 'Now, what do you say we let these horses free and show the kingdom what a *true* leader looks like? How would you feel about a race?'

'*Can* we?' The group had been riding at a sedate pace so far, keeping each new round of horses from tiring too soon along the long journey.

'Why not? We'll change steeds soon enough, at our next stop. Why don't we see how fast you can move without Lady Fauvre standing over you!'

'Ros? What's going on up there?' Behind her, Giles's voice rang with an unhidden warning.

She knew that tone. She'd heard it again and again for the last six weeks, ever since they'd first moved into Raven's Roost.

Don't walk too fast. Don't say what you think. Never fight back. Don't make trouble. Don't ...

She scooped up the red squirrel from her pommel, ignoring his chattering outrage at the indignity, and passed him swiftly to the closest of the duchess's guards.

'You want to see how fast I can go?' She clapped her heels against her horse's sides, sending him tearing across the open landscape. 'Just watch me!'

For once, for this glorious moment, she was free – and the Duchess of Solenne's whoop of laughter followed her like a blessing.

16

Unbelievable. Giles stared after his sister as she galloped into the distance with their family's oldest enemy.

She'd heard him call out to her – he *knew* she had. And yet ...

Riding on a sleek black horse beside Giles, the Duke of Lune *tskd*. 'It appears,' he said regretfully, 'that Her Highness no longer listens to anyone – not even her own loving brother.'

Show no weakness! Giles's jaw snapped shut. 'It is *fine*.' He'd played the role of a happy, confident prince for six weeks already. He wouldn't fall down on it now. 'My sister will never turn down any opportunity for a race, that's all. She's a born warrior.'

'Mm ...' The duke's brow furrowed as he watched Ros

and the duchess disappear around the green bend of the next rambling hill. 'An admirable quality for a girl in the wilds, perhaps, but for a princess with the eyes of the royal court upon her and our family's enemies all on the hunt for vulnerabilities they might exploit …'

He sighed. 'I had hoped the latest rumours might have exaggerated Princess Rosalind's dangerous volatility. If she truly is too reckless and driven by hot temper to respect even her own brother any more …'

Giles's teeth ground together behind his smile. 'It's not a problem.'

Of course Ros didn't respect his opinions. Over the last two days, that had become excruciatingly obvious. He still didn't understand how that had happened, but anyone could see it – because his infuriatingly stubborn sister never bothered to hide her emotions for the sake of *anyone* else's feelings, not even when they were family.

But why was she so furious at him? *And why won't she listen to me, so I can explain?*

'Your Highness …' Lune lowered his voice, and his guards closed protectively around them, shielding their conversation from the duchess's guards and from Lord Edmund, who rode among them with his shoulders hunched and his head lowered in what looked like despair. 'You know my loyalty to our family's cause. I have fought for nothing else for decades. So you must know how deeply it pains me to have to give you this warning.'

Giles lowered his voice too, horribly aware of all the silent, listening guards around them. 'I promise, you have nothing to fear. My sister is the most loyal person I know. She would *never* betray our family in any way.'

'Of course not – but do you really imagine that she couldn't be betrayed herself, merely by trusting the wrong person?' The Duke of Lune tipped his head meaningfully in the direction of Ros's gleeful, thoughtless race with the duchess. 'Look how easily Solenne has already played upon her competitive instincts. I must admit, I *had* hoped that your mother would see fit to teach the princess some self-control and a more royal mode of behaviour for the sake of our entire family's reputation and safety, but as she has apparently neglected to do so …'

The duke shook his head, raising one elegant hand when Giles opened his mouth to argue. 'No, you must allow me to speak this bitter truth to you now, out of the love I have always borne for our family. As you know – as I warned you myself, weeks ago! – our situation at court is perilous indeed. You were wise enough to heed my earlier advice and hide your own less palatable qualities from the court, but I fear the rest of our family has not been so cautious. Between your mother's scandalous reputation and the uncontrolled – even brutish – behaviour of your sister, we shall soon reach a tipping point at which we lose all hopes for the support of the highest lords of this kingdom … and for our family's survival.

'If the princess cannot be brought to see reason and modify her behaviour, then we must find a way to close her away from public view – or else, I promise you, that point of vulnerability *will* be used against our family.'

'*Close her away?*' Giles finally managed to break through, his voice rising. 'What are you talking about? Ros doesn't need to be imprisoned. She's—'

'She presents a serious danger to our family's control of the throne, and I believe you know it.' Lune gave him a grim look as their horses trotted steadily forward. 'Or had you not heard any of the rumours that have been circulating?'

Lady Fauvre's face yesterday, so full of fear as she'd passed them on …

'So long as she keeps on wildly swinging around that lethal sword and flying into rages that terrorise her poor ladies-in-waiting, those whispers will only grow more dangerous – and if we do not find a way to halt them, they *will* weaken your other sister's reign irreparably. Do you really think the court could ever maintain faith in a ruling family that allowed such *animalistic* behaviour in its own princess?'

'Animalistic?' Giles had to whisper the word. His head was suddenly spinning, even as his stomach vibrated with the snoring of the hedgehog in her makeshift pouch, just one more piece of damning evidence of his family's ties to nature.

If anyone suspected …

If anyone had guessed the truth of his and Ros's true origins …

'*Animalistic*,' Lune repeated calmly. 'Wild. Uncivilised and uncontrolled. In other words …' He gestured once more ahead of them.

The thick leather reins of Giles's horse bit into his palms as he squeezed hard, desperately fighting to keep his balance. *Show no weakness. Don't let them see …*

He wanted so badly for Lune's words to be mere nonsense to ignore. But he couldn't discount them, not when they so closely echoed everything Lady Fauvre had confided in him with such sorrow yesterday. And he couldn't forget his own vow to the spirits: to love this land and to listen to its needs and to protect it with all his skills. Cordy *had* to hold the throne, for the land's sake as well as her own.

Still, he would never sacrifice one sister for another. The thought of losing Ros even more than he already had was unbearable. There had to be another way – but only if they worked together to find it.

'Thank you for your warning, cousin.' His voice was a mere rasp of sound. 'I'll talk to her, I promise.'

... *No matter what it takes.*

Ros might not *want* to listen to him any more, but Giles still knew without a doubt that any sacrifice was worthwhile for their family's protection. That had been true when he'd given up his music and true again last night, when he had escaped Raven's Roost by betraying Wincester's trust. It remained just as true today, in the open air and sunshine.

Still, as sick dread curled up through his gut, Giles knew that his next sacrifice might hurt even more than his earlier ones.

That night, hot smoke twirled up from the Duchess of Solenne's campfire, rough stones poked into the soles of Rosalind's boots, grass smudged the legs of her borrowed tunic, and she felt more at home in herself than she had in weeks. The little squirrel had scampered off when she'd first sat down, disappearing along with the hedgehog to hunt for their own suppers, but he hadn't left her alone. Welcoming voices surrounded her like an embrace as she sat cross-legged between the duchess and the captain of the duchess's guard, sharing a cheerful meal of plain, dried meat, crusty bread and tart apples with the rest of Solenne's guards and her uninteresting nephew.

Lord Edmund hadn't said a single word all evening, sitting hunched and brooding, deep in thought, but Rosalind hardly even noticed his doleful presence as the others swapped hilarious jokes and glorious stories of battles and hard journeys past. Rosalind soaked in every word like healing medicine ... and saved up that feeling of fellowship to bolster her for the battle that was waiting to be fought tomorrow.

The duke and duchess might be longtime enemies, but they'd organised this journey with the skill of leaders who'd spent all their lives fighting campaigns across this landscape. Today, they'd allowed only the briefest of halts to collect fresh horses from waiting stables along the way. By the time they had finally agreed on a site to pitch their camp, they'd left the last farms and villages behind. The rocky hilltop where their tents perched now, in two carefully separate circles, marked the midpoint of a familiar series of hills that rolled into the thickly wooded slopes of Mount Corve ... where Raven's Nest was waiting for their arrival.

Even as she sat surrounded by perfect companionship, Rosalind could feel it looming behind her back like a perilous beacon, calling to her and threatening her in equal measure. It was as if the ancient spirits who'd retreated there hundreds of years ago already had their eyes fixed upon her, plotting how best to make use of her for their next schemes.

She'd never seen any of those spirits in fleshly form, but she could never forget the feeling of their presence: overwhelmingly magical, unpredictable and *other*. They'd been the ones who'd helped her mother transform her shape from animal to human when Rosalind was still a newborn. Then they'd revealed that truth to her and her triplet siblings in a life-upending vision at Raven's Nest … and her second unwanted transformation, from fierce knight-in-training to princess, had taken place a scant few days later.

Rosalind was only just starting to reclaim her true self now, after six weeks of misery and doubt in Raven's Roost. She wouldn't cower away from those spirits when her sister needed her – and of course she would keep the vow that she had made to them to protect the land – but she *would not* let herself be transformed against her will ever again, no matter what they wanted.

Watch out, she silently warned those spirits, and deliberately kept her back to them.

Fortunately, that gave her exactly the view she wanted. Two different campfires had been set on this hill: one for the duchess and one for the duke, with only smoke daring to trail between them. Red flames from both fires crackled steadily and sent hot sparks flying up through the dark, giving just enough light for her to keep an eye on her brother's shadowy figure from a safe distance.

Lune might be the worst kind of snake in human form, but Giles ought to be safe enough for now with so many other people gathered around the two of them. No doubt she'd hear his bell-like voice rising up soon enough in one of his beloved ballads or comic songs, the kind he used to sing at home all the time. Her brother could never resist the opportunity to charm everyone around him, and once he'd started singing, no one in the world could resist him.

So she wasn't prepared to see Giles rise to his feet beside the duke's campfire and stroll casually away into the darkness beyond the tents.

Rosalind gaped in disbelief. Had he lost his wits?

One of the duke's guards stood up to follow him, and she started up from her seat on the grass immediately – but the duchess reached out a hand to stop her.

'Never fear,' Solenne murmured. She gave a subtle nod to a guard on Rosalind's left, who slipped silently into the darkness, heading in the same direction. 'Trust me, Princess. I won't allow either you or your brother to be left alone with any of Lune's hired knives on this journey. That's why my party joined yours in the first place – to guard your back on this secret mission, whatever it may be.'

Shadows shifted across her strong-boned face in the flickering light of the fire as she took a swig of the hot, spiced drink in her clay mug. Her eyes met Rosalind's over the mug's rim. 'Of course, I'd be happy to offer more assistance too. Anyone travelling to Mount Corve can only have one destination in mind – and Raven's Nest is a perilous pilgrimage even for a royal. If my advice would be of any use to you, I'd be more than happy to give it.'

'Thank you.' Rosalind put her own half-full mug down on the grass between their feet and said, with true regret, 'I wish I could tell you all about it.'

The Duchess of Solenne had managed so many battles; she would have been the perfect person to consult, now that Rosalind knew she'd been on her side all along. But when it came to her family's safety, Rosalind could never trust anyone else to stand guard.

So she slipped away into the darkness herself a moment later, leaving behind the warm circle of firelight and companionship, and stalked with deliberate care around the back of the clustered tents in pursuit of the brother she'd been avoiding all day.

Giles might think it was wonderfully romantic to

wander around in the wilderness at night to dream up new ballads, but—

'*Stand.*' His voice pierced the darkness and slammed her to a halt.

It was Giles's voice, the same voice she'd heard tens of thousands of times across their lifetime, raised in laughter or debate or ridiculously catchy, impossible-to-forget songs.

N*ever* had she heard him speak in this tone. She tried to take a step forward. She couldn't. Her muscles were locked.

He had enchanted her.

'What do you think you're doing?' she whispered. He was alone; he must have given the others the slip. 'It's *me*, you fool!'

'I know.' He stepped closer, his face still shrouded in darkness. 'I froze both of the guards in sleep already. They won't overhear anything we say or even realise what's happened when they wake. Why do you think I drew you out here?'

'You – what?' Rosalind's jaw dropped open. 'You knew I'd follow? You mean, you *tricked* me?' Humiliation bubbled up her throat, shattering every good feeling of hope and faith and strength that had shored her up all evening. 'I was trying to protect you! And you *dared* to use your magic on *me*?'

They had never used their magic on each other. Not *ever*. That was the whole point of the magic that they held: it was for *protecting* their family, not attacking it.

Perhaps Lady Fauvre was right and Rosalind was stupid after all – because somehow, she had never even imagined that he would.

'I didn't want to have to resort to this,' he snapped, 'but we need to talk, and you wouldn't listen to me. So—'

'So you decided to do it anyway? To *make* me do whatever you wanted?' Her whole body shook internally with the urge to lunge forward, to pound her fists into the ground and make the whole hilltop shatter, but her skin didn't move a single inch. Every muscle and bone was locked in place, out of her control.

She couldn't even let out the scream building deep within her without alerting the Duke of Lune and all his men to her vulnerability.

Tonight, for the first time in so many weeks, she had felt free. Now here she stood, trapped more completely than ever before – and, as always, it had been done to her by *her own family*, choosing *their* needs over hers once again.

'I don't know why you've been so angry lately,' Giles began in a low, careful murmur, 'but I have to tell you—'

'*Enough!*' Rosalind couldn't shout without alerting the

others, but she spat out her words with all the fury in her broken heart. 'I am *done.*'

'Done?' He paused. 'With what?'

'Done with you and everyone else making me feel worthless!'

'What are you talking about?' He shook his head, his shadow stirring in the darkness as he stepped closer. 'I've never—'

'Do you think I'm that much of an idiot?' she snarled. 'I hear it *every single day* from Lady Fauvre. What a terrible disappointment I am as a princess. What a clumsy, stupid, unroyal oaf, who should have stayed in the woods forever to let the rest of you be free of me. What a horrible *brute* I am! How much the whole court laughs at me every day, and how tragic it is that I'm around to embarrass all the rest of you. How much you *all* secretly wish I wasn't a part of the family, and how you talk about it with her!'

'Wait.' Giles's voice wobbled. 'Ros, hold on a minute. Lady Fauvre never actually *said* any of those horrible things to you, did she? Not really?'

'You think I would lie about it?' Her laugh turned into a sob, which made everything so much worse. 'I have spent *six weeks* being tormented every day for every single tiny detail about me that is wrong and stupid and unladylike and laughable in a princess. And it's not just her! All her cronies titter at her constant jokes about my worthlessness whenever the rest of the family isn't there to hear them. Yesterday, she called me *an animal in a dress!*'

'But – but why—?'

'I have endured *every moment of it*,' she ground out, 'because I am loyal to the family. I *love* our family. That's why I've agreed to everything! I'm not like you – I don't care about the pomp and finery. For you, it was easy. You didn't have to give up anything you cared about. But for me—'

'Didn't have to give up anything? *Me?*'

'But now I'm *done!*' She shout-whispered her final words, drowning out his interruption. 'I am sick and tired of letting everyone else tell me who to be no matter what I think or feel about it. I'*ll* decide who to be from now on. And you will *never* use your magic on me again!'

She still couldn't move a muscle below her neck – but her magic had never been controlled by her physical muscles. Now it crashed out in a wave of furious energy and slammed into her triplet's body, sending him flying off his feet.

He cried out in shock. His own magic lost its grip and she was free. Her heart ached as she stepped forward and saw him lying sprawled awkwardly on the bare, rocky ground.

She had only ever wanted to *protect* her family.

'Don't worry,' Rosalind said flatly. 'I won't follow you again. Next time, you're on your own.'

Without another word, she strode back to her tent, on the Duchess of Solenne's side of the encampment. Once she was safely inside, she curled her knees up to her chest to form a tight, defensive ball under her blankets, leaving her sword in easy reach by her side. She was ready to defend herself against intruders … but she couldn't stop her chest from hurting all night long.

17

In Giles's dreams, he was a sleek red fox, racing on four legs to the top of the highest hill to sing out his panic and despair to the moon and to every animal around him, summoning aid to save them all ...

But no sound came out of his throat, no matter how hard he tried.

He had lost his voice.

In Rosalind's dreams, she was a warrior hare who had been savaged by a predator too powerful to defeat. Now, she was dragging her way back to her burrow, wounded and bleeding, with enemies lurking in the darkness on every side.

In Cordelia's dreams ...

But Cordelia wasn't dreaming any more.

18

Giles woke, for the first time in memory, without a single note of music in his head. It felt as empty and aching as his chest, where all his shining hope and certainties had resided only a few days ago.

Ros didn't lie to anyone. *Ever.* That, at least, he still knew to be true – but that meant that every awful story she'd related to him last night had really happened, back at Raven's Roost. Worse yet, she hadn't trusted him enough to tell him about any of it as it was happening.

Why would she trust you with anything any more? his conscience whispered. He groaned, rolling over to press his forehead into the thin pillow that protected him from the bumpy tent floor … but it couldn't protect him from the truth.

He'd been so determined to have her do what *he'd*

thought was right, he had broken her trust last night to force it. It wasn't the first time he'd betrayed her either.

How could he have been so taken in by Lady Fauvre's wicked lies about his sister? No wonder Wincester hadn't heard any of those terrible rumours before she'd arrived. *She* was the one spreading all of them herself! Perhaps *that* was the explanation for why she'd spent so much time flitting 'helpfully' from one royal household to the next – all the better to spread her poison.

But why had she even wanted to in the first place? Giles had no idea, but the Duke of Lune had obviously been as thoroughly deceived as he had. Lune's warnings about Ros yesterday had almost exactly echoed the vicious taunts from Lady Fauvre that Ros had passed on last night.

He had to find a way to convince their powerful cousin that Ros wasn't the menace Lune imagined – but first, he had to do something even more important.

He needed to apologise to his sister … and pray to all the ancient spirits that she would forgive him after all.

The hedgehog hadn't returned from her hunting expedition by the time he'd stumbled to bed last night, heartsick and despairing. So there were no interruptions as he threw on a clean outfit from his lute case and ran his fingers through his thick hair to tame it into respectability.

Closing his eyes, he took a deep breath, forcing his

body to stop jittering with nerves. *Remember: you're still surrounded by enemies!*

His lips stretched into a false, performing smile. His shoulders straightened. He knelt to undo the thick ribbons that held the tent door closed, then stepped out into surprisingly chilly, damp air …

And knew immediately that something was terribly wrong.

The grass outside his tent was brown. Where it had stood thick and vibrant green yesterday, it now lay flat and dry and crackling under his feet, while a dark grey sky lowered overhead.

The change was *everywhere*. All the wildflowers that had been joyfully scattered across the hillside were dead now, crumpled into withered remnants.

It was bizarre – no, *inconceivable*. There was no reason or way for such a drastic shift in the landscape to happen so quickly … *unless* …

Dread pulled at Giles's gut as he slowly, reluctantly raised his gaze past the line of tents around him, beyond the newly barren brown hills that rose before them, all the way to the thickly wooded slopes of Mount Corve.

Even as he watched, a diamond-shaped patch of greenwood near the very top of the mountain faded to a dead brown before his eyes.

Cordy!

Giles was running before he could even stop to think, the damp, heavy air clinging to his skin like a mourning veil.

He couldn't be too late to save his sister. He *couldn't*!

'Ah, cousin. Just the person we were looking for.' Strong fingers closed around the right sleeve of his velvet doublet and yanked him to a skidding halt just ten feet before the line of tethered horses. The Duke of Lune's dark eyes glittered as he smiled thinly down at Giles, flanked by his men. 'I believe we're ready for the most important secrets to be shared with the rest of us, if you please.'

'There's no time!' Giles yanked desperately at the duke's iron grip. 'We can't talk now. We have to get to Raven's Nest!'

'Not quite yet, I think.' Lune's voice was soft, but his grip was unyielding. 'I take it *you* understand what's occurring with the land around us, Prince Giles. Why don't you enlighten the rest of us?'

'I ...' Giles's gaze darted around the tightening semicircle of grown men, all with looming, broad shoulders and stony expressions.

'Get your hands off the prince!' *That* was Ros, shouldering her way through the circle of armed men without any signs of fear – and with an angry squirrel standing on her shoulder and the Duchess of Solenne following just behind, flanked by her own armed followers, men and women alike.

'Princess. Of course.' Lune lifted his hand off Giles's arm.

Beside the duchess, Edmund hugged his arms around his narrow chest, his gaze fixed on Mount Corve, and his expression as pale and horrified as if he'd seen a ghost.

'I hope you weren't threatening Prince Giles, Lune.' Solenne raised one haughty eyebrow, ignoring her nephew.

'Not at all. I was, however, hoping we could all be gifted the truth of this mission without any more hints or roundaboutation.' The duke met her gaze full on. 'Unless *you* think it wise for us all to pretend we don't see the signs of a land in mourning?'

'The land is *not* in mourning!' Giles's heartbeat thundered in his ears. 'Can't you see? It's *suffering* – but we're on our way to fix it. That's why we have to hurry!'

The duke and duchess exchanged a long, silent look as their followers visibly braced themselves for battle.

'Don't worry. *You* don't have to come if you don't want to.' Ros sneered up at the duke, the squirrel on her shoulder scolding an angry accompaniment to her words. 'The duchess already promised to help.'

'So I did.' Solenne lowered her strong chin in a nod. 'My household knights and I are perfectly capable of escorting both children to Mount Corve without any assistance.'

The duke's upper lip drew back, giving him the look of the wolf that symbolised his duchy as he glared at her. 'If you think I'd trust *you* to deal with them on your own—'

'We swore an oath,' said the duchess firmly. 'Remember?'

'*Everyone* swore oaths!' Giles said desperately. 'When my sister first took the throne, you all promised—'

'Agreed,' the duke said, cutting him off. 'So long as the Raven Queen holds the throne, you and I hold a common cause.'

So long as the Raven Queen holds the throne. Giles blew out his breath and sent his prayers to the spirits on the dying slopes of Mount Corve. *Please let her hold the throne. Let her hang on another hour, at least!*

'Then let's go!' He started for his horse, and the adults broke into controlled chaos behind him, rapidly sweeping up the camp.

The sweet, steady sorrel mare that he had collected at their last stop was tethered just beside Ros's larger steed. As he saddled her, he sensed Ros's familiar presence coming up behind. His shoulders relaxed. 'Thank you,' he said fervently. 'Without your help—'

'I didn't do it for you.' She saddled her own horse with tight, efficient gestures.

The hedgehog waddled up between them, snorting loudly and looking from one to the other of them as if she felt all Giles's agitation about the invisible wall that had appeared between him and his sister. He knelt to scoop up the little creature, but her snorts only turned into demanding squeaks as she tried to pull him in Ros's direction, and he couldn't think up any way to reassure her.

Words and music had always come so easily to him; he'd always known just how to lighten a situation with a song or calm one of his relatives with a joke. Now, though, he hardly even recognised the cold stranger who stood beside him. 'Ros …'

She yanked the last strap into place. 'We don't have anything more to say to each other. And it's *Rosalind* to you, from now on.'

'But I want to—'

'You *always* want to talk me into things! But I told you: I don't have to listen any longer.' His sister stepped away, her expression as hard as stone. 'Neither of us had any choice about what happened when we were born, but we can both make our own choices now. So we'll rescue Cordy together, but from now on, save your performances for the people who *want* to hear them.'

'But—'

'Your Highnesses!' Edmund hurried up to hover anxiously between them, his fingers winding around and around each other. 'I beg of you,' he whispered. 'We must talk, now!'

'Just give us a minute first.' Giles waved him back. 'I need privacy with my sister—'

'No, he doesn't.' Ros kept her eyes on Edmund as she untied her horse. 'What did *you* want to say?'

'Ros—'

'Prince Giles was right in what he said about the land!' Edmund's gaze darted frantically from one triplet to the other as he spoke in an anxious whisper. 'This *isn't* the way it traditionally mourns a ruler; I've read all about that in the old scrolls. But if *that* isn't the cause, then the only thing I can think of …' He broke off, squeezing his eyes shut as if in pain. 'I mean, it can't be possible for the land to be actually *dying*, not unless – but I mean, that wouldn't have happened, it just couldn't have – but if I don't even *tell* you, then—'

'Your Highnesses!' The Duke of Lune strode up from behind Edmund while the Duchess of Solenne closed in from the opposite angle. 'Shall we be on our way now?'

Ros propelled herself on to her horse's back with easy grace as Edmund flinched back, lips sealing shut. 'We're ready,' Ros said firmly.

Giles looked from her ice-cold expression to Edmund's silent, panicked figure … and mounted his horse without another word, sliding the protesting hedgehog into the pouch around his stomach and leaving the other boy to find his own safe way behind them. There was no time left for private conversations or theories any more.

The dead grass crackled warningly under the horses' hoofs as they set out. Giles fixed his eyes on the fading magical woods of Mount Corve while the hedgehog squeaked unnecessary warnings up at him from the half-closed pouch. More and more brown patches spread across the mountainside ahead with every passing minute … but there *was* still plenty of green around the heart of Raven's Nest. They *could* still be in time to save Cordy. He knew it – and he hung on to that truth like a lifeline pulling him in the right direction.

But the hedgehog's warnings only grew louder and more frantic with every step.

Rosalind refused to be intimidated by that stupid know-it-all of a mountain. She kept her fierce glare fixed on the shifting colours of its slopes as they taunted her over every rise and fall of the endless hills.

Rosalind didn't care how many trees turned brown

with defeat before her eyes. *She* wouldn't give up. She would save Cordy, and then … well, then they would all see!

The Duchess of Solenne rode beside her like a thrilling promise of the future. If only Rosalind trained hard enough, she could be as powerful as the duchess one day. Solenne might even agree to train Rosalind herself! The thought was a bubble of hope that loosened her tight chest … until she imagined Mother's reaction.

Oh, how her whole family would hate that idea!

They can't stop me any more.

She glowered ferociously at the mountain ahead as yet another patch of trees turned a dull, dead brown.

Don't you dare give up on Cordy already! She shouted the mental order at all the waiting ancient spirits, despite knowing it was useless; she had never been the sister that they'd listened to. ***I'm on my way to help, and I have a plan!***

They'd left all human-made roads far behind. No iron gates or stone walls protected the slopes of Mount Corve and Raven's Nest itself from trespass. Instead, the wooded mysteries of the mountain were surrounded by a thick circle of shimmering, unnatural white mist that rolled in an endless path along the ground, shielding Mount Corve's lower slopes from intruders and sparkling with inner light and ancient, predatory magic.

No ordinary soldier, no matter how fierce, could ever fight their way through with a sword. This mist was a barrier that would only allow entrance to visitors who possessed royal or magical blood – as both the duke and duchess, unfortunately, did. Rosalind and Giles *might* be able to convince both potential enemies to stay behind at the moment of their own crossing … but even if they did, that would only lay them open to unexpected sneak attacks later, beyond the mist.

As their party pulled up in front of the shining, shifting barrier, their horses stamped and whickered, hanging back nervously from the unnatural mist. Giles slid down to the dead grass on the ground in a graceless rush.

'My sister and I will go in. The rest of you, *wait here*.' He started for the barrier at a run.

Still mounted, Rosalind shook her head and looked directly at the Duke of Lune, baring her teeth in the semblance of a smile. *I'm on to your schemes!* 'You should come in with us. *Both* of you,' she added, nodding to the duchess.

'Ros?' Skidding to a halt on the brown grass just before the wall of mist, Giles stared back at her. 'I mean … *Rosalind*?' His lips puckered on her full name, as if he'd bitten into a lemon. 'What—?'

'We need them both with us. *Trust me.*'

She *wasn't* stupid, no matter what he or Lady Fauvre thought. All the lines of this tangle had stretched out in her head and sorted themselves into the same perfectly balanced solution that she had first uncovered in the stables of Raven's Roost.

Out of the duke and the duchess, she knew which one *she* trusted, but another set of overriding truths was clear: one of them wanted to kill her family, while the other was loyal. One wanted to stop her and Giles from saving Cordy; the other didn't know Cordy had even been attacked. Most importantly, as all Corvenne knew, the two of them were mortal enemies.

Who could ever be a better guard to set against the other's treachery?

The duchess gave Rosalind an approving smile and nodded her acceptance, jumping lightly down from her black stallion and tossing her reins to one of her household knights. 'Well played, Your Highness. It will be my honour.'

'Your Highness ...' Behind his aunt, Edmund sat hunched on his own horse, his expression haunted. 'Actually – I would strongly suggest—'

'Of course you should join us, Edmund,' said Solenne. 'Everyone from the high families ought to make a pilgrimage to Raven's Nest at least once before they come of age. It's a tradition for all our young ones.'

'Particularly when they're angling for the throne,' Lune muttered.

'Are you afraid of a mere stripling now?' The duchess snorted.

'Enough!' Giles's voice silenced all of them. His red hair stuck out in wild, inelegant hanks around his chalk-pale face as he stood before the wall of mist, shivering visibly with panic. 'We haven't time for this nonsense! If you want to invite them along, *Rosalind*, so be it. I won't try to stop you! You don't care what I think about anything. But I'm going! And I'm not waiting for *any* of you any more.'

He turned and leaped with his long legs into the shimmering white mist. It closed around him with an audible sucking sound and devoured him before Rosalind's eyes.

A small, wordless sound jolted out of her chest.

'Well then.' The Duchess of Solenne strode forward across the dead grass, her sword hanging by her side and her nephew trailing unhappily behind her. 'For the crown!'

'*For the crown*,' echoed every man and woman in the clearing in a resonant chorus.

That familiar sound shook Rosalind from her

paralysis. Breathing hard, she scrambled off her horse, ignoring the urgent complaints of the squirrel, who still clung to her shoulder. 'Just get off if you don't like the way I'm moving!' she finally snapped as he gave her hair an angry tug and tried to yank her round to face him. 'Don't keep bothering me now!'

This was her chance to prove herself to the kingdom and save her sister. She had no time for distractions!

Steeling herself against the squirrel's piercing yells of outrage, she strode between the duke and the duchess into the shimmering mist and let it swallow her.

19

Everything was white, blindingly white, even behind Giles's eyelids, which he'd pressed tightly shut when he had leaped into the mist. Giles had been through this terrifying barrier before. He knew to expect the wet white air that tried to choke him with every breath and the strange, icy shocks that shot along his skin with each new step he forged forward – the sparks of his magic coming into contact with the enigmatic powers of the mist itself.

This time, he even understood why, as white filled his vision, he still *knew* that thick, copper-coloured fur was trying to poke its way out from underneath his skin.

Cold mist thickened against his face, forming the shape of a pointed snout and ears beyond his ordinary human features. This barrier was prying deep inside his soul to force out his darkest secret: the form he'd been born into, before he'd been, first, transformed into a boy, and then paraded in front of the kingdom as an elegant prince.

It didn't matter. ***I might not have royal blood, but I have magic. You can't keep me out of here!***

The mist sank icy tendrils into his skin, trying to reshape him into a form he didn't want. He gritted his teeth together and focused on pushing his chilled human legs forward even as the mist filled his ears with a wild language of barks and howls he refused to recognise. ***That's not me!***

Ever since he'd finally learned the awful truth, he'd thrown everything into proving there was nothing left of that wild, orphaned fox cub he'd once been. Now, Giles was the perfect prince that his family and the kingdom all needed him to be.

So he stiffened his spine against that feral chorus that so nearly made sense … that he *would* understand, if only he gave in and allowed his body to melt into the mist's prompting—

'No,' he whispered with his cold human lips and tongue. But the sound was swallowed up by the mist.

Last time, he had travelled through this barrier with his sisters. Now Ros had pushed him away and Cordy was far away and fading. There were no anchors left to hold him steady against that call …

Until he caught hold of something he had almost forgotten. Deep beneath his skin, a *second* truth was also buried: a rival language that belonged to him alone, no matter what his form.

My music! Giles had forced himself to resist its call for weeks. Now, he grabbed for it just in time and set it free:

Copper fur in the mist
You can't name me.
Tooth and claw, wild past,
You can't claim me …

Cold, wet mist plunged vengefully between Giles's lips, choking him as he sang. He gagged and coughed, again and again, as he stumbled forward. Still, he kept on singing in his head, louder and louder against the fury of rising barks and howls that clawed his skin, fighting to take back his body.

Never! They might be fierce, but they couldn't intimidate him. Giles had dealt with two stubborn triplets all his life. He knew better than to give in to any other wild creature who thought they should be in charge of him.

I *write my own songs*
I *sing my own way*
I *write my future*
I—

'Ahh!' The mist released him with an explosive **snap** that sent him tumbling forward, out of control. He landed hard on his knees on cold, moss-covered rocks, shivering convulsively in the shade of overhanging, leafy branches.

The last time he'd visited this clearing, that shade had been a deep and mysterious green. Now, it was *dark*. Dark and foreboding.

Panting, Giles clung to the damp, mossy earth. The hedgehog that he carried, reawakened by his fall, poked her long nose out from his pouch's opening with a grunt of complaint. 'Sorry,' he whispered breathlessly.

His hands were utterly filthy, soil lining his fingernails, but he couldn't have cared less. They were *his* hands, not a fox's paws. They could play lightning-fast scales on a lute or write dreamy ballads with a quill pen.

They were his, and he was himself, still, after all.

'… I'll *have my own say.*' He sang the final words of his verse softly, like a lullaby, as he rose painfully to his feet and raised his arms in a luxuriant stretch.

Bright, thick copper fur spilt over the right sleeve of his dirty blue doublet, overflowing.

Giles clapped his left hand over it with a smack that sounded like an explosion. He barely even felt the sting of contact or heard the anxious grunting of the hedgehog in response.

He couldn't—

He had to—

He—!

THUMP. It was the sound of a large adult body landing on the ground close behind him.

He closed his eyes.

He was out of time.

Ros had – inexplicably – invited Lune and Solenne through the barrier. One of them was trying to kill their sister. Neither of them could be allowed to witness this.

He *had* to get to Raven's Nest in time to save Cordy. That was all that mattered now; it was all that he had left. He couldn't return to Raven's Roost like this, but if he could just get to Raven's Nest before anyone else suspected, even Ros …

I *can do this.* He had performed the role of a human prince for over six weeks already.

He yanked his sleeve up over his right wrist, desperately shoving the lush fur into hiding as a second thump sounded behind him. An instant later, third and fourth thumps sounded in near unison.

Stretching his lips into a wide smile of welcome, Giles turned around to greet them.

Something was wrong, and Rosalind knew it the instant she saw her brother's face.

Giles's blue eyes were manic over his beaming smile. His hands were trembling. 'Everyone ready?' he said brightly.

Her right hand dropped to the hilt of her sword. Her gaze darted around the clearing as she knelt on the cold ground, gathering her breath.

That stupid, sneaking mist had sunk its nosy tendrils deep underneath her skin this time, pulling up every shameful fear and doubt that she had fought so hard to keep hidden ... everything about herself that she least wanted to be known.

Why should your family trust you to protect them any more? Why not give up and run back to the wilds? Save yourself from more shame and failure!

But she was *not* the coward the mist thought her to be – and Rosalind was here to save her sister, not herself. So, she had gritted her teeth and charged through without faltering, using the strength in her powerful leg muscles to force her way through the mist as it thickened and pushed her back at every step.

Only now did her certainty slide away from her.

Giles looked so alone ... and so terrifyingly breakable.

The squirrel on her shoulder tugged at her hair, chattering fiercely as he jerked his head towards her brother. Was *that* what he'd been yelling at her about before? She didn't need him to remind her: *Family protects family.* She wasn't the one who'd broken that rule in the first place! *Giles* was the one who'd shattered it into pieces last night.

Still, the squirrel wasn't wrong: infuriating or not, Giles *was* her brother. The little creature on her shoulder was practically pushing her forward now, overwhelming her with his noisy determination … and she wasn't sure she wanted to resist him any longer.

She *definitely* wasn't ready to forgive Giles. She might never be – but she didn't have to forgive him to keep him safe, did she?

Drawing a deep breath, she gave in to the squirrel's urging, stood, and took her first slow step towards her brother.

That hard, false smile on Giles's face widened horribly enough to make her flinch. For the first time she could remember, he turned pointedly away from her, dismissing her without a word.

Ugh! Rosalind slammed to a halt, ignoring the squirrel's protests. If Giles didn't want her protection, she wouldn't force it upon him. At least *someone* here still liked and trusted her … and it was time to get moving anyway. The duchess was already on her feet, hands planted on her hips and a smile curving her lips as she surveyed the shaded clearing. She looked as if she were preparing for battle and planning to enjoy it.

On Rosalind's other side, the Duke of Lune rose to his feet with sinuous grace, his hooded gaze moving from the blackened leaves over their heads to the knotted, twisting spines and branches of the moss-covered ancient trees around them.

Only Edmund still knelt on the damp ground, breathing hard. Sighing, Rosalind walked over to help him up – but he shook his head and didn't accept the hand she held out to him. 'Princess,' he said hoarsely, 'if we could have a word in private—'

'Oh, I think we're past the point of requiring privacy.' The duchess cocked her head at the high wall of mist that shimmered blindingly behind Edmund, blocking the world outside. 'No one out there can see or hear us any more. None of them can even enter these woods. In other words, we're finally safe to share all our secrets. Don't you agree with me, Lune?'

'For once –' the duke's lips twisted into a sneer – 'I actually do.' He gestured to Giles, turning his back on the duchess. 'Shall we? You did say there's no more time to waste.'

Unease thrummed through Rosalind's chest. *Something's wrong.* Something about the tone of Lune's voice … 'Wait for me.'

'Not a chance.' Giles didn't even bother to glance back at her as he answered, already starting for the treacherous, root-studded slope between the trees, at the far end of the clearing. 'Don't come too close to me!'

Rosalind's breath hissed out with pain. What did he think she was planning to do? Attack him?

'Come, Edmund.' The duchess strode briskly past her kneeling nephew. 'There's no point fretting now we're finally here, on the brink of Raven's Nest itself. You're not afraid of a bit of old magic, are you, Princess?' Smiling, she clapped Rosalind on the shoulder.

The red squirrel shrieked with alarm, but the approval on the duchess's face was just what Rosalind most needed. She scooped the noisy creature off her shoulder to make space as Solenne stepped up comfortably beside her.

'Let's just fix your collar before we present ourselves to the ancient spirits of this place, shall we? You do want to make a good impression.' The duchess nudged Rosalind around to face the wall of mist and smoothed down the back of her tunic with efficient maternal care. It was the same gesture Alys had made a hundred times back home, when she'd been *tsk*ing over the state of Rosalind's battered training gear.

For just one moment, Rosalind let her eyes fall closed as she sank into that familiar comfort, ignoring the frantically wriggling squirrel in her arms …

But Cordy needed her *now*, not in five minutes. 'I'll be fine. Let's just go!'

'One ... more ... moment ... .' The duchess held her steady with a firm hand on the back collar of her tunic, humming with concentration.

To their right, Edmund made a wordless sound of protest. Frowning, Rosalind glanced over.

He was staring after her brother with a look so full of dread, it made her breath catch in her throat. She squirmed in the duchess's strong grasp, craning her neck at a painful angle to follow Edmund's gaze.

The duke was striding after Giles like a wolf closing in on his prey, closer and closer with every purposeful step. As Rosalind watched, Lune reached into a velvet pouch and pulled out something that glinted gold in the dim light between the trees.

Is that a knife?

'No!' She lunged forward – and nearly choked as the duchess yanked her back into place with shocking force, leaving her coughing and sputtering.

'Sorry, Princess. I'm not quite—'

'*Giles!*' Rosalind screamed as the duke reached out for her brother, still so close and yet so horribly out of reach of her protection.

Giles started to turn ...

And something cold and hard clamped shut around Rosalind's neck, closing with a *click*. 'There!' said the duchess. 'Now, *that* should do nicely.'

Freezing ice raced across the surface of Rosalind's body, sucking up all the magic that flowed along her skin. It felt so *wrong* that nausea swelled up in response through her chest and her throat until the whole world spun in dizzying circles around her, black dots dancing wildly before her eyes. As if from a great distance, she felt her arms drop to her sides, heavy and sluggish, losing their hold on the burden they had carried.

The red squirrel screamed with fear and anger as he slipped towards the ground ... but Rosalind couldn't help him. She staggered and fell hard to her knees as the muscles in her legs gave out entirely.

Giles needs me!

She forced her head up, fighting desperately against the sickening weight around her neck. Blinking through the dots that blurred her vision, she caught sight of her brother just as he fell into a crumpled heap less than fifteen feet away from her, gold glinting horribly around his neck.

The two most notorious enemies in Corvenne nodded to each other.

'You were right,' the Duke of Lune told the Duchess of Solenne. 'Our secrets *should* be safe now.'

20

Dappled shadows shifted back and forth across Giles's limp fingers as his right cheek rested against the damp, cold soil. Angry voices sounded nearby in a muddle of sound, but his brain felt too sick and chilled to untangle any of it. Instead, he simply watched the shadows shifting across his skin while waves of nausea rocked through him and the hedgehog wriggled frantically in her pouch against his stomach, making the nausea even worse.

He hoped, distantly, that she hadn't been hurt when he'd fallen. He was sure he'd tried to curve his back and land in a way that would keep her small body safe – but it was only now that he could even feel his own legs again. He still couldn't move them. He'd lost all sense of them in the first shock of what had happened.

But what exactly *had* happened? He swallowed hard, fighting to think through the nausea.

His neck. Something had closed around his neck, smooth and cold. Ros had called out first – to warn him? Or ask for help? – but he'd been so desperate to reach Raven's Nest in time, he hadn't paid any attention to what was happening behind him until it was too late.

And then …

The Duchess of Solenne's voice sliced through his daze. 'It's a magic-suppressing collar, Princess. I admire your grit, but there's simply no use trying to fight its effects.'

So *that* was what was around Giles's neck – the same kind of golden cage the Duke of Lune's mages had devised for Mother when she had been held prisoner. No wonder he felt so ill and drained!

But—

Wait. The duchess had been talking to Ros, not to him.

Ros! Panic surged through Giles's veins, shattering the languor that had gripped him. He pushed himself up on to one elbow, breathing hard and persevering until he could finally look back across the clearing to where his sister knelt with a red and furious face and wicked gold around her neck. Edmund huddled miserably in the background with his hands over his face, and …

'You've been working *together*?' It made his head spin even worse, but Giles couldn't stop turning between the smiling duke and duchess, the shock of revelation every bit as disorienting as the collar around his neck. 'But everyone knows the two of you hate each other!'

'Fortunately,' drawled the duke, 'we won't need to associate for much longer. As you'll learn when you grow older and wiser, Your Highness, some goals matter enough to merit a bit of compromise along the way.'

'Goals like *killing our family*?' Ros's words came out in infuriated pants. As Giles watched, she lunged upward, reaching for her sword – but then staggered, losing her balance completely.

The duchess caught her just in time with one hand on her elbow. Ros jerked away from Solenne's touch, and the red squirrel on the ground nearby added a noisy stream of abuse, but the duchess only smiled indulgently. 'Don't talk nonsense, Your Highness. Neither of us wishes to kill your entire family! Lune is a relative of yours himself, remember? This is only one more round of the political game – and unfortunately for your sister, she ended up on the losing side of the battlefield. Without enough supporters to counter the two most powerful players, the poor girl never stood a chance.'

'Cordy has the whole land of Corvenne on her side.'

Giles pushed himself three tooth-gritting inches higher, powered by fury, and the hedgehog wriggled her pointed nose up out of his pouch, grunting angrily in chorus. 'She's the rightful Raven Queen!'

'And that, you see, is the problem in a nutshell,' Lune said regretfully. 'In taking the throne, she upset the age-old balances of power that have worked so well for all of us until now. You should have seen her at every meeting of the Council of Dukes! She rides roughshod over everything we tell her, and for the most unreasonable of causes. Giving back our land to grimy peasants when we've firmly claimed it in battle? Those creatures can't even read or write, yet your sister would treat them like our equals. Worse yet, she uses the power of the land to overrule every one of our rational arguments. What else *could* we do but remove her for the sake of good governance?'

He aimed a tight smile at the duchess. 'There is, as you say, some natural distaste between the duchess and myself. However, it became rapidly apparent to us both, soon after your sister's coronation, that we shared common ground after all.'

'And are all the other dukes partners in this treachery?' Ros snarled.

'Those fools?' The duchess laughed. 'Why, as far as they know, Lune and I have never shared a civil conversation in our lives. Even our own followers have no idea! Why do you think we had to wait until we were out of sight of them to finally sort all this out?

'No, we found it *far* more practical to rely on a single trusted acquaintance as our go-between, for the sake of political discretion. You'll learn soon enough, Princess, that it's wiser *not* to involve weaker-minded folk in any plans that matter … at least, not if you want to avoid unnecessary bloodshed.'

'*You* wanted to avoid unnecessary bloodshed? Ha!' Giles's laugh came out more like a sob as his fingers dug into the damp soil, fighting to keep him upright. 'What about the archivist? I saw the blood left behind when you abducted her!'

'*What?*' For the first time, Edmund spoke up, lowering the hands that had covered his eyes and staring at his aunt in open horror. 'You tried to kill Margotte too?'

'Of course not, Edmund.' The duchess shook her head in weary exasperation. 'She is perfectly safe and comfortable; she just couldn't be trusted not to tell the prince what he wanted to know when he came asking too-cunning questions.' She gave her nephew a contemptuous look. 'Don't look so horrified! I didn't make you do any of the dirty work, did I? I *knew* you wouldn't have the stomach for this.'

'But it is my fault, isn't it?' Edmund rose slowly, unhappily to his feet. 'I'm the one who researched the way the crown's magic actually worked. If I hadn't told you the connection I'd discovered—'

'Oh, don't make yourself into a martyr.' The duchess snorted. 'Trust me, *no one* gives you credit for this plan. How many times have you rattled on at the supper table about some tedious new finding in the archives? Half the time, I don't even bother to listen. It just so happened that *this* time, you'd finally come across something I needed in order to solve my own problem.'

'You mean, the problem of how to kill a queen who was protected from magical attacks and had all the land's powers at her disposal.' Giles breathed in deeply through his nose, fighting down the nausea as he pushed himself the rest of the way up into a crouching position, freeing the hedgehog to clamber from her constricting pouch. 'So, what was the connection Edmund found?'

'Sacrifice,' Edmund said hollowly. His eyes were still fixed on his aunt's face as he slowly shook his head. 'There was a great sacrifice made by the spirits of the land, when the Raven Crown was first created, to finally bring peace for everyone.'

Giles nodded, ignoring the hedgehog's anxious grunts as she circled his crouching figure again and again. 'The fact that they allowed the wearer of the crown to control the land's magic, you mean.'

'No.' Edmund shook his head. 'That *is* the bargain that's been kept for as long as the crown has been intact – but there was a greater sacrifice made in the very beginning, to establish the magical connection *and* prove to the humans that the spirits would never break it. The whole castle was built as a symbol and reminder of that ancient sacrifice.'

'Raven's Roost?' Giles frowned. What about the structure of that huge, rambling castle, with its two outstretched wings, main body, and … ?

His eyes widened. 'Wait,' he whispered. *Wings and a body* … and hadn't the archivist even said that the archives were located directly above its *heart*?

There *was* something peculiar about that castle, wasn't there? Something that had struck him as odd from the very beginning.

'All those ravens,' he said. 'Ravens *everywhere*.' Even the name …

'No one ever thinks about it any more.' Edmund turned to Giles, his voice suddenly eager with the shared discovery. 'It's simply taken for granted nowadays. But once I read about that first great sacrifice made by the spirits of the land – sending one of their own to act as the physical conduit between the crown and the magic of the land *and* serve as a hostage too …'

Giles's mind was racing furiously, almost overcoming the nausea of his magical collar. 'We've almost reached Raven's Nest,' he said. 'But the castle is named Raven's Roost.'

Of course, a raven was meant to live in its nest; that was its true home. But a roost … now, that was where it might settle for a time, perhaps to sleep, when it was too far from its nest.

And if it was no ordinary raven but an ancient spirit of the land, channelling all the land's magic into its ruler …

'Delightfully neat, isn't it?' The Duke of Lune laughed lightly, an appreciative smile curving his lips. 'And yet, I missed it too, for far too long. In all my own research, it never occurred to me that the bond between ruler and land would be quite so physically *present* – nor so easy to break, once one put one's mind to it and followed the clues to find the source.'

'It's underneath the castle, isn't it?' Giles said numbly.

That ancient presence Cordy had talked about – the one she'd been so certain about feeling deep below her, the one that had taken the first brunt of the attack …

'That ancient spirit,' he finished. 'It's been sleeping

under Raven's Roost, directly below the archives, all this time.'

And he had deliberately ridden *away* from it in his hunt for answers.

He didn't know how he'd ever live with the answers he had found.

'Not for much longer, I expect.' The duchess shrugged. 'I couldn't get near it myself – it has its own barrier, like the one around this mountain, formed by the spirits at the same time. It only allows in certain visitors.'

'A *barrier only family can* ...' Rosalind's voice was choked as she quoted the only part of the scroll they had found. The squirrel clambered up her clothes like a tree, shrieking angrily at the adults nearby.

'Exactly.' Lune smiled thinly. 'I *am* part of the queen's family, little though any of you seem to truly believe it. So, it wasn't difficult for me to pass through that barrier. And luckily –' he nodded at the collar around Giles's neck – 'my mages know very well how to suppress magic. While the ancient magic of this land is *far* more powerful than yours, it is still susceptible in the right circumstances. A golden sword, infused with my mages' casting, couldn't kill even a sleeping ancient spirit outright ... but it *could* send a paralysing poison neatly through its veins. And as that spirit was the living conduit between the land and the Raven Throne, once the poison began to spread …'

'You're actually proud of what you've done. You little worm!' Ros was still half bowed over her knees, panting and sickly-pale, but as she stared at Lune with the angry red squirrel on her shoulder, she radiated so much disdain that Giles's own shoulders straightened in response. '*Traitor.*'

The duke's voice hardened. 'You should take care how you speak to me, *Your Highness*, now that I don't have to play at courtesy any more. Without your sister's vast powers to protect you, you will find that life at court is about to become *very* different for you.'

'What do you mean, *different*?' Giles demanded. 'Aren't you going to kill us both?'

The duke and duchess, incredibly, both laughed at his words.

'Oh, Your Highness.' Lune shook his head, still chuckling. 'You have so much still to learn about royal politics.'

'I promised the princess I'd keep her safe, and I meant it. Have no fear, Your Highness.' Solenne nodded firmly to Ros. 'I knew I liked you from the moment I first saw you on the battlefield.'

'So you'll let her go?' Giles let out his breath in a whoosh of relief.

'Nonsense! I'd never waste all her potential. No, I'll be her regent. Once she and Edmund are old enough to wed, there will be *no* stronger contenders for the throne.'

'*What?*' Ros bellowed.

Giles's mouth dropped open.

'No!' said Edmund, jerking forward. 'I won't do it. I mean that, Aunt!'

But the duchess was only looking at Ros. 'I know he's not much of a catch in some ways, but trust me: together, you'll form an unbeatable partnership for power. And if you can toughen him up for me along the way? Well, then, we'll *all* be grateful.' The duchess smiled. 'I look forward to fighting side by side to win your kingdom.'

Ros stared at Solenne in silence, her face stricken.

'I wouldn't be too certain of that!' Lune's voice snapped like a whip. 'I believe you'll find, with our family already on the throne, that Prince Giles is far more likely to be accepted as the true heir. Under *my* regency, as soon as Queen Cordelia's sad passing is announced—'

'We'll just sort that all out on the battlefield, shall we?' Solenne bared her teeth at him. 'We shouldn't have long to wait. Our truce only lasts until we leave this mountain.'

'But we can't!' Edmund turned on her. 'Aunt, we *cannot* do this. You don't understand. We have to fix everything, before it's too late!'

'*Enough.*' She rolled her eyes. 'You've never had the guts to make the hard choices, but I do – and I swore to your father that I'd put you on the throne. So I'm not interested in hearing any more of your mewling about principles or—'

'I am talking about *magic.*' For the first time since Giles had met him, Edmund spoke over his aunt, his voice clear and certain. 'You still don't understand, either of you! It's not only the queen or that spirit whom you're poisoning right now. Lune, you fool – *and* Aunt Solenne. You two are going to destroy the whole land with your scheming!' He waved his long arms frantically. 'I *know* what the throne means to both of you, but can't you see what's happening? Queen Cordelia isn't the only one who's dying! Look around you.'

A withered black leaf broke off from the thick canopy overhead and began to curl its winding way down between them as if in answer.

Sick to his stomach, Giles watched it fall. When the hedgehog started nibbling at his right sleeve, he didn't even try to resist. His body had finally adjusted to the collar; he could move again to stop her, but what would be the point?

He had no magic any more. He was half the kingdom away from the ancient spirit who needed his help and the sister whose rule he'd sworn to defend. He had trusted the wrong voices all along. He'd tried so hard, but he had utterly failed as a prince and as a brother.

In despair, his gaze sank down to his shaking hands ... and he caught a glimpse of illicit copper fur, exposed once again by the hedgehog's worrying of his sleeve. His breath caught in his throat.

Maybe he wasn't out of options after all.

He couldn't access his family's magic any more. The duke had made sure of that. But Giles knew something about himself that even the duke and duchess didn't, and the mist had forced him to stop hiding from it.

'Ros.' His voice was a rough whisper.

His sister met his gaze across the dying clearing and raised her eyebrows as the other three argued heatedly together.

This time, he didn't ignore the open question in her face. It was too late for anything but the full truth between them, just as it should have been all along.

'I *trust you*,' he mouthed to her. '*We can do this. We just have to let go.*'

It was time to make their own greatest sacrifice.

Their family's magic might be hopelessly out of reach, but the spirits still in Raven's Nest weren't dead yet. Maybe those spirits *were* already dying along with their land as

Lune's terrible poison spread, but theirs was the ancient power that maintained the barrier around Mount Corve. If it still stood, so must their magic.

All he and Ros had to do was surrender to it.

The Duke of Lune was shouting directly into Edmund's face now. Edmund trembled like a birch tree in high wind but kept arguing anyway, while Solenne stood a watchful guard over their debate.

Bracing himself, Giles pulled up his right sleeve by a further telltale inch. His sister's eyes fixed on that copper fur and widened.

Then she took a breath, nodded firmly, and squared her shoulders.

Despite everything, relief washed through Giles like a healing potion. They were finally united once again ... and together, they were *never* truly powerless.

Ros's strong fingers counted down the seconds against her left knee, out of the others' sight. *Three ... two ... one ...*

Now!

Giles leaped forward, leaving the hedgehog behind. He forced his legs to hurtle faster and faster across the damp, uneven ground, despite the wild lurching of his belly and the waves of dizziness and nausea that the collar sent through him with every footfall. He aimed a zigzag course across the clearing, swept along by his sister's battle roar, and ignoring every shout from their enemies. All his focus was on that looming wall of ancient, perilous mist that he had barely escaped only fifteen minutes ago.

He had to get back inside.

Closer, closer …

A sudden thump sounded behind him – the sound of bodies in combat. He hesitated—

'Giles, *faster!*' Ros yelled.

With a final, desperate push, he flung himself forward, stretching his long legs to their limits.

Footsteps crackled against the fallen leaves behind him. Fingers brushed against the back of his tunic as he jumped …

And then he landed, at last, in that shimmering white wall of mist. This time, Giles didn't even try to resist.

Instead, he allowed it to transform him.

21

The moment Giles started forward, Rosalind *lunged* – but not in the same direction.

She might have found herself lost when it came to courtly politics, but when it came to battle strategy, her head was crystal clear. With three enemies between her brother and the wall of mist, he'd never reach it without her help – and she would *never* leave him behind to be imprisoned.

So she roared with rage and threw herself forward, the red squirrel's sharp hind claws digging deep into her shoulder and his front claws clinging to her hair. Tears streaked down Rosalind's face as she scooped up her sword from the damp, dark moss where it had fallen. Nausea from the golden collar swept through her body in protest, but it couldn't stop her any more.

It was *nothing* to the memory of that fur on Giles's wrist: the symbol of everything she was about to lose and everything he had somehow lost already, without her even realising it.

He was the one who had fitted in at court from the beginning. He should have been able to live there in peace and sing his heart out for everyone.

She wouldn't let anyone stop him now.

Rosalind landed with a thud against the Duke of Lune, slamming the blunt hilt of her sword into his side before he'd even finished turning towards her. She didn't need any magic to fight *him*. She didn't even slow down as he crashed to the ground with a cry of shock and pain. She was already spinning around, ready for a far more dangerous foe.

'Giles, *faster!*' She yelled the warning as she ran.

The Duchess of Solenne had almost caught up with Giles already with her long, steady strides. Her expression was perfectly calm and focused as she reached out to grab the back of his tunic with one calloused hand—

Until Rosalind's sword sliced through her sleeve.

It was only a scratch. But Solenne jerked away for an instant – which was all that Giles needed.

He leaped into the mist. Rosalind's eyes widened until they burned, desperately fighting to absorb every final detail ...

And then the mist swallowed his body whole.

A convulsive shudder rippled through her body. Rosalind's heartbeat thudded in her ears. The hilt of her sword shivered in her hand.

She was alone, surrounded by enemies. *Alone.*

Rosalind would never hear Giles's stupidly beautiful singing voice ever again. Cordy was already dying in that stone maze of a castle. Mother and Alys and Connall were gathered around her, so very far away …

'That was an entirely useless piece of theatre, you know.' Lune's voice was sour as he levered himself up from the ground, wincing and cradling his side. 'Our soldiers will stop him within a yard. Without his magic, even *he* won't be able to talk them out of loyalty.'

'You don't know my brother.' The reminder steadied Rosalind's grip around her sword hilt. 'You have never understood either of us.' She lifted the heavy sword in preparation, carefully balancing her weight across both feet. She'd sworn to protect her family, and she would.

She couldn't see inside the endlessly shifting, shimmering mist. But it couldn't be much longer before—

'Krr-krrrrt!' The squirrel on her shoulder shouted out in gleeful triumph as a bolt of copper-red fur shot out from the wall of mist. It raced past them on four legs up the wild slope of Mount Corve, darting between knotted tree trunks, sailing over moss-covered rocks, and disappearing into the deep shadows within seconds.

A bright golden collar – still firmly closed, but now empty – fell out of the wall of mist in its wake and landed on the mossy ground with a soft, anticlimactic *thump*.

'What the—?' Lune gaped, his head swinging between the discarded collar and the vanished fox.

'*You* said those collars would stop all their magic!' Solenne whirled around to point an accusing finger at him. A thin trickle of red blood leaked out along the rip in her tunic sleeve, but she ignored it.

'The collars work! Something else must have gone wrong. Their sister was supposed to be the only one of them who could shapeshift!'

Rosalind's lips stretched into a fierce grin, despite the spearpoint of loss that twisted in her chest. 'I told you you didn't understand us.'

'You little—!' Breathing hard, Lune yanked his sword free from its sheath.

'Careful.' The duchess shifted between the two of them, one hand on the hilt of her own sword. 'You may have mislaid your own pathway to the throne, but you won't steal mine.'

Tension vibrated between them. Rosalind was certain

that their blades would cross – until the duke let out an explosive sigh and slid his sword back into its sheath.

'There's no time to decide this. We'll *both* lose everything if Prince Giles reaches Raven's Nest before us and rouses those final spirits in time to act. The Raven Queen's not dead yet, remember!'

'So, we'll keep working together until she is.' Solenne curled her free fingers in a casual gesture of invitation to Rosalind but kept her warning gaze fixed on Lune. 'Your Highness, if you would please walk in front of me, with Edmund just behind …'

Rosalind let out a choke of disbelieving laughter. 'You think I'm actually going to *help* you?'

The duchess shrugged. 'You know you can't stop us without your magic. All credit to your fighting skills, Princess –' she smiled faintly as she glanced down at her torn sleeve – 'but with that collar on your throat, you're outmatched by three to one. You'll never manage to kill us all.'

'I don't have to.' Rosalind lifted her chin. 'I only have to slow you down long enough for Giles to find those spirits.'

'Oh, this is absurd!' Lune turned away with a hiss of air through his teeth. 'I'm not waiting around any longer. Just tie the girl up and let's go!'

Perfect. Rosalind's lips curved with ferocious satisfaction as he contemptuously turned his back on her – underestimating her as usual. 'Now!' she whispered, and scooped the one companion she still trusted off her shoulder.

Over the years, Rosalind had trained herself to throw just as well left-handed – and the furious red squirrel was only too eager to make this leap. His arms, legs and claws stretched out wide in perfect flight, and he landed exactly where she'd aimed him: on the nape of Lune's undefended neck.

The elegant duke howled with shock. Knocked hopelessly off balance by a biting, scratching whirlwind, he fell forward and landed, hard, on one of the sharp-edged rocks that covered the slope. One last grunt escaped him – and then he lay sprawled on the ground, unmoving and unconscious.

'You counted wrong,' Rosalind told the duchess. 'Two to one now.'

The duchess's laughter filled the shadowed air. 'Well done, Princess. Well done, indeed.' She clapped her hands together, grinning widely. 'I cannot even tell you how satisfying that was to watch!' She nodded to Edmund, who'd hung back, silent and miserable throughout, as the red squirrel scampered back across the ground to Rosalind.

'You see why I'm determined to see you two wed? This girl will make a queen to remember!'

Rosalind didn't relax her grip on the hilt of her sword. 'My sister is *already* the queen, and I will never help you.'

Solenne's smile turned rueful. 'You still haven't learned the most important lesson of all, have you, Princess? I tried to tell you before: this is all a game. Remember those fireside tales of battle that you enjoyed so much last night? Those were moves on a playing board to win or lose power – because *that's* all that matters in the end. It's what defines us as warriors! And *that* was your sister's mistake: she chose to ally with the weak, not with the strong.'

Rosalind stared at the duchess in disbelief. 'My sister isn't weak. She holds the whole land of Corvenne!'

'But she never understood that to hold *on to* power, you have to please the powerful.' Solenne shook her head wearily. 'Trading favours for peasants who could do nothing for her? Ranting about their *rights* to the dukes who own their lands? Of course she lost everything! She deserved to … and now that we're here at endgame, there's only one side strong enough to win. That's the side where *you* belong.'

'I have never belonged at court,' Rosalind said tightly.

'What rubbish.' The duchess snorted. 'Court is just

another kind of game to play. Trust me, I can teach you all the rules. You would have mastered them yourself by now if it hadn't been for all the poison Lady Fauvre's been dripping into your ears.'

'She said a real princess—'

'You mean, *herself*, in her dreams?' Solenne barked a derisive laugh. 'Or hadn't you worked that part out yet? If we choose to stand back and let Lune come to power, her fantasy may well come true. Do you *really* want to let that happen? Or would you rather ally with me, here and now, to ensure that that serpent *never* touches the throne and spreads her poison across the kingdom?'

Smiling, the duchess held out one strong hand. 'Come. The game's already been lost for your sister; there's nothing more you can do to win it back for her now. All the old magical bindings will come undone upon her death, which means that *everything* will be in play, for the first time in centuries. No more kings or queens chosen by the land without any care for how we feel about it. We choose our own rulers for ourselves from now on. Fight for yourself in this next round of the game! Prove yourself to the kingdom. I know you can do it!'

It was an invitation and a challenge, and Rosalind *hated* the fact that it sent a shiver of anticipation racing across her skin. 'You just locked up my magic in a collar,' she pointed out, sliding a slow and careful step closer to the wall of mist. 'Are you really trying to say that you would teach me to win real battles?'

'Of course.' Solenne's grin was triumphant. 'That collar is only a temporary measure, until you're ready to accept that I can give you everything you've ever wanted and been told you had to hide. Trust me: *no one* in my household will ever criticise you for your strength. Instead, we'll *train* it – and once the two of us start fighting side by side, we'll be unbeatable.'

The confidence in her tone was more than exhilarating. It was everything Rosalind had yearned for:

Acceptance. Approval. The *certainty* that she was enough, exactly as she was, and that Lady Fauvre had been wrong, wrong, wrong after all.

And yet …

'What will we do when we win those battles?' Rosalind asked, without lowering her sword. 'What will we use our strength for, in the end?'

'What will we *use* it for?' the duchess repeated blankly. 'Well … we'll *keep* it, obviously, unlike those last few useless kings. We'll cement our power and crush our enemies and rule Corvenne for decades!'

… And there it was.

'That's not what I want *at all*,' said Rosalind. 'I've spent years training already. But I trained to be a knight – and knights are supposed to use their strength to *protect* weaker people, not to crush them underfoot. That's the whole point of becoming strong, isn't it? To *use* your strength for the people who need it, like those peasants whose lands you stole. Cordy was right. They *do* deserve someone to stand for them against the people who hold more power!'

'And how very high-minded and noble that all sounds.' Solenne rolled her eyes. 'When you're older, though, you'll understand—'

'No, I won't.' Rosalind had been through enough transformations. She *knew* now, without a doubt, who she was at her core, beneath them all. Shifting another inch closer to the mist, she kept her gaze fixed on the duchess, who had nothing to offer her after all. 'I won't change my mind about what's right and true, and it wouldn't show *strength* to abandon my family just because they're losing. That's only *fear* – fear of weakness, and I'm sick of giving into it.'

Finally, she understood what the barrier of mist had been trying to tell her as it forced her to confront all the fears that she'd been hiding … and allowing to control her. '*That* was why I didn't tell my own family what Lady Fauvre was doing. I was afraid they would all think I was weak for being hurt. I was wrong.' She took a steadying breath even as she took another careful step to the side. 'I am strong enough to know that I don't have to pretend, any more, about who and what I am. I'm even strong enough to fail.'

'Well, that's all very pretty and philosophical, but in *reality* ...'

Rosalind used her final, sliding step to turn to Edmund, who had been watching them both in horrified silence from his position by the wall of mist, scarcely a foot away from where she stood now. 'You're not weak either,' she told him, ignoring Solenne's increasingly irate rant behind her. 'Thank you for trying to warn me and my brother. We should have listened to you – and I shouldn't have paid any attention to all the nonsense your aunt said about you. Strength *isn't* just about muscles and training with swords, no matter what she's tried to make you think. It's about being brave enough to do the right thing, even when it's hard and scary. *You* tried to do that, which means you're stronger than her and Lune together. You should use that strength before it's too late.'

'I ... I will.' Edmund nodded, green eyes huge in his pale face. 'But—'

'Enough of this!' The duchess sliced her hand through the air, cutting off her nephew's words. 'You two may want to stand around and wring your hands over principles, but I'm here to tell you—'

Rosalind had listened long enough.

The duke was beginning to stir on the ground, with a faint, grumbling noise, but Giles was safe from recapture by now. She'd done what was necessary for his safety. Now, it was her turn.

She dropped her sword to the ground, ignoring the clatter of metal against stone. She wouldn't be needing it again.

The red squirrel chattered anxiously, tugging at her hair. 'It's all right,' she whispered. 'This time, I know what to do.'

She put one hand on his back to keep him safe …

And then she turned and threw herself into the ancient, shimmering wall of mist with the squirrel cheering raucous approval all the way.

This time, Rosalind chose her own transformation.

22

The fox knew how to run for his life on four legs, no matter how muddled everything inside him felt.

There were enticing smells everywhere, trying to lead him astray, but he didn't slow. The chase was on, hunters were close behind, and he couldn't duck into a den for safety. He had to reach the top of the mountain, because …

Because …

Deep inside his mind, beneath the languages of smell and taste and instinct, something else was calling: a strange-familiar voice. It sounded strangely human, not fox at all, yet somehow it still felt like *him*.

He shook his head hard, as though to dislodge a buzzing insect from his tufted ears. This voice was inside him, though, not flying around his head. It couldn't be dismissed so easily, and it wanted him up at the top of this mountain.

Never mind. The land smelt better in that direction anyway. *Safer. Stronger.* The air tasted like … like …

Like a song, whispered that impossible, intrusive voice, in a language that he should never have understood. It began to hum alien, human music in his head.

He shivered with alarm and confusion. *Something isn't right.* Those humans with their heavy, looming bodies had fallen behind, but now a terrifying realisation was chasing him instead, and it felt far more perilous than any mere hunter.

He ran even faster to escape it.

The hare didn't feel any such confusion. *Her* mind and body had always been more firmly entwined than her brother's; shifting forms couldn't alter that solid, lifelong connection. Now that she'd shaken off that nasty metal collar that smelt of bad human magic, she felt as fresh and clear as ever … and unlike her brother, she had never feared the animal side of her nature.

Her clever nose twitched as it sniffed the air for clues. Her towering ears tilted. *Fox. That way!*

A strong, fierce hare like her didn't fear any fox, but her first instincts still shouted to avoid it, just in case.

She quashed them instantly. *Family. Mission. Protect him against all danger!*

Foxes were fast runners … but hares were faster. Her long, powerful legs pushed hard against the ground and propelled her off her big, furry back feet with ease. She leaped high into the air and shot past the astonished humans in the clearing beyond only a moment later.

Whatever form her body took, *she* never sidled or sneaked. She ran fast and she ran hard into the shadows of the dying forest, leaving the fallen sword, the collar and the humans far behind.

Inside that clearing, the three abandoned humans argued heatedly.

Metal swords were drawn.

Vicious threats were made.

Ruthless new schemes and plots were hatched in desperation.

And they were all so intent on their own human dilemmas that not a single one noticed that no troublesome squirrel had re-emerged from the magical mist. Neither did they notice the small, sleepy hedgehog as she waddled quietly over to a large, mossy rock and then seemingly vanished into it.

At the very top of Mount Corve, in the legendary, mystical sanctuary of Raven's Nest, the last of the ancient spirits who had been born to the land's magic were no longer resting.

They were hurting.

They were raging.

They were, very slowly, dying. Which meant that they were more dangerous than ever …

And now they were waiting.

23

The fox grew wild with panic and confusion. That impossible voice inside his head wanted him at the top of the mountain, no matter what. But the smells on every side were so distracting!

It was too bright outside for any reasonable fox to keep running, wasn't it? He ought to be hiding and sleeping by now. But whenever he tried to dart into a safe-looking hollow, the voice in his head started shouting with terrifying force.

He let out a desperate whine …

And a fierce warrior hare leaped in front of him.

He startled backwards, paws scrabbling against the ground. Hares this large were hard to kill and not sensible to fight. His body and mind agreed entirely as he veered to run around her.

She leaped in front of him again! This time, she stomped commandingly on the ground with one big foot. Was she trying to frighten him away?

'*Grr!*' He peeled back his lips from his sharp teeth, arched his back and snarled menacingly. His tail curved into a clear warning. He was sensible, yes, but he wasn't a coward. He'd show this hare he could *not* be threatened, then find a nice den to rest in until dark, and—

THUMP!

The hare's strong right front paw slammed into his chest, startling him into falling. He rolled back up on to his feet with a growl. *Enough!* Crouching down, he prepared for an attack of his own …

And then the hare's foot started drumming on the ground. Something about the rhythm made him pause.

Thumpthump-thump … *thumpthump*-thump …

The fox tensed, belly still pressed to the damp ground and ears tilting to catch every nuance.

Why did that rhythm sound so familiar?

Thumpthump-thump*thump* … *thump*thump*thump* …

That sound felt as if it were drumming inside his chest. As if it were trying to tell him something important …

And then that strange voice in his head, which had been so frightening and angry, suddenly became soft and warm and tender instead. It crooned human words that matched the rhythm of the hare's foot. Words that the fox somehow, incredibly, understood.

Little ones, go to sleep; it is time now for dreaming …

That lullaby meant *sleep*.

That lullaby meant snuggling in with his triplet brother and sister, safe and warm in their very first bed while their mother sang all of them to sleep and then …

Ohhhh.

Sinking back into himself, Giles looked through fox eyes into the face of the fierce wild hare before him, and he knew her at once. Of course he did.

Who else would ever think to reunite with a punch?

He leaned forward to sniff his sister. With a huff, she sniffed him back, checking him all over for injuries. Finally, they rubbed faces, and rightness washed through him along with her reassuring scent.

Rosalind was *family*. She always would be, no matter which form either of them wore.

Now that they were together again, though, they hadn't any time to lose. The mountain slope still stretched high above them, and Giles could actually *feel* the land dying beneath his paws, plants withering all around him with the scent of rot and doom.

Luckily, now that his mind and body were working

together again, he could sense something else as well – something his human body never would have told him.

He could smell the vivid green of the vegetation above, where the spirits themselves were waiting. But their power wasn't limited to that single spot. He could feel it beneath and around him too, resonating through every dying stem and even coursing through his own four furry legs.

Humans forgot about the ancient spirits when they couldn't see them. In fox form, though, Giles felt their power tingling all around him, and it made connections pop and spark in his brain.

Yes, it had taken a pilgrimage all the way to Raven's Nest itself for the triplets to gather the broken shards of the Raven Crown. But that had never been the only place where the spirits could respond to Cordy. She had made her own great sacrifice to them on a battlefield outside the walls of her capital city. Giles and Ros had made their own promises there too, and seen the Raven Crown sealed in acceptance.

Giles had never shared Cordy's magical connection with the land. Now, though, as he finally accepted his fox form, he felt closer to the land than he ever had before.

He wouldn't wait a moment longer.

Tipping back his head, Giles planted his paws in the

damp soil and let his first, forgotten language, of barks and yips, flow out in desperate song.

The hare was ready when they came. Unlike her brother, she was always prepared for battle.

Thousands of blackened leaves suddenly flooded down upon them from every side of the canopy overhead, whipped by a dozen angry winds into a smothering cascade. The hare leaped in front of Giles without a second's pause. She stood strong on her haunches and boxed them away from her brother's snout with steady, non-stop punches.

Everyone in this kingdom knew by now that Rosalind wasn't charming, courtly or persuasive. But that was all right, because her brother was – and she was here to fight for him to be heard, their two skills complementing each other perfectly. Now, he howled and yipped with all his might even as leaves cascaded over his back and rose around his paws. With Rosalind keeping the air clear around his mouth, nothing could stop his wordless cry for help.

The wind shrieked and roared in fury. Rosalind couldn't see her brother any more. He was lost in the torrent of leaves that poured over her in wild circles and violent gusts. Still, she didn't need to see him to know exactly where he was.

Her paws kept moving.

Giles's pleading song kept pouring out against the gale, filled with a powerful and eerie beauty.

The wind slowed. The flood of leaves became a flurry, growing thinner and thinner. It circled lazily again and again around the two of them, until the last black leaf finally dropped to the ground. The stillness was startling. The wind had simply stopped.

Rosalind lifted her nose to sniff the air as Giles's song grew softer and more tentative. The branches above them were bare.

Had they done it? Were the spirits ready to hear them?

Something hard slammed into Rosalind's back. Hissing, she spun around, placing herself in guard position before her brother.

A clump of mossy earth ripped itself free from the ground and hurtled towards her with vicious accuracy. Dozens followed. Rosalind used her long legs to jump, again and again, to knock them aside from Giles's face. They battered against her sides and stuck in horrible, heavy clumps to her thick fur, making it harder to move quickly.

Giles kept singing through every new blow that hit his unprotected flanks, but his voice grew weaker and weaker.

Why aren't the spirits listening? They'd never acted this way before. Didn't they *want* to help him and make things better, to save Cordy and the dying land? Didn't they understand that *they* would die too, if she and the land weren't saved?

If only Cordy were here now! In the old days, she could have turned into a giant bear and stood over the others to protect Giles's song. Even now, she would have battled tooth and nail for her family with her earth-shaking powers *and* bare fists, if necessary.

That was how it was always supposed to be: the three of them against the world. *That* was how they'd won that last great battle outside Corve's city walls. Rosalind and Giles had never been meant to fight alone without their triplet by their sides.

A new blow slammed against the side of Rosalind's head. This time, it hurt so badly that she let out a high, shameful squeal. Warm blood dripped down against her sensitive whiskers. There had been a sharp rock hidden in that clump of soil!

Another clump arrowed past her as she reeled with pain. Shaking her head, she leaped as fast and as high as she could.

She didn't catch it. Giles's song cut off with an unbearable, high whine of pain.

Red rage flooded through Rosalind's body.

No one touches my triplets! Never again!

She didn't care what the ancient spirits threw at her. *Nothing* would stop her now from—

Oh. *Oh.*

How could she have forgotten how all this had started in the first place?

No wonder the spirits were so angry. She, of all people, should have recognised their response. That wild, protective fury – and the truth that she and Giles had only just discovered about the first target of the duke and duchess's poisonous attack: the ancient spirit who'd been lost to the humans as a hostage and a symbol of good faith all those centuries ago.

Rosalind set all four paws on the earth. Rough soil sailed past her, but she didn't attack. Instead, she closed her eyes and projected her thoughts with all her might to the spirits who embodied the magic of the land.

We're not the ones who hurt your lost one. But if you listen to us now, we can help you to save him! It's not too late. I promise!

The missiles stopped. There was a long, tingling silence.

Then the voices of a dozen different, inconceivably giant animals, deafeningly loud, screamed through the earth and into her head:

*YOU TWO ARE LIARS! YOU'LL NEVER LIE TO US
AGAIN!*

Rosalind's eyes shot open. She jumped to the side with long hare legs – but it was too late to escape. A white mist swept from the ground to fasten around her and her brother alike, tighter than any binding ropes.

The earth fell away beneath her, and she was lost.

Giles could see nothing in the white mist that surrounded him – not Ros nor his own paws before his face. He was buffeted on all sides by rage and pain and words that echoed through his head from a dozen different voices in a language so ancient, it was universal:

We trusted you, and you broke your vows! Now our brother is dying.

We haven't broken our vows to you, Giles yipped. *You're wrong!*

A blast of wordless fury slammed into him – and then an image splashed suddenly, vividly, across the mist before him: three ragged children, dirty and bruised, standing together on a barren hillside above a valley full of soldiers. Each lifted a single silver piece of a broken crown up towards the sky while their free hands clasped each other's shoulders. As one, they chanted their joint promise.

We swear to love this land and to listen to its needs and to protect it with all our skills. We three seal ourselves to the land of Corvenne ... forever.

And we did! Giles protested. *We gave up everything. I gave up my music.*

I gave up being a knight. Rosalind's voice emerged from the white mist, raw with a pain that twisted through him. How had Giles not realised just how miserable she'd been?

So you both confess that you broke your vows!

What? The injustice was overwhelming.

How dare you? Rosalind's voice throbbed with rage. *If I could find my sword right now, I'd—*

Wait! Giles cried.

In the mist before them, that scene from their memories was playing over and over again.

We swear to love this land and to listen to its needs and to protect it with all our skills. We three seal ourselves to the land of Corvenne ... forever.

Giles had changed his whole life for that promise – but now, for the first time, he saw it in a different way.

'Ros,' he whispered in the animal language that they shared, 'what if we've had it wrong all along?'

We swear to love this land and to listen to its needs and to protect it with all our skills ...

On that first journey across the countryside, he and Ros *had* both fought with all the skills they had. Once

they'd won, though, they'd moved into Raven's Roost …
and everyone there had immediately started telling them
exactly how true royals should behave.

Giles had worked so hard to follow those traditional
royal rules. He'd given up practising magic; he'd even
given up his music.

And he wasn't the only one to have made a sacrifice.
All those weeks of watching Ros look miserable in long
skirts, turning herself into a princess instead of a
warrior …

All those weeks of being separated from their sister …

What if that was the *opposite* of what the spirits had
wanted them to do?

What if it was his family's most unusual,
ungovernable and outrageous truths – all the same ones
that made them so scandalous as royals – that the land had
truly needed from them all along?

'We didn't win Cordy the throne by acting like
traditional royals,' Giles said, 'did we?'

At his words, the scene in the mist before them
changed.

There was Ros, standing before him and Cordy with
her sword, using her magic with her weapon-craft in a blur
of incredible motion, shredding a cloud of enemy arrows
with her sword.

The scene shifted again …

There was Giles, holding an entire valley of soldiers enthralled with his song – a song born of all the pain and wreckage that the human wars had wrought upon the land. Grim adults had flung aside their weapons and fallen to their knees in tears when they had heard it, carried to them all in utter clarity with the force of his personal magic.

'Ohhhh!' Rosalind's animal voice was a groan of longing and bittersweet triumph.

'That was why we needed to seal the crown with her,' Giles whispered. 'It had to be the three of us together as we truly are. Always!'

The spirits had chosen Cordy as the land's queen. But somehow, through all the confusion and ground-shifting of the past six weeks, Giles had forgotten that the spirits had *also* chosen him and Ros from the very beginning, when the two of them had first been sent as day-old orphans to their new family's home. The spirits didn't just need Cordy after all. They needed Giles's passionate, persuasive music and Ros's magnificent martial skills to keep Cordy safe at court while *she* used her power to guard the land.

Please, he said into the mist, *forgive us. We didn't understand! But we do now, and we will never make that mistake again. Ros was right: we do know how to save your brother. Look in my memories if you don't believe me! You'll see that it's true.*

The scene before him changed again as ancient magic ripped through his mind, and Giles bit back a shout of pain. It rifled through his memories with raw force, yanking out one painful moment after another. Ros and Giles fighting in the dark … Golden collars clamping shut around their necks …

Then the Duke of Lune's smug voice was narrating once again into their ears exactly the wicked methods he had used.

We can pull out the enchanted sword from your brother, said Giles, *but only if you get us back to him in time. We can't travel quickly enough on our own, no matter which bodies we wear.*

There was a long, shuddering silence as the mist pressed closer and closer. Finally, the spirits spoke.

To push you both across the kingdom would take all the power that we have left. Can you be trusted to keep this vow?

A true knight doesn't lie about her vows, snapped Ros, *and I'm never giving up my knighthood again. Look in my mind if you need proof of that!*

There was a huff of … could it be *laughter* around them? From the spirits?

No need for that, fierce one. Not any more.

The mist shifted, showing a hare and a fox, faces touching in love and trust and unity.

Now, follow the guides that we sent you once more – but this time, do not fail us.

Guides? Giles said. *What gui—?* 'Ahhh!'

The mist was gone, and they were falling deep, deep into the earth as the mountain opened up beneath them. Screaming, Giles flailed out with all four copper-furred legs.

Something prickly brushed against his paw pads with a quiet snort of reassurance.

A familiar loud, demanding chatter sounded nearby.

And then they were flying, flying through the darkness, with the hedgehog and squirrel leading the way … just as they had always been intended to do.

24

Deep within the earth below Raven's Roost, a single, vast chamber had been built with walls of the same stone as the castle high above. The floor was plain, packed earth, all the better for magic to flow freely; only a single, narrow doorway shrouded in mist led to the long-forgotten hidden stairwell and the busy human realm above. Of course, the ancient one who slept in that secret chamber could never make use of such a tiny, mortal passageway – but long ago, it had been agreed that that magical mist would allow none to pass but the family members of the current Raven ruler, as a guarantee of safety on all sides.

After all, who wouldn't protect their own family?

For hundreds of years, that barrier of mist had been left undisturbed as the human world carried on above the sleeping spirit's chamber. It was a prison, yes, but a chosen one, ensured by human pledges of protection.

Only days ago, though, that mist had been reopened by an enemy with the blood of the royal family running through his veins … and everything had changed.

Now the ancient, immortal one was no longer sleeping. It was in pain, it was trapped, and it was dying, with no witnesses to its agony in that silent chamber.

The barrier of mist was once again shut. The Raven Queen high above it was trapped as still and as helpless as the spirit itself, their shimmering, unbreakable connection transformed into a lethal trap.

The land beneath it was still screaming as it faded …

And then, for the first time in all those silent centuries, the packed earth of the chamber's floor suddenly *erupted*, flinging four different creatures into the dying spirit's presence.

Soil sprayed over Rosalind's face as she landed hard, tucking her body into a ball and rolling with the impact.

Her tall, sensitive hare ears bumped painfully across the hard-packed earth, but it was her human pair of arms that closed around the leggings of her newly human legs as she rolled herself across the makeshift floor, trying not to bump into Giles along the way. The spirits had altered her body during the journey, pulling and prodding uncomfortably at her limbs as they'd sent her flying through a tunnel of earth beneath the kingdom ... but as she blinked stinging dirt from her watering eyes, Rosalind realised why that partial retransformation had been necessary for her mission.

There were no human torches or lamps in this cavernous room; there was no need for them. Green-and-gold light beamed from the giant black figure who filled the chamber, emanating a power so intense, it pulsed in fierce, tangible waves through the cool air, beating against Rosalind's skin until she had to fight just to summon her own breath as she stared in stunned, open-mouthed wonder, barely aware of her fox-furred brother pushing himself up with human arms to a kneeling position on the dirt floor nearby.

Those massive, folded black wings before them could surely shake down the entire foundation of Raven's Roost if they were ever unfurled. This titanic creature who lay so still before her could never be called a mere raven: every animal instinct in her morphed body told her that this had to be *the* Raven, the original spirit who had spawned all the tiny, mortal imitations of its eerie, glowing glory.

She had never felt such awe before, not even when she'd seen her own sister wear the mended Raven Crown.

If she weren't already on her knees, Rosalind would have sunk to them in wonder … but that wasn't what the spirits had sent her here to do.

The Raven's great head was flung back in agony against the dark earthen floor. Its wings were stiff as death. Its tall black chest, high above the ground, did not rise or fall. The ancient, eerie and powerful spirit was paralysed in the same position that Cordy had clenched into on her own bed …

And a lethal golden sword protruded from its chest in a sight so wrong that bile shot up through Rosalind's dry mouth in response.

Treason!

Murder!

It was a betrayal of *everything* her family stood for.

As she knelt, staring, the little red squirrel leaped with frantic impatience across that vast black, shining body. It raced around the sword in panicked circles, as if Rosalind couldn't see the abomination for herself. '*Muk-muk-muk-KWAH!*'

'Don't worry.' Rosalind's voice was hoarse with effort. 'I know what I need to do.' And she would need all her human strength to do it.

The spirit's power pulsed in overwhelming waves through the close, underground air, buffeting her body like a storm. She hadn't travelled so far and fought so hard only to give in at this final hurdle, though … and by now, she knew exactly where her true mission had always lain.

'I *never* give up,' she promised the dying ancient spirit and the squirrel who shrieked his impatience on its body as she pushed herself up from the ground. 'This is what I was born to do.'

Protect the land and my family, forever.

Every step forward seemed to carry the dragging weight of a thousand stones. Every painfully sucked-in breath was a hard-won victory.

After the last six weeks, Rosalind knew how to endure pain without forgetting what mattered. More than that, she understood her own value in the world – and that she could not be quashed into surrender, *ever*, no matter how much pressure was brought upon her.

So she strode with unstoppable force through those powerful waves of green-and-gold, and she climbed – wincing, but determined – up on to the vast, shining chest of the Raven spirit, grabbing hold of coarse feathers that tingled with magic against her hands and stood stiff beneath her sturdy boots.

Breathing hard, she finally knelt atop its still chest and wrapped both hands around the leather-bound hilt of the gold sword that was leaking its poison through the Raven spirit and, through it, into her sister and the land.

That gold, no matter how carefully enspelled, couldn't suppress her own magic without touching her skin, but even the hint of its power through the leather hilt she held sent repulsion shooting up through her arms and body, making her whole body shake.

'Watch out,' Rosalind warned the squirrel, who was peering and chattering anxiously over her shoulder. She waited for him to scamper backwards, out of danger, and then she closed her eyes as he finally fell silent.

The sound of her own heartbeat filled her ears. She drew a deep, nauseating breath, working to find her focus as Mother had always told them to do whenever it came to their magic—

And then the memory of her mother's calm instruction was overwhelmed by a far more recent memory, spat from a voice that had never tried to help her: '*You bumptious little fool!*'

Rosalind's eyes popped open as she jerked backwards, her hands falling away from the hilt of the sword. More and more of Lady Fauvre's remembered words flooded through her ears, making her suddenly, horribly aware of exactly how small and insignificant she really was as she perched like a bug atop the shining ancient spirit.

How had she ever dared to think that she could help it?

'None of your little play-weapons, if you please.

'Useless.

'Common.

'The whole court is laughing at you, you know!

'Did you ever really imagine you could … ?'

'Muk-muk-muk-KWAH!' the squirrel shouted, rising up on his hind feet to bellow his reminder directly into her ears.

Rosalind let out her breath in a rush of pure relief.

It was exactly what she'd needed.

Clenching her jaw, Rosalind tightened her hands around the leather-wrapped hilt even as the sickening memories continued to swamp her. *It doesn't matter what anyone else thinks any more. I know who I am, and the spirits know it too.*

No matter what form she wore, Rosalind would always be a *warrior. A knight. A sister. A protector.*

And *that* was all the focus that she needed.

She drew her shivering magic up through her body until it flooded her waiting arms with power – and then she *pulled* with every single bit of her strength.

Rosalind's hard-trained muscles strained until she groaned with effort. Her family's magic roared within her.

The poisonous blade of the golden sword shifted, inch by inch, higher and higher, with torturous slowness … and then came free with one final, painful drag.

'Ugh!' Rosalind flung it to the closest patch of empty floor. As it thumped harmlessly on to the packed earth, she half slid, half jumped off the Raven's massive chest and landed hard on the opposite side of its body from the sword.

'There!' she told the Raven, shaking out her aching arms. 'You should feel much better now.'

But that primordial, glistening black body still didn't move.

Green-and-gold light and magic continued to pulse steadily through the air, but the Raven's chest neither rose nor fell. It remained as frozen as a statue.

'I don't understand.' Frowning, Rosalind looked past the awe-inspiring mass of the spirit to the small pile of disrupted earth where her brother still knelt, half-fox and half-human boy, pale and staring, covered in dirt and copper fur and washed in rippling waves of green-and-gold light.

Giles was the one who had always found his way with ease around the maze of their new life while she had struggled endlessly. She was ready for him to lead the way again. 'Why didn't it work?'

Giles stared at the beautiful, shining spirit and felt all his wonderstruck awe transmute into heavy, dull despair.

It wasn't moving.

He'd been so certain that Ros was doing what the spirits had wanted – exactly what the two of them had been sent here to do. The spirit *wasn't* dead yet. It couldn't be. It was still shining! Its powerful magic pulsed around him, filling the air with a pressure so intense that he could hardly breathe through it.

Yet it still didn't shift from the same pose that Cordy had frozen into earlier, when she'd mirrored its great wound and the poisoning of their shared magic. If its soul was somehow trapped deep inside itself, where it had retreated to hide from that terrible poison, then Cordy's must be too, high above this eerie chamber.

And if Cordy didn't wake up soon …

'*Wake up!*' Giles screamed at the ancient spirit. His voice cracked into a sob. 'Just wake up.'

The red squirrel chittered a ferocious reprimand at him for his insolence from atop that huge black body. Standing beside it, Ros crossed her arms and raised her eyebrows. 'I thought you were supposed to be the diplomatic one?'

Giles tipped his head forward into his hands. 'What's the point?' He'd tried *so hard* to be a diplomatic prince for weeks, taking so much care never to offend or frighten anybody, and all that effort had come to this. He couldn't pretend to cheerful confidence any more … or hide from the truth frozen directly in front of him.

Something nudged at his leg, jolting him momentarily free from the cloud of misery that had settled over him. 'Wha—? Oh, it's you.' He smiled weakly down at the hedgehog who had bumped against his leg with her small nose and was sniffing him. 'I'm sorry, little one. Maybe if we'd realised earlier that you two were here for us, not for Cordy, and that the spirits had sent you for a reason …'

'That's it!' Ros's dirty face brightened. The red squirrel spread out his arms and legs and leaped off the Raven to land on her shoulder as she continued, 'The spirits sent guides to *both* of us, remember? Of course I couldn't wake the Raven on my own.'

Giles frowned, struggling to pull his thoughts free from their fog. 'You think I should have helped you pull out the sword? But—'

'Giles, *think!*' his sister demanded. 'What did we just vow, all over again? The spirits didn't send you here just to watch me use my powers. They sent you here to use *yours*.'

Giles's eyes widened. 'But—'

Ros and the squirrel both let out identical grunts of exasperation. 'Honestly!' she said. 'I never thought I'd see the day when *you* had to be talked into a performance!'

'I haven't sung for anyone else in weeks!' he protested. 'Not except …' He swallowed hard.

The memory of Wincester's betrayed expression tore at him; the reminder of just how dangerous his power could be.

'Lune told me not to, weeks ago,' he finished in a mumble.

'Well, of course he did.' Ros snorted. 'He wanted you *weak*, as Lady Fauvre did me.'

'Really?' Giles thought back to all those 'helpful' cousinly moments of advice, shared only when the rest of the family wasn't there to overhear them.

For the last six weeks, Lune had done everything he could to convince Giles – *so* patiently, kindly and tactfully – to swallow his own voice until it nearly disappeared, to hide every note of his beautiful music, and to feel ashamed of all the magic that he had inherited.

Had it really been a ruse all along, meant to turn Giles into a helpless political pawn? To make Giles forget that his own power could be used for good – and that he possessed the strength within himself to stand for his family and their kingdom?

'Of course he did.' The realisation came out in a deep groan. Giles locked eyes with his sister as he rose to his feet and saw rueful understanding in her gaze. 'I should have told you all the sly things he said to me so that you could have helped me to see through his trickery.'

'And I should have told you about Lady Fauvre.' She shrugged. 'We're here now, and I've done my part. It's time for you to do yours … if you still remember how.'

The hedgehog nosed encouragingly at his leg, and Giles suddenly remembered all the times that she had worked to lead him back to his lute and his music. It was time for him to lead the Raven back now.

The music in his heart struck two deep, resonant chords in preparation, filling his body with a sense of rightness for the first time in so long.

His sister was waiting. Even the squirrel had fallen silent.

Drawing a deep breath, Giles stepped forward, set hands covered in copper fur against the Raven's shining chest, and finally began to sing.

25

The Raven Queen had been lost in the darkness for so long. She couldn't fight. She didn't dare to even try to move. There was nothing left of her any more but a desperate, curled-up shield of defence around one last, defiant spark of flickering light: that single piece of her spirit that still remembered a different name, a different life, and loves beyond the crown that bound her and had doomed her. The moment that she let go and allowed any careless unfurling of her thoughts beyond that shield, she *knew* that the darkness of her poisoned bond would sweep in and extinguish the tiny light forever.

In the past, she had fought to save an entire kingdom. Now, all that she could do was endure the smothering darkness, fight every weary temptation to unclench and give in, and protect that single kernel of light that remained within her ...

Until a familiar, golden peal of sound suddenly floated through the darkness to wrap around her shield like an embrace.

> *Wings in the night,*
> *Carry me home.*
> *I've travelled so far,*
> *No more shall I roam ...*

The Raven Queen had never heard that song before, but the light inside of her that was still Cordelia would *always* recognise that unique and unmistakable singing voice.

It meant *love*. It meant safety and squabbling and a loyalty that would never break.

It was an anchor and a beacon, and it was the only thing left that could have convinced her to trust any promise of safety outside her shield.

> *My family is waiting,*
> *Their arms open wide.*
> *My heart hears them calling!*
> *There's no need to hide.*

Slowly, instinctively, she began to unfurl.

There *were* voices and movements nearby now, weren't there? How had she not noticed them before? The more attention she paid to them, the louder they became.

She couldn't make out individual words, not yet, but she knew every one of those agitated voices. They were the voices of her family – and other voices, too, that came from deep inside. She could hear the land again! The agonising block between them had vanished.

The poison is gone.
It's time to awake.
Spread your own wings,
Your throne to retake!

Slowly, tentatively, Cordelia stretched out her physical arms and legs on the wide bed underneath her. All the human voices around her immediately cut off. A hushed silence fell over the room.

Inside her head, the voices of the land erupted into a sudden, deafening chorus of joy and celebration.

You're back!
lovelovelove
We have you!

lovelovelove
You are saved!
lovelovelove
We are saved!
lovelovelove
We—

DANGER! TREACHERY! SAVE US NOW!

A single high, cracked voice screamed in warning with all its might, and Cordelia jerked upright in alarm. Her eyes were closed, but she knew exactly where that cry had come from – a patch of land far away in Raven's Nest, that spot where the deepest of magical secrets were protected.

Those secrets were meant to be guarded by the powerful, ancient spirits of Corvenne – but something had changed in the time since she had lost the land's voices. Now, those spirits were suddenly, horribly vulnerable – and they needed her help *immediately*.

Eyes still closed, Cordelia sank deep into Corvenne and saw everything clearly. The spirits had used up their own powers, somehow, in a great act of sacrifice. They would need time to recover. In the meantime, they could no longer protect themselves or anyone else …

And those same traitorous enemies who had attacked

her and the land were now striding up the slope of Mount Corve to Raven's Nest for one final act of betrayal.

'*Cordelia!*' Mother's voice was urgent and demanding, only a few inches from her face.

But Cordelia would never be trapped by other people's expectations of her again. It was time to show all Corvenne exactly what made her the true Raven Queen … and what would happen to anyone who *ever* tried to hurt the land that she guarded.

The trees were shivering all around Raven's Nest, shaking blackened leaves like a last line of defence across the two adult humans who stalked through them.

The boy who hurried after those adults threw his own words forward like another kind of shield. 'It's still not too late to think better of this madness! We can all go back, even now. Just lay down your arms and—'

'Put a gag on your nephew or I will, Solenne.' The Duke of Lune's predatory gaze swept across the gaps between gnarled tree trunks ahead, fixing on the overgrown path towards the central clearing where the air shimmered and blurred, obscuring whatever lay inside. 'If he rouses them with his whining …'

'*Enough*, Edmund!' The duchess snapped the words without slowing, one hand already on the hilt of her sword. 'There's no going back for any of us now that the princess and prince are free. If the Raven Queen survives to learn what we've done, *none of us* will last another week. Even for you, that must make this decision simple!'

'But it doesn't. Don't you understand?' He scrambled to catch up with her. 'If you do this, you'll destroy the whole land for good! The ancient scrolls all said—'

'But *we'll* survive.'

'That doesn't make it right!'

'Oh, really?' His aunt unsheathed her sword as she stepped through the final tangle of trees, breaking every frantically outstretched branch in her way.

A rounded wall of shimmering green-and-gold light filled the outer edges of the sacred clearing, dazzling Edmund's vision and making him gasp as he fell back in wonder.

Aunt Solenne snorted. 'Save the philosophy for your time-wasting friends in the archives. In the meantime, I'*ll* do what needs to be done.' She sliced her sword, with a sudden, sharp gesture, through the wall of light before her. When the blade met no resistance, she nodded briskly and strode into the light, vanishing an instant later.

Lune lingered a moment longer, smirking. 'You might as well wait here, boy. It's time for the adults to take back control of this kingdom – and we all know you couldn't stop us even if you *were* truly royal enough to try.'

Edmund's hands knotted into pathetic fists as his throat locked into all-too-familiar choking knots. He knew – he'd always known – that he was seen as a useless weakling by his aunt as well as by her enemies. He had given up long ago on changing any of their minds.

But as he watched Lune's black tunic disappear behind that shimmering, mystical wall of light, Princess Rosalind's remembered words suddenly echoed in his ears:

'It's about being brave enough to do the right thing … You should use that strength before it's too late.'

'Maybe I can't stop you both,' he muttered, 'but I can *try*.'

Taking a deep breath, he hurled himself forward into the dazzling green-and-gold wall of light.

When he emerged on the other side, panting, he found a broad, flat clearing stretching impossibly far before him, strands of mist curling and retreating around his feet below the brooding grey sky. This space was surely – surely! – too large to ever fit atop Mount Corve … but then, Edmund had studied the history of Corvenne for years, back when he'd feared that he might have to rule it. He knew that, when it came to the magic of Raven's Nest and the ancient spirits who lived there, very little was impossible.

Still, he had to blink and blink again to take in the massive shining creatures who filled that impossible stretch of space.

A glowing white stag five times the size of any he had seen in any woods; a terrifying black wolf; a giant fox; a huge red squirrel ... even as his disbelieving gaze passed over them, he was mentally cataloguing them against a different list from memory. *Yes*: these were all but one of the creatures who'd been painted dancing on the tiled floors of Raven's Roost's archives. They were the remaining ancient spirits of Corvenne ...

... And they lay helpless and unmoving on the mist-blanketed ground as his aunt and her lifelong arch-enemy stalked towards them.

Aunt Solenne stopped before the furred and glowing neck of the first spirit's body: the great stag.

The Duke of Lune stepped up beside her. 'One at a time? Or—'

'Both of us together. No more tricks.' She bared her teeth at him in a cold smile. 'I want history to remember that we *both* made this decision.'

'Together, then, in equal guilt and in equal reward later.' He raised his sword as she raised hers. The light from the ancient spirit shone into both of their faces, but their blades never wavered. 'Three ... two—'

'No!' Crying out, Edmund darted forward, elbowing his aunt out of the way and grabbing the duke's lean wrist …

And lightning crashed down from the sky, opening a massive crack in the earth just behind them.

From out of the earth flew an enormous, shining and fully awake spirit in the shape of an immense black raven. It swept into the sky to hover so close that Edmund's hair blew in the wind from the beat of its glorious black wings, and his eyes stung with the impact. Two familiar human figures waved frantically from its back.

'Come along!' Princess Rosalind beckoned impatiently – and Edmund, gaping, realised that she was talking to him. 'We're here to take you home. You don't need to be here for this part.'

'But—'

Edmund's voice was overtaken by another that echoed from the sky and the earth and the wind, all at once, in an overwhelming roar of sound.

'We are all bound by the ancient contracts, and you will never threaten this land again!'

He knew that voice. He had heard it once before, at the coronation of the Raven Queen. Then, he had stood carefully out of her sight, knowing that she would hate him the moment she realised who he was. Still, he had soaked in every detail.

Queen Cordelia had stood a full four inches shorter than Edmund. Her dark eyes had looked wild in her pale, pointed face, and his aunt's friends had whispered behind him that she was *'half feral … a ridiculous choice!'*

He'd winced in empathy for her as she was paraded down the hall by the dukes and the duchess, the latest victim of their schemes. Yet, when she had finally spoken her vows, her voice had echoed with an extraordinary, inhuman power – the same power he was hearing now.

When the celebrant had finally spoken the ritual words, *'Rise now, Queen of Corvenne,'* the entire building had shaken with the land's unrestrained celebration, and Edmund's legs had gone weak with relief.

He had known in that moment with glorious certainty that all the stories in the scrolls he'd devoured had been true. He was finally, *miraculously* free from the threat of the throne that had broken apart his family, killed both of his parents and chased him all his life.

'**Surrender**,' the magnificent, disembodied voice of the Raven Queen commanded. '**Now.**'

'Aunt Solenne!' Edmund jerked himself out of his trance to start forward just in time. '*Please*. Surrender to her quickly! Cast yourself on her mercy, and—'

'You will *always* be such a disappointment!' His aunt snarled the words as she lunged forward.

Her sword arced through the air with lethal speed …

And a second hole opened in the earth beneath her feet. She was gone an instant later, her blade falling with her into endless darkness.

The grass sealed shut above her, green and blank, as if she'd never stood atop it.

A sob burst from Edmund's lips as he sank to his knees.

The Duke of Lune dropped his own sword as though it had burned him and smiled widely up at the sky. 'Thank goodness you've arrived at last, my dear cousin!' he called up to it. 'I fought hard to defend you, but the duchess and her nephew threatened me and held me prisoner, so I had to pretend—'

Edmund's head shot up. '*In equal guilt and in equal reward!*' He shoved himself to his feet. For the first time in his life, he felt no fear as he glared at the man who'd killed his mother in battle. 'Those were your words! I heard them myself!'

'Ah, but who would be foolish enough to trust *your* memory?' The duke shrugged gently. 'I, on the other hand, am Her Majesty's family by blood—'

'I trust his word,' Prince Giles called down from above.

'So do I.' Princess Rosalind nodded firmly. 'He's one of our only true friends.'

'I … am?' Edmund blinked up at her.

She shrugged, her expression mulish. 'I told you before, didn't I? You're the bravest person I've met since we came to court.'

'*And* he knows more about the ancient scrolls than almost anybody else,' said Prince Giles. His wrists were free of fur now – or perhaps that earlier glimpse had been only a trick of the light, playing on Edmund's eyes? 'Cordy, he's going to be a *wonderful* ally. He's loyal to the bone and knows everything there is to know about the history of this kingdom.'

The Duke of Lune let out a low hiss of outrage. 'If you knew all that his family has done to ours—!'

'No one is responsible for the family they were born into.'

Queen Cordelia's voice echoed around the clearing, and Edmund found his eyes filling with sudden tears at the strength and compassion in it. Her words rang through him like a blessing, soothing over all the fears and terrible losses of his past.

So many relatives had been killed in those stupid, endless wars; so many nights, he'd been shaken awake in the dark so that he could race across the kingdom in mortal danger, all because the adults around him were fighting yet again, and he was just one more powerless pawn in their games …

'We all make our own choices,' the queen's voice continued. 'My family is chosen, and lying traitors are no part of it. So tell me truthfully, Lune. Are you loyal to the crown?'

'But of course!' Lune's smile broadened with satisfaction, his shoulders visibly relaxing. 'Always. You know I would do anything to serve you, my dear cousin.'

Clouds massed together in the sky overhead, a storm preparing to strike. 'Good,' the queen's voice whispered. 'Then you will prove that loyalty by staying here to guard the spirits from any further treachery, forever.'

'What?' Lune's face twisted. He lunged to scoop his sword up from the mist-covered grass, but thin, strong saplings shot up from that grass to encircle his legs, pulling him back as they grew with impossible speed. They twined around and around his tall body to form a tangled cage of bark. Green leaves burst into abundant life all around him, smothering his protests. Branches closed around his contorted face to seal him in and cut off his voice forever.

The Duke of Lune would never threaten anyone again.

Edmund lowered his head as green life sprouted in joyous profusion all around him and starflowers burst in triumph through the ground's blanket of white mist.

'I'm so sorry, Your Majesty,' he whispered. 'I couldn't stop them.'

'***But you tried. You cared more for what was right than what was expected.***' The queen's voice was quieter now; more distant, as if her attention was being called away from this clearing. Still, her final words resonated through him. '***Rise now, Duke of Solenne. This land and I both need you to fight for it and for our people.***'

Swallowing, Edmund pushed himself up to his feet. His eyes burned. His chest ached.

'*You will* always *be such a disappointment …*' He couldn't bear to look at the patch of thriving ground where his fierce, terrible and beloved aunt had fought her final battle.

He knew what she would think of him now … but what he thought of himself mattered even more. He bowed deeply despite the grief in his heart, and he let the bitterness of generations slide away from him. 'I'll do my very best to serve you and the land, Queen Cordelia. I swear it.'

'Are you coming or not?' Princess Rosalind demanded from the great raven's shining back.

He hesitated. Could he really ride with them after all that had transpired? All that his aunt had done?

The raven bent its own large head to look at him.

Those ancient, starry eyes were filled with a grave understanding that made him shiver … and take a final step forward.

Beyond them, the other, giant figures were beginning to stir.

'Truly, there's no more time to waste,' said Prince Giles with a rueful smile. 'Remember, you still need to rescue your friend the archivist … and we have one more battle left to fight.'

26

Rosalind had never expected to return to Raven's Roost on the back of the original Raven of Corvenne. Its black feathers radiated beams of green-and-gold light around her tightly gripping fingers, and its magic pulsed like an earthquake through her chosen, human body with every beat of its great wings around her. Town and villages, castles, woods and farms raced past below in such a blur of awe-inspiring speed that she had no time, after all, to recover from her last battle and prepare for her next before the Raven began to circle down over the high towers and ramparts of Raven's Roost – which, from this high in the air, was all too clearly spread out in perfect raven shape beneath them.

She had *definitely* not expected the entire court to be gathered atop the castle ramparts, waiting in all their most glittering and intimidating finery for her and her brother and Edmund to arrive. That vast flat roof atop the castle's east wing, where she and Giles had sat alone together under the stars only two nights earlier, was fully occupied now. Dukes of the realm stood proudly on the flagstones before the ranks of royal ladies- and gentlemen-in-waiting, who stood in their turn before all the other nobles who'd managed to crush their way into an eager mass beyond. Lines of royal guards flanked the side walls too ...

But as the Raven dropped in one final, stomach-tilting rush, the sight of one small, familiar figure standing before all the rest eclipsed every nerve in Rosalind's churning belly. 'Cordy!'

She scrambled and slid off the ancient spirit's massive back, dropping even before it had landed on the far edge of the flagstones, and she landed with a thud that rocked through her weary bones ... but it only slowed her for a moment. '*Cordy!*'

Ignoring every gasp and whisper from the elegant assembled court, she hurtled forward—

And Giles, every bit as heedless as her of courtly protocol, for once, reached their sister at exactly the same moment, so that all three triplets ended up pressed against each other in one tangled mass of embracing arms and love and overwhelming relief.

Everything was finally as it always should have been … and Rosalind was still brimming with joy as she elbowed Giles a minute later. 'Hey! Watch out for my foot.'

'Watch out with your elbow! Haven't you done enough sword-fighting for one day?'

'If you two don't *both* watch out—!'

'*Ahem.*' Alys stood above them next to Mother and Connall in a protective shield of bodies that hid the triplets' tear-streaked faces from the avidly watching court … but tears sparkled in Alys's green eyes too, even as she attempted a reproving frown. 'Remember,' she whispered, 'we're all on show up here. There will be time for a real family reunion later.'

'And we'll have a *very great deal* to talk about as soon as we're alone, believe me.' Mother looked as if she'd aged a decade since Rosalind had seen her last, dark eyes shadowed and a new streak of silver shining in her thickly piled black hair. Her whispered words might have been fierce, but she couldn't seem to stop stroking all three of the triplets' shoulders in quick, frantic pets, as if desperate to convince herself that they were all truly back within her grasp and safe again. 'You two especially, you little *scoundrels* – I could not *believe* that you—'

'What *did* you do, exactly?' Holding himself correctly still and stiffly ducal, Connall didn't reach out to touch

Rosalind or Giles, but Rosalind could feel the effort that it cost their protective older brother to restrain himself in front of all their onlookers. His warm, dark gaze ran again and again over both of them. 'You both need healing. Those bruises—'

'Later,' Rosalind said. 'We have things we need to tell you first.'

'Can it wait until we're in private?' Alys glanced past them at Edmund, who was hanging back a polite few feet, his gaze lowered. 'Cordelia will need to address the court very soon – I can feel them getting restless. And as she's well again and tells us that the conspirators have been dealt with—'

'Not all of them,' Giles said.

'*What?*' Mother's voice rose.

'Shh.' Alys put one gentling hand on Mother's arm even as her own face tightened. 'They'll tell us as soon as they can, Kathryn. Remember, like it or not, we're still in full view of the court. We *all* have to behave like the royal family of Corvenne.'

'Not any more,' Rosalind said. 'That's part of what we have to tell you.' Taking a deep breath, she stepped back and met her queenly sister's gaze. 'You know that we'll support you,' she promised, '*always*. But we can't act like a regular prince and princess any more. We—'

'Oh, I know.' Cordy's grin looked more natural and familiar than anything Rosalind had seen from her in weeks, that essential wildness sneaking through in a glint of pure mischief. 'I talked to the spirits too, before you got here. Did you think you were the only ones making plans? Why do you think I summoned everyone up to the roof in the first place?'

'Cordelia … ?' Connall's eyebrows rose. 'What are you three scheming?'

'Oh, you'll see.' Lifting her chin, their sister turned to address her next words to the most powerful assembled group of nobles in Corvenne, with Rosalind and Giles by her side and the great Raven poised behind them at the very edge of the roof, shining and unmistakable. When she spoke, all her earlier gleeful mischief was gone – but the power of the land rumbled through her booming voice, making the whole castle tremble and the court fall silent. '**A great wrong has been done to the spirits of this land – but there are three here now who fought to defend them.**'

Turning to Rosalind, she gestured imperiously – and Rosalind obediently sank to her knees, bowing her head with all the heartfelt respect that her queen deserved. She felt her sister's hand press lightly against her short hair … and then Cordy's voice boomed once again over her head:

'For your heroic service to the kingdom and your exceptional skills, I name you my own personal knight. Rise, Sir Rosalind.'

Rosalind's head jerked back. She stared up at her sister, open-mouthed ... and saw her beloved sibling and her true queen combined in the glowing smile Cordy gave her.

Whispers and hisses of shock – and, yes, a few titters too – rose up from the watching crowd, but this time, Rosalind didn't even think to flinch away from them. Instead, she leaped to her feet and said as loudly as she could, 'I will protect you and our kingdom *forever*! I swear it.'

'I know,' Cordy whispered in her own familiar voice. 'And you can start training tomorrow with the captain of my royal guard. But you both need to know that from now on, no matter what anybody else thinks of it, I'll be taking *much* more time in private to listen to the land – so that next time, I won't miss any of its warnings.'

'I understand.' They would both keep their promises to the spirits – but from now on, they would do it together, as they had been meant to all along. Feeling lighter and stronger, both at once, Rosalind rose to her feet and stepped aside to let Giles take her place.

More tears glinted in his bright blue eyes as he knelt

down before their sister, but he smiled up at her, his golden performer's voice perfectly pitched for the watching crowd. 'It is so very good to see you again, Your Majesty!'

Then he dropped his voice to a cheeky whisper. 'Just, please, Cordy, don't make me a knight. If I have to start sparring with Rosalind, you know I'll be bruised bloody!'

Rosalind rolled her eyes in company with the rest of their family, but Cordy's voice was steady and filled once more with the echoes of the land that had chosen her. '**We look forward to hearing the splendid tales of your adventures … as Corvenne's new high royal bard.**'

'But he's a *prince*!' That squawk of horror came from somewhere in the assembled noble crowd; when Rosalind turned to glower ferociously at its source, she found only rows of guilty, close-mouthed faces, with no one willing to step forward and take the blame.

Cordy didn't turn, but her voice echoed around them, and the whole castle shivered as she spoke. '**This kingdom has been ruled for *far* too long by kings and queens and dukes and duchesses who only wanted to drain it dry for their own benefit. From now on, Corvenne will be ruled by those who actually *serve* it and our people.**' Nodding, she dismissed Giles and looked past him. '**Step forward, Duke of Solenne.**'

Edmund had been hanging back, one hand resting on the Raven's great wing as if for reassurance, but Rosalind was glad to see him bravely step forward now. He swallowed hard but met Cordelia's eyes as he knelt before her. 'Your Majesty.'

'**We thank you,**' she said, '**for your service on behalf of our kingdom. We look forward to our families working in friendship from now on**.'

'*What?!*' The Duke of Arden started forward from the crowd, his face purpling with outrage over his big black beard. 'But his aunt—!'

'Was a traitor. We know.' Cordy was half his size, but even without the land echoing through her voice any more, she still seemed to be looking down her nose at him. 'Your friend the Duke of Lune was a traitor as well, but we aren't punishing you or any other innocents. Both Lune and Solenne have received just punishment for their crimes against the ancient contracts of this land. Neither of them will be returning to this court.'

'They didn't act alone in their crimes though.' Giles's voice rang out clearly as he stepped up beside Rosalind. 'They had an accomplice here at court.'

A wave of shocked whispers rolled around the assembled company, and Rosalind saw Mother reach out to grip Alys's hand tightly. Giles met Rosalind's eyes, and she nodded firmly, ready to support him in any way he needed as he navigated deadly court politics for both of them.

But she still wasn't expecting what he said. 'Sir Rosalind, would you care to be the one to tell our company who this co-conspirator is?'

'Me?' She stiffened. For weeks, she'd been humiliated by Lady Fauvre's malicious descriptions of how constantly these courtiers laughed at her ineptness. Now, Giles expected *her* to be the one to convince them? 'But …'

'You don't need to be courtly or elegant,' he whispered fiercely. 'Just tell your truth and let them see for themselves how strong you are. I'm not speaking over you any more!'

For a moment, Rosalind genuinely feared that she might cry in front of everyone. She had needed *so badly* to hear that from her triplet brother for so long!

But she was the queen's knight now, and Giles was right. She *was* strong – and she wouldn't let anyone convince her otherwise ever again.

So she squared her shoulders, crossed her arms, planted herself in front of the entire gossipy court and said flatly, 'Lady Fauvre is the traitor.'

Voices broke out in horror and shock all across the roof, but Lady Fauvre's voice pierced all the rest. 'How *dare* you make such a vile accusation! Everyone *knows*—'

Rosalind simply closed her ears to all the nonsense and kept talking. 'The Duke of Lune and the Duchess of Solenne told us that they'd trusted their plans to just one person – someone they both knew well, but for different reasons. Solenne knew her because they'd grown up together, and Lune was secretly courting her.'

Rosalind could have kicked herself now for not having guessed earlier that Lune was Lady Fauvre's mysterious suitor, even before the Duchess of Solenne had confirmed it. That black wolf that Lady Fauvre had been embroidering in her antechamber had been the very image of Lune's howling family mascot. 'So she conspired with them both to kill the Raven Queen *and* destroy the land's magic, all in hopes of one day becoming Queen of Corvenne herself, after we were all dead.'

More gasps sounded as she finished – but this time, none of them were aimed at Rosalind or her family. The assembled nobles drew aside in a horrified rush of withdrawn skirts and noisy whispers, and left Lady Fauvre standing all alone.

She jerked her chin upward, cheeks flaming. 'Of all the most blatantly ridiculous rubbish—!'

Pulling free of Alys's grip, Mother stalked across the flagstones like oncoming doom, sweeping past the line of powerful dukes without a pause. Hisses of panic sounded from several of the retreating nobles as she drew upon her magic, making the air prickle and spark with power around her as if a dark storm were approaching.

'Shall we attempt a simple truth spell, Lady Fauvre?' she demanded. 'If you played no part in my daughter's murderous attack, you will wish to prove your innocence to everyone gathered here. Won't you?'

Lady Fauvre raised a hand to her mouth, her gaze darting frantically around the watching crowd. 'I – Well, that is … Oh! Your Grace, the truth is, it was all so dreadful! The duke forced me into everything against my will, and the Duchess of Solenne always simply *terrified* me. So—'

Rosalind gave a loud, derisive and entirely unroyal snort.

'Oh, *fine!*' Lady Fauvre's eyes flared with anger. She twisted around to glare at the crowd. 'Can any of you truly blame me? What kind of royal family do we want for our kingdom? One that cares about tradition and respect – one that we can be truly proud of? Or –' her lip curled into a sneer as she raked her gaze over Rosalind's muddy leggings, bruises and wild hair – 'one that produces a so-called "princess" like *her*?'

Humiliation swelled through Rosalind with hideous familiarity, trying to lower her eyes and hunch her shoulders in admitted shame. All those calculating courtly faces turned towards her, all of them poised for social judgement …

Then Giles's voice rang out behind her. 'My sister Sir Rosalind risked her life to save all of us!'

Mother snapped, 'My daughter Sir Rosalind fought to save this kingdom and our family … and she *won*.'

'My sister,' growled Cordelia, with the ferocity of all the wildest animals in the land, 'is the princess chosen by the ancient spirits *and* my knight, a title she earned for herself.'

'My sister is a hero.' Connall's grave voice was as controlled as always, but he set his hands proudly on both Rosalind's and Giles's shoulders as he spoke, and that protective warmth washed through Rosalind like a healing balm. 'Whereas *you*, Lady Fauvre, are a traitorous worm. Guards?'

Two of them stepped up with alacrity, and not a single member of the court uttered any protest as Lady Fauvre was marched away.

In the last six weeks, Rosalind's Mistress of the Bedchamber had tried to take everything from her – her new home, her family and her pride. Now, surrounded by the people she loved most, Rosalind held her chin high and wore her grubby clothes and bruises with pride … as any knight should after a successful battle.

Well done, young one. The voice that resonated with sudden, shivering force through her head was unfamiliar but unmistakable. Rosalind jerked around to find the ancient Raven spirit watching her, its big head cocked, and its closest dark eye sparkling with infinite, ageless stars. **You are a worthy guardian for our land. You keep your promises, and so shall we**.

It nodded its shining head, first to her, then to Giles, and finally, deeply, to Cordelia. When it spoke again, Rosalind could tell from their faces that the other two could hear it too.

I will return now to my sacrifice deep below, to honour our old agreements.

'No!' The word burst out of Rosalind's mouth before she could stop it. Just the thought of this beautiful, powerful spirit, who had flown them with such thrilling speed across the kingdom, being shut back inside that dark and stuffy underground chamber, so far from all the rest of its family, forever …

'Wait.' Frowning, Cordelia stepped forward and held out one hand.

The Raven carefully dipped its massive head so that its lethally sharp beak brushed gently against her fingers. Combined, their power pulsed through the air in rolling waves, tingling against Rosalind's skin.

Have no worries, young one. Long ago, I agreed to remain beneath this castle as proof and hostage for my family's commitments. I bound myself by my own choosing in order to end the terrible wars. I shall not betray my vows – or you.

'I said, *wait!*'

Giles said, 'You really *don't* know Cordy yet, do you?'

The Raven's head tilted in confusion.

'Families are supposed to *stay together*,' said Cordelia. 'The last thing I would ever want would be for yours to be kept apart.' She lifted one arm. 'Go! Your brothers and sisters need you, and you can maintain the connection between me and the land just as well from Raven's Nest. You were only ever here as a hostage to prove that your family would keep their promises – and *we* won't break any of ours while you're gone. I'll trust your vows without binding you any longer.'

For the first time in her life, Rosalind saw an ancient spirit stunned into silence.

'She really means it,' Rosalind told him helpfully. 'My sister would *never* keep a wild creature captive. She's mostly wild herself, you see.'

'Oh, shut *up!*' Cordelia groaned, sounding suddenly far less like a grand and magical queen and far more like their familiar triplet who always became hilariously grumpy when teased. 'I'm not wild *any more*.'

'We-e-ell ...' Giles snickered.

The Raven bowed its head deeply. Then its great wings swept out around it with a sudden rush of air that billowed across the rooftop, knocking everyone backwards. An instant later, it launched its massive body upward to wheel high and free above the castle, glowing with dazzling power in the bright blue sky. Its voice boomed through the ears of everyone on the castle roof and throughout the whole crowded city of Corve below, to be repeated throughout the kingdom in dozens of ballads and stories across the decades:

'The spirits stand with this Raven Queen and her family, now and forever.'

Rosalind stood side by side with her triplets on the high roof of Raven's Roost, and she knew without a doubt that she belonged there.

27

Giles didn't return to his own quarters until much, much later that day, long after the sun had finally lowered in the sky. There had been so many stories to share with his family, so many loving lectures to endure, and so many ferocious hugs to savour.

So many plans were still waiting to be made. A whole new future lay spread out before him. Who knew where it might carry him? He'd sworn to stand for the whole of Corvenne as its national bard. He couldn't imagine that *that* would mean staying in one castle forever. Once he was a grown adult, he might well end up travelling through the kingdom with his songs, just as he'd always dreamed of doing. Never before, though, had he imagined carrying official news of the Raven Queen to all her people, and bringing back their stories and hopes to her.

He was humming the beginning of a brand-new tune as he opened the outer door to his antechamber.

Then he came to a dead halt.

His Master of the Bedchamber was sitting alone at the low table by the door, playing a solitary hand of cards. He looked up calmly as Giles entered.

'Wincester?' Giles's voice came out as a strangled squeak.

'Your Highness.' Carefully, Wincester shuffled the deck back together and then gestured towards the empty chair on the other side of the table. 'Congratulations on a successful journey.'

Giles forced his feet forward and let the door shift closed behind him. He sat meekly in the empty chair before his legs could give out.

An impatient snort sounded just beside his feet. 'What's – oh, *you*!' His throat tightened as he scooped up the little hedgehog, whom he hadn't seen since he and Rosalind had woken up the Raven. He'd assumed that she would have returned to the wilds – but she had been waiting for him here after all, even after his great task for the spirits had been completed. No doubt Rosalind was reuniting with her own squirrel too.

He ducked his head over the hedgehog's prickles to mask the fresh tears in his eyes as she settled herself firmly into place.

'I am sorry,' he said at last, when he thought he finally had control over his voice. 'Wincester, I am *so* very sorry.' He forced himself to look up and meet his Master of the Bedchamber's gaze. 'You were the only one at court I trusted. I never, ever wanted to hurt or frighten you if I could help it! But of course I'll understand if you no longer want to attend me. You won't get into any trouble for it, I promise.'

Wincester looked at him steadily across the table. 'Do you truly think that I would run away from my sworn commitments simply because I was frightened?'

Giles shook his head slowly. 'No. But I would still understand. And I wouldn't call it running away, just … realising –' he took a deep breath, bracing himself – 'I'm not the prince you thought I was.'

The spirits had allowed him and Rosalind to return to their chosen bodies once they'd awoken the Raven, but he would never forget what he had felt in fox form. He refused to feel ashamed of where he'd come from any more.

He might wear the body of a human, but he still carried all the cleverness and sensitivity of the fox who ran and yipped inside him, just as Rosalind would always share the warrior nature of her hare. Every part of him combined to make him the loyal brother that he was, along with the fabulous bard he would become. From now on, he would draw on every single piece of himself to shape the music that was his and always would be, no matter what form he wore.

'No, you are not.' His Master of the Bedchamber rose to loom over the small table. 'Have you eaten yet, Your Highness? Or would you like me to summon food for you now? I assume –' he heaved a long-suffering sigh as he glanced at the happily snuffling hedgehog on Giles's lap – 'your small *creature* will want some sustenance as well. And perhaps a litter tray.'

'Well, yes, but …' Giles stared up at him, baffled. 'I don't understand. What's going on? Don't you hate me for what I did before I left?'

Wincester's brows lowered into a thoughtful frown. When he spoke again, his voice was quiet. 'When we first met, I thought you were a kind and clever boy, trying his best to adapt to a lethal court and protect his family from its dangers.'

'Um.' One of Giles's knees started to bounce anxiously up and down beneath the table, making the hedgehog grumble. 'And now?'

'When we first met,' Wincester continued inexorably, 'I had hopes but no great expectations that you would ever survive to adulthood, *or* that you could keep your conscience if you did. I've lost too many young princes before, you see.' He bent his lanky body into a low, respectful bow. 'Thank you for proving me wrong and saving our kingdom despite my best efforts to hold you back, Prince Giles. I promise I won't underestimate your strength again. And it seems that you were, indeed, right.' His lips curved into a small smile. 'I could come to love a wild creature after all.'

'Oh. *Oh*.' Giles blinked furiously as he stood and bowed deeply in return, taking care not to let the hedgehog wobble. 'I promise I won't ever use magic on you again either. We'll trust each other from now on.'

'Excellent.' Wincester nodded solemnly. 'And now?'

'Now?' Giles shook his head, his mind whirling.

He finally had the safe home he'd always wanted.

He had a whole future full of dreams and a loyal hedgehog making herself at home in his arms.

And *now* … ?

His lips curved into a wide and mischievous grin. 'What else?' he asked. 'You have to hear my latest song!'

That night, ivy crept up the castle walls once more, because the Raven Queen was dreaming. In her dreams, just as in reality, she was surrounded on all sides by her family, rooted and shaded by the ferocious strength of their love ... but she drew her own deepest power from the land below, and she stood strong, claiming all the space that she needed to move and grow.

She was the Raven Queen, and she always would be – but she would never again let herself or anyone else forget that she was still Cordelia too.

Her triplets were also dreaming in their own chambers. Rosalind leaped and boxed with wild joy as a fighting hare, training every bit as hard in her dreams as she soon would in real life under the guidance of Cordelia's captain of the guard. As a fox, Giles yipped and sang his contentment to the moon in a language he no longer wanted to forget.

Their whole family slept in safety as ivy crawled through Cordelia's windows to embrace her in hopeful, new green life ...

And the spirits of the land slept safely too.

~The End~

ACKNOWLEDGEMENTS

Thanks so much to all my generous writer-friends who beta-read chapters for me along the way: Jenn Reese, Patrick Samphire, Holly Webb, Deva Fagan, Ying Lee, Tiffany Trent and Heidi Heilig. Your help meant so much to me!

I owe special thanks to Jenn, Holly and Deva, who read and cheered on every single chapter of the first draft as I wrote it – and to Jenn and Ying for reading and cheering on every single chapter of my ground-up rewrite afterwards. Your words of encouragement all made *such* a difference to me as I drafted and redrafted this novel across an extraordinarily difficult few years!

Thank you to Jamie Samphire, who let me read several chapters out loud to him, which helped an awful lot. Thank you to Lili Trent for being my first kid-reader for the entire book and for giving such an enthusiastic response! Thank you to the members of InkMusketeers and Memory & Reason, whose generous support every single day got me through some of the hardest moments of 2020–2022. Thank you to Patrick Samphire for endless support and generous critiques, and to Ollie Samphire for being my nighttime-walk buddy throughout and for helping me to remember how playful and fun story-creation should be.

Thank you to Molly Ker Hawn, amazing agent *and* friend, for supporting me fiercely and being an incredible professional partner. Thank you to Lucy Mackay-Sim, Ellen Holgate and Carla Hutchinson for being so patient, generous and understanding as one family health disaster after another delayed my deadlines again and again. I hope you all know just how much I appreciated it!

Thank you to Pétur Antonsson for another absolutely gorgeous cover.

And, oh, thank you to Lucy Mackay-Sim, Gen Herr and Carla Hutchinson, whose patient series of edits helped me finally find my way through all the tangles. I feel very lucky to have worked with all three of you!

I've also been really lucky to have so many great people working on this book at Bloomsbury. Thank you to Fliss Stevens (Managing Editor) for beautifully managing the desk-editing process, Veronica Lyons for sensitive, thoughtful copy-editing, Eugénie Woodhouse for careful proofreading, Jearl Boatswain (Children's Campaign Assistant) for enthusiastic marketing, Isi Tucker (Publicity Assistant) for the wonderful publicity, Stephanie Amster (Creative Director) for designing the amazing cover, Jet Purdie for fabulous chapter artwork and Michael Young (Production Manager) for brilliantly overseeing the book's production.

HAVE YOU READ

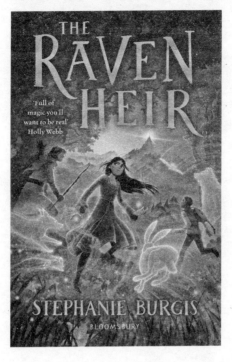

The first epic fantasy about triplets Cordelia, Rosalind and Giles

'Warm, immersive fantasy storytelling' – Hilary McKay

'Such a wonderful book. Exciting, welcoming, and full of magic you'll want to be real' – Holly Webb

Turn the page for a sneak peek …

1

Beyond the castle's moat, the deep, dark forest was shot through with trails of sunlight, tracing golden paths of possibility. Robins sang from hidden branches while swifts dived and darted over the sun-dappled water. They were all wild with the first taste of summer, and so was the dark-haired girl who sat, bare feet dangling against stone, on the windowsill of her tower bedroom, watching them fly.

Inside the castle, her mother and her older brother, Connall, were busy in the herbarium as usual, casting stinking enchantments to protect their home against the world. Cordelia's triplet sister, Rosalind, was loudly bashing mock enemies in the first inner courtyard, using the latest long stick that she'd adopted as a sword. Their triplet brother, Giles, strummed a lute soulfully in his tower bedroom high above, windows left open to spread his endless wailing song through the warm air.

But outside the castle, the birds were free, and so could Cordelia be, if only—

No! Catching herself leaning forward, she forced herself to stop before wings could sprout from her back.

She couldn't turn bird and fly out into the sunshine. *Not today.* She'd promised Mother never to do it again without Connall's supervision, even though that was a *ridiculous* rule. It meant only going out once or twice a week, when she wanted to fly free every day. They lived all alone in the centre of an enchanted forest. Who could possibly hurt her among the trees? And why would they want to?

But those were questions that Mother would never answer, like everything else about their family's past ... and the last time Cordelia had given in to temptation and flown free on her own for one delicious, stolen afternoon, Mother had cast a cloud of dark smoke to wrap tightly around her window for an entire week in punishment. So Cordelia only sighed and tipped her head back now to soak in the gorgeous warmth of the sunshine on her face and the vast, familiar murmuring of the deep forest around her ...

Until harsh voices called out suddenly in the distance.

She jerked upright, eyes flying open. No animals in the forest made sounds like that! Sixteen-year-old Connall's voice was the closest she could think of – but even his wasn't nearly so deep.

'Mother?' she whispered.

If her mother had been paying attention, she would have heard that whisper through the tug of connection that she'd laid upon all her children. Spellcasting must have taken all her focus, though, for Cordelia still sat, uncertain and unanswered, on her windowsill a minute later when the first grown men she'd ever seen burst through the trees into the narrow clearing beyond the moat, wearing armour that clanked and flashed in the sunlight.

'There!' The first one strode forward, as big and hulking himself as the raging bear painted on his shield. A great black beard jutted out beneath his iron helmet. 'The sorceress's castle – and no dragons guarding the gate after all!'

'None that we've seen … *yet*.' The man who answered was lean and poised, like the wolf who snarled on his own shield – and he looked every bit as ready to spring. His head turned, predatory gaze sweeping the clearing. 'We may have slipped past her outer shields with our ploy, but that's no guarantee of our safety from now on.'

Cordelia held her breath, unmoving on her perch, as more and more armoured men and women flooded out of the trees behind the first two. Each of them carried a shield with a wolf or a bear in one hand and a long, sharp-looking sword in the other, and they took up position behind their two leaders.

Too late to change into a bird for safety now! She should have slipped inside before, if only her insatiable curiosity had allowed it. Her feet and arms were nearly as pale as stone, though, and her comfortable old linen gown – carefully ripped along the sides to allow herself proper adventures – was a deep green that matched the ivy on the walls. Perhaps they wouldn't notice her?

'No dragon,' said the leader of the wolf-knights, 'but a little spy watching us with big eyes for her mistress. You, girl!' he called out. 'Tell the Dowager Duchess she has visitors!'

The Dowager Duchess? Cordelia stared at him.

There were no duchesses in their castle. No one lived with their family at all except for Mother's friend Alys, who looked after the goats, argued with Mother over what to plant in the kitchen gardens, and was almost always covered in dirt up to her bony elbows.

On long winter evenings in the great hall, after Giles had finished singing his latest ballads, Mother would often

4

summon up a pile of tiny scented silk-bound books to read out loud to all of them. Cordelia had heard of elegant, powerful duchesses in those pages, along with queens and countesses and fiercely beautiful knights in armour ... but none of them sounded anything like Alys.

'The girl's obviously simple,' said the leader of the bear-soldiers. 'No sense looking for any help there.' Shaking his head, he cupped his big hands around his mouth and bellowed, 'Sorceress, reveal yourself! Or we'll attack!'

Cordelia winced. Mother wasn't going to like that threat at all!

For one long moment, silence hung over the clearing. Even the birds in the forest stopped calling. They were wise enough to hide in times like these.

Then Cordelia *felt* Mother rush towards them through the castle, grabbing out for the whole family at once – not her usual gentle brush against their thoughts, but a hot, frantic swipe.

CORDELIA!

I'm fine! Cordelia hastily pushed her own thoughts back at her mother. **But there are men at the gate. They—**

The great silver portcullis flung itself open, and her mother exploded through it. She was still wearing her stained working apron from the herbarium, and more than half of her long dark hair had twisted free of its constraining plait. But Mother never needed to look tidy to be imposing.

Long weeds from the bottom of the moat shot up and wove themselves together to build a living drawbridge for her to stalk across in fury. Bobbing shapes beneath the green moss and lily pads burst upward as she passed, revealing venomous snakes, long and coiling, heading straight for the invaders. They swam as fast as shadows, and the closest soldiers jumped back, shouting at the sight of them.

I should have thought to change into one of them, Cordelia thought wistfully.

It was too late to hide among the water snakes now. Mother's voice snapped through Cordelia's head as she stalked forward:

Get off that windowsill *now*. Out of sight!

U*gh!* Cordelia scrambled back into her bedroom and sank obediently to the floor beneath the window ... for a moment. Then she lifted herself just enough to peer outside.

It wasn't as if she was in any danger now that Mother was here. If anyone would simply take the time to *explain*—

'Make way!' A hard push shoved her aside, and Rosalind took her place. 'I want to see!'

'Go somewhere else!' Cordelia shoved her sister back, hard. 'You've got your own room!'

'But *you've* got the best view.'

'Out of the way, runts!' Giles skidded in behind them, panting, and squeezed his way into the middle. 'I couldn't hear anything from my tower.'

'Not over the sound of your own voice, you mean,' muttered Rosalind.

Cordelia snorted in agreement.

'Shh!' Connall stepped into the room behind them. '*Quiet.*'

It was a spell, not an order; the lips of all three triplets sealed themselves shut against their wills. Cordelia gritted her teeth, Giles sighed through his nose, and Rosalind punched out wildly, her face reddening with rage – but their older brother ignored the blow, leaning over all of them with his gaze intent and his light brown hands braced around Cordelia's windowsill.

Now Cordelia couldn't even see what was happening through her own window! In her family, she could never keep *anything* for herself.

She could still hear their mother's voice, though. '… bellowing at *my* door as if you had *any right* to intrude on my home after all these years?'

'Duchess.' That was the leader of the wolf-knights, his

voice smoother than his friend's. 'We apologise for the rudeness of our greeting. We fought long and hard to reach your gate, and our manners were strained by the journey.'

'My *patience* has been strained more than enough.' Mother's voice was colder than Cordelia had ever heard it. 'State your business and begone, all of you.'

'Alas, we bring grave news that will not be dismissed so easily,' said the wolf-leader. 'King Edmund – long rest his soul – is dead.'

Cordelia felt Mother's gasp; it was a ripple of unease that billowed through their connection, sending a disconcerting chill through Cordelia's body before Mother snapped her emotions tightly shut, closing herself off from everyone. 'And?' she demanded. 'What has that to do with me?'

'Your game is over, sorceress,' snarled the bear-leader. 'You've lost. You won't hide the heir from us any longer! And if it were up to me, I can tell you—'

'It is time, madam,' interrupted the wolf-leader, 'to return to our kingdom at long last so your child may rule over all of us.'

ABOUT THE AUTHOR

Stephanie Burgis grew up in a big, noisy, loving family in Michigan, USA. These days she is a dual citizen of the US and the UK and lives in South Wales (land of dragons) with her husband, the author Patrick Samphire, and their children. She loves to write books about history, magic, families, bravery, dragons and chocolate! *The Raven Throne* is Stephanie's fifth book for Bloomsbury.

Three magical adventures about acceptance,
family, friendship – and dragons!

Read the whole series …

AVAILABLE NOW

Prim and proper nineteenth-century England is definitely not the place for magic . . . but that's not going to stop Kat Stephenson!

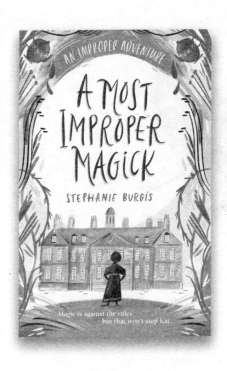

Join Kat in her Improper Adventures today . . .